Praise for *Girl in Disguise*

"If you love historical fiction, you're going to devour *Girl in Disguise*. The time, the place, the girl—this book takes you on a thrill ride with the first female detective, making her way by pluck and luck through the seedy streets of nineteenth-century Chicago, finding her place in a male-dominated world."

—Melanie Benjamin, *New York Times* bestselling
author of *The Swans of Fifth Avenue*

"Greer Macallister brings the original Miss Pinkerton roaring back to life in this electrifying tale. *Girl in Disguise* is a rollicking nineteenth-century thrill ride, complete with clever disguises and coded messages, foiled plots and hidden agendas, lies, indiscretion, and forbidden love. Kate Warne is a scrappy, tough-as-nails detective who did a man's job for the first time in American history. She lives and breathes again in this riveting novel."

—Amy Stewart, *New York Times* bestselling
author of *Girl Waits with Gun*

"With cunning, guile, and a dash of desperation, Kate Warne charms her way into the old boys' club of a mid-nineteenth-century Chicago detective agency and soon finds herself catapulted into a world of spies, rogues, and double-crossers. As she dons and sheds all manner of disguises, Kate discovers that she has a knack for subterfuge—and more than that, she likes it. Inspired by a real-life story, Greer Macallister has created a fast-paced, lively tale of intrigue and deception, with a heroine at its center so appealingly complicated that she leaps off the page."

—Christina Baker Kline, #1 *New York Times*
bestselling author of *Orphan Train*

"Macallister is becoming a leading voice in strong, female-driven historical fiction. Exciting, frightening, and unspeakably moving, *Girl in Disguise* reveals what one courageous woman endures to enact justice in a nation at war, and change the course of history."

—Erika Robuck, national bestselling author of *Hemingway's Girl*

"All hail a mighty woman in a man's world! Greer Macallister aims her pen at Kate Warne, the first female Pinkerton detective, and hits the mark with this rousing, action-packed adventure. A book that brings to light a commanding and little-known contribution to American history."

—Sarah McCoy, *New York Times* and international bestselling author of *The Mapmaker's Children*

"*Girl in Disguise* cleverly unearths the story of Kate Warne, the first female Pinkerton detective. Fast-paced, subversive, and with rich prose, it's everything a historical mystery should be. In the end, it will leave you stunned. And then you will want to read everything else Greer Macallister has ever written."

—Ariel Lawhon, author of *Flight of Dreams*

"I was absolutely ensnared by *Girl in Disguise*, Greer Macallister's unflinching investigation of what it means to be true to yourself while living a life of deception. Mysterious Kate Warne, who fought perception to become the first female Pinkerton detective, is just the kind of courageous, ingenious, fierce character I love. I could not stop turning pages as she dons disguises; tells lies; rubs shoulders with lady spies, hardened criminals, double agents, and President Lincoln; and manages to uncover the truth—not just about the crimes she investigates, but her own heart. Chock-full of fascinating ripped-from-the-headlines period details and intriguing historical personages, I drank this book down in a single shot."

—Erin Lindsay McCabe, *USA Today* bestselling author of *I Shall Be Near to You*

"The ride Macallister takes us on is a grand one… At the end, you might find yourself rooting for the story so much, you'll make your own disbelief disappear."

—*Columbus Dispatch*

"Macallister is as much of a magician as her subject, misdirecting and enchanting while ultimately leaving her audience satisfied with a grand finale."

—*Dallas Morning News*

"In her historical fiction debut, Macallister…has created a captivating world of enchantment and mystery that readers will be loath to leave."

—*Library Journal*

"Like her heroine the Amazing Arden, Greer Macallister has created a blend of magic that is sure to delight her audience. *The Magician's Lie* is a rich tale of heart-stopping plot turns, glittering prose, and a cast of complex, compelling characters. Reader beware: those who enter Macallister's delicious world of magic and mystery won't wish to leave!"

—Allison Pataki, *New York Times* bestselling author of *The Traitor's Wife*

"A suspenseful and well-researched tale of magic, secrets, and betrayal that will keep you guessing until the end."

—J. Courtney Sullivan, *New York Times* bestselling author of *The Engagements, Commencement,* and *Maine*

"*The Magician's Lie* is riveting, compelling, beautiful, frightening, evocative, and above all, magical. Don't miss this immersive novel of suspense and wonder from an exciting new voice in historical fiction!"

—international bestseller M. J. Rose

"A riveting read with suspenseful turns, *The Magician's Lie* takes you on an engaging and atmospheric journey through storytelling and illusion. Greer draws on raw emotion and leaves you questioning just how much is left behind the curtain."

—Sarah Jio, *New York Times* bestselling author
of *Goodnight June* and *Blackberry Winter*

"In *The Magician's Lie*, Greer Macallister has created a rich tapestry of mystery, magic, and lost love. The novel drew me in with its lush details and edge-of-your-seat plot. The tale of the tragic Amazing Arden, a female magician, will have you questioning how the truth of a tale can be different than the material facts, and how what you feel can be stronger than the soundest logic."

—Margaret Dilloway, author of *How to Be an American Housewife* and *The Care and Handling of Roses with Thorns*

GIRL IN DISGUISE

GIRL IN DISGUISE

GREER MACALLISTER

sourcebooks
landmark

Published by Sourcebooks Landmark, an imprint of Sourcebooks, Inc.
P.O. Box 4410, Naperville, Illinois 60567-4410
(630) 961-3900
Fax: (630) 961-2168
www.sourcebooks.com

Library of Congress Cataloging-in-Publication Data

Names: Macallister, Greer, author.
Title: Girl in disguise / Greer Macallister.
Description: Naperville, Illinois : Sourcebooks Landmark, [2017]
Identifiers: LCCN 2016007221 | (hardcover : alk. paper)
Subjects: LCSH: Warne, Kate, -1868--Fiction. | Pinkerton's National Detective
    Agency--Fiction. | Women detectives--Illinois--Chicago--Fiction. | GSAFD:
    Mystery fiction. | Biographical fiction.
Classification: LCC PS3613.A235 G57 2017 | DDC 813/.6--dc23 LC record avail-
able at https://lccn.loc.gov/2016007221

Printed and bound in the United States of America.
WOZ 10 9 8 7 6 5 4 3 2 1

CHAPTER ONE
THE FIRST DISGUISE

August 1856

L ike any Chicago tavern in deep summer, Joe Mulligan's stank. It stank of cigars smoked the week before, months before, years before. Tonight's smoke pooled against the basement ceiling in a noxious cloud. I acted like I smelled only roses. The woman I was pretending to be would have done the same.

I was also pretending the sharp tang of men's sweat surrounding me didn't terrify me. These were not good men. But I wasn't a good woman, not tonight. My mission was to ignore the smoke and the sweat, blind a bad man with a wicked smile, and wring out his secrets. There would be no second chance.

So I breathed as shallowly as I could and made my way through the crowd to the bar. Men's bodies brushed mine, hips and hands and God only knows what, lingering on my shoulder and everywhere below. My nerves frayed, and I stumbled. With anything less at stake, I would have fled Joe Mulligan's as if it were on fire. But I needed the money. The money would save me.

"Drink?" snapped the barkeep.

I squared my shoulders and answered him as the woman I was pretending to be.

"Well, I sure am thirsty," I said, lowering my head as if sharing a confidence, "but I'm waiting on a friend."

Empty glass in hand, he looked me over. The low-sweeping neckline of my claret silk gown and the pale expanse of décolletage it artfully framed. The intricately curled hair piled atop my head, shot through with ribbons. The coy smile, all lips, no teeth. I saw recognition flash in his eyes.

"Do your business, but don't make no trouble," he said and moved on down the bar to a knot of raucous, rowdy men. The first gate, passed. Now, I was just waiting.

And waiting.

At least thirty long minutes crawled by, and with each one, my relief drained away. The same disguise that had fooled the bartender fooled the patrons. Man after man took turns perching on the red leather stool next to me. They bent close. Their mouths offered drinks and conversation, but their eyes made it clear what they really wanted.

I hadn't expected to be the only woman in the place. This late at night, the slatterns of Chicago did a brisk business in establishments like Joe Mulligan's, which is why I'd chosen this place and time. I'd known how it would look and what they would think. But the practice was turning out to be much harder than the theory. Every man had to be skillfully parried away. A single slip would waste the night. The effort exhausted me.

"Oh, sir," I was saying to the latest one, fluttering my fingers at him, "you do me a kindness. But I really must insist you leave that seat free for my companion."

He leaned closer, breathing almost into my mouth, and slurred, "I'll be your companion, sugar."

I swallowed my disgust and kept my voice steady. *Be pleasant*, I told myself. *Cheerful. Bland.* "He'll be here any minute, I'm certain of it," I said and gazed over his shoulder hopefully. As if in answer, the door to the outside creaked open.

Rumbles of laughter sounded as half a dozen men guffawed

their way down the stairs into the tavern. I recognized my target immediately. He wasn't the tallest of them, nor the most handsome, but it was clear he was in charge. His smirk showed he was the one who'd told the joke everyone was laughing at.

Henry Venable, better known as Heck, was a sallow man with deep-set, hooded eyes. He wore a hat worn soft with age. The rest of his clothes were so new they practically gleamed. If I were closer, I'd be able to see my reflection in his shoes. He looked, unmistakably, like he'd recently come into money. Which the Pinkerton Detective Agency and the First Eagle Savings Bank believed he had, several weeks before, with the help of three accomplices and four shotguns. Eyewitnesses had given a description that matched Heck's, but it wasn't enough. The best way to prove he'd done it was to find the money. He'd spent some of it, clearly, but rare was the man who could spend five thousand dollars in less than a month without leaving some kind of trail. The rest had to be hidden somewhere.

I had to find out where.

Easy, easy, I told myself. I couldn't shove my way over to him right off the bat. I had to get him to come to me. Somehow.

Still laughing and jostling one another, the six men took their seats at a booth in the corner, much farther away than I would've liked. I was too far off to catch his eye, and it would look odd if I changed my seat for no reason. Given that, I sidled down the bar and forced myself to slide onto an empty stool next to a stoop-shouldered man. I sat much closer to him than I needed to and dangled one foot close to his.

"Evening," I said.

He glared at me through bleary eyes, clearly three sheets to the wind already, maybe four. Well, that wasn't all bad. He couldn't cause me trouble if he slipped out of consciousness. I hoped.

"Evening," he slurred, barely able to manage even the two required syllables.

"What're you drinking? Looks delicious. I sure could use a drink myself," I said and gestured to the empty bar in front of me.

He managed to raise two fingers to the bartender, who came right away—clearly, this was a regular—and said, "'Nother round, Jim."

"Coming right up."

I edged even closer to him and peeked over my shoulder as discreetly as I could toward Heck and his men. All seated, and some looked restless. Good. There were still possibilities.

My ever-drunker neighbor half raised his glass of bourbon to me. I took a sip and nearly choked. It took all my concentration not to gasp at the burning, searing sensation. I'd have to get better at that. Any man in possession of his faculties could easily see I wasn't used to strong drink. Tonight, this one's faculties were thoroughly drowned, but that was luck on my part, not skill. If I made it through this night, I'd put it on my list of things to learn.

Finally, one of Heck's men eased out of the booth. As I'd hoped, he came toward the bar, into the larger-than-usual space on my far side. He flagged down the bartender and rattled off a complicated order. As soon as he was done and his elbow was resting on the bar next to me, I ignored my marinated neighbor, as I'd planned, and leaned over toward him, my décolletage almost spilling out onto his arm.

"Evening," I said.

He nodded back silently. He was a striking man, with blue eyes like ice under his thick black brows, but there was something cruel about his face. Something cold. Locked away.

I'd have to generate enough warmth for both of us. "Say," I nearly purred, inclining my head toward the booth, "would you mind introducing me to your friends there?"

"Yes, I'd mind very much," he said, turned square toward the bar, and then ignored me as if someone were paying him a goodly sum to do so.

Damn it. The wrong target, I supposed, but what was I to do? I was beginning to panic in earnest. Heck was only ten feet away from me, but he might as well be ten miles if I couldn't get myself into his orbit. I had it all planned out. Delicate fingers laid on his arm. Breathless, admiring questions. He was known as a boaster with an eye, and other parts, for the ladies. If I was in the right place at the right time—which I was so, so close to being—I could get him to boast to me. Then I'd have what Pinkerton wanted, and in turn, he'd give me what I wanted: a position as the first female operative of the Pinkerton National Detective Agency, at full salary.

But it all depended on Heck, and to get to him, I had to get through this man-shaped woodcut first. And all he was doing was staring at the barkeep, waiting.

We stayed like that a few minutes. My brain worked madly, thoughts zooming and swooping around my skull, but I had no good ideas. It could all fall apart this easily. *Damn it. Damn it.* The drunk on my other side finally laid his head down on the bar; he'd be no help.

At last, another man rose from the booth and joined Blue Eyes, standing close to both of us. His hair was drenched with brilliantine, and his small, sad mustache was little more than a pencil line above his lip. "Boss wants to know what's taking so long."

"See for yourself," said the taller one, inclining his head in the direction of the culprit, who was hard at work pouring coppery brown liquid out of a silver shaker into six matching coupes. "Ragman's taking his sweet time."

The new arrival inclined his head toward me. "Looks to me like you're caught up in conversation."

"Heavens no," I said, pivoting my body toward his. "This clod couldn't make conversation if I spotted him both ends of the sentence. Are you more of a...talker?"

"I could be," he said with a wolf's leer.

"Then perhaps I might join your party?" I smiled, but not too wide. Softly, sweetly. Let him think me a sheep.

"Sounds good to me," he said.

"No," said the first man.

"You're no fun," said the second.

"That may be," said Blue Eyes. "But no need for the boss to get distracted. There's business to be done."

"Aw, plenty of time for business when the sun rises," Mustache replied. "Tonight, I think he's more in the mood to celebrate, if you catch my drift."

"I like to celebrate," I said.

"I bet you do," both men said in unison, with very different inflections.

With much clattering and fanfare, the bartender finally poured the sixth drink and pushed the glasses across the bar. Mustache immediately grabbed one in each hand. The elegant stems looked especially fragile in his fists. He carried them over to the table, where his arrival was greeted with appreciative hoots.

I assumed Blue Eyes would follow, but instead, he grabbed my elbow sharply and growled in my ear, "What are you playing at?"

"What?"

"Walk away," he said. "Right now. Walk away."

"No," I hissed, but my heart pounded.

"All right, then. Come with me."

"I'll scream," I said.

"You do that," he said, cool as the far side of the pillow.

He was right. A scream would call attention my way, but what for? What man among these would rush to my side? I scanned their faces. Heck Venable and his crew were hardly the only wrongdoers here, and some were doubtless worse than mere robbers. First Eagle had been knocked over with no fatalities. There were things far worse than money to steal. I was likely better off taking my chances with Blue Eyes, as poor a prospect as that seemed.

Mustache returned for the rest of the drinks. "You helping?" he asked, clearly confused.

"Naw, you take 'em. I'll be back in two shakes," said the taller man, shifting his grip on my elbow around to the inside, so it looked less overtly threatening. His long, rough fingers moved over the delicate skin on my inner arm, and I couldn't suppress a shiver.

"Oh, I see," leered Mustache.

Annoyance crossed his face, but Blue Eyes said, "Don't drink mine. I won't be long."

"Sure."

I wished I could think of something to say to Mustache that would result in him getting me away from Blue Eyes, but my mind was a blank. I never should have taken such a risk. Never should have come here. I didn't even protest as the taller man hauled me to my feet.

"This way," he said, steering me up the stairs. I dragged my feet as much as I dared, and a new wave of terror swept over me. Upstairs was the hotel. That was a key reason Joe Mulligan's was particularly popular with the whores of Chicago: convenience.

His hand was locked around my arm like an iron cuff. He didn't relax his grip at all, even while using his other hand to unlock the door of a room that I assumed to be his. My throat was dry, and my head swam. *Damn it, damn it.* I'd disguised myself as a prostitute to crack the case, believing it the best, if not the only, way to achieve my aim. Now, unless a miracle happened, I'd have to choose between certain exposure and an unthinkable act. Blue Eyes was clearly expecting me to follow through on my disguise. Unless I wanted to give up all hope of ever gaining the confidence of Heck Venable and prying loose his secrets, I'd have to deliver on my unspoken promise and do what prostitutes do.

With one more tug, he pulled me inside the room and shut the door.

CHAPTER TWO

SOMEONE HAS TO BE FIRST

O nly three days before, I'd knocked on the front door of the Pinkerton National Detective Agency offices on Washington Street and, hearing no answer, swung the door open to step inside. I could feel the perspiration collecting like rainwater between my shoulder blades, trapped under the charcoal shirtwaist I'd selected to convey seriousness. I knew he wouldn't consider me if I looked frivolous. He might not consider me anyway.

It was a muggy, sun soaked day outside, but in here, it was dim. A neat, white arrow painted on the wall pointed me up a set of stairs. No wonder no one had heard my knock. The stairs were narrow and rickety, and they carried me up into the unknown.

Three floors above the steaming Chicago pavement, I took a moment to wipe my brow before I knocked on the inner door. An indeterminate reply—was it *go ahead* or *go away?*—came through the door in a muffled bass. I heard the answer I wanted and went inside.

Nearly the entire room was taken up with a heavy oaken desk the size of a draft horse, dwarfing the man who sat there. I knew him in an instant. Allan Pinkerton. Twenty years my senior, with thinning reddish hair and a full beard, looking very much like the portraits I'd seen in the newspaper, alongside stories of daring exploits that brought dangerous criminals swiftly to justice.

A decade before, as a cooper harvesting wood for barrels

from the dense forests outside Chicago, he'd stumbled onto a counterfeiting operation hidden among the trees. He reported it to the authorities and won himself a position in the city's police department. In his version of the story, the work suited him but the politics didn't, and after a handful of years, he opened his own private detective agency. He'd been publicizing his many successes ever since. If he had failures too, neither the *Tribune* nor the *Daily Journal* was quick to say.

I waited for a moment to catch his attention, but he was scribbling furiously in a ledger. Too busy to waste his time on me? Fully unaware of my presence? It couldn't be the latter, and I wouldn't accept the former. At last, I cleared my throat.

When he saw I was a woman, he stood. We took each other's measure in a long moment.

It seemed fitting that he'd been a cooper, so closely did he resemble a barrel. Solidly built but not gone to fat, despite his age. Shirtsleeves rolled up, exposing freckled, thick forearms and meaty hands that would have looked more at home on an ax handle than a fountain pen. In the heat, he'd shed his jacket and hung it on the back of his chair, where it hung crookedly, like a dark flag. My attention settled on one last, essential detail—his look of impatience—and I braced myself to make my claim.

"Mr. Pinkerton, my name is Kate Warne," I said, trying to sound like a woman who had never perspired in her life. "I've come in answer to your advertisement."

"Advertisement?"

I unfolded the newspaper in my right hand, belatedly noting a black smear on my gloves from the cheap ink. I spread the paper over the desk and pointed to the words.

OPERATIVES REQUIRED—for Pinkerton's National Detective Agency. Intelligence and tenacity required foremost. Generous salary commensurate with personal danger. Apply in person to Mr. Allan Pinkerton, Washington St. at Dearborn St., Chicago.

Impatiently, he asked, "I see. On whose behalf?"

"My own."

"You," he said, saturating the word with disbelief. "You want to apply for a position as a detective?"

"Yes, sir, I do."

"See, now, Miss…"

I supplied the name. "Mrs. Warne."

"Mrs. Warne," he said, his Scottish brogue extending the sounds of my name into an oddly appealing hum. "Women are…not encouraged to apply."

I jabbed at the newspaper with my finger again. "The advertisement doesn't say."

"Because it doesn't need to. I have never hired a female detective, and I don't mean to start today."

For just a moment, I faltered. Perhaps he really would turn me away. A rivulet of perspiration made the plunge from my shoulder blades down the small of my back, pooling under the lacing of my corset.

"Someone has to be first," I said with all the force I could muster.

Blessedly unaware—I hoped—of my physical situation, Pinkerton rubbed one freckled forearm absently and put on a look of concern.

"Brass tacks, ma'am. Detecting is dangerous work. Criminal. Violent. How could I place a delicate female such as yourself in harm's way? How could I explain such an outcome to your husband?"

"My husband is dead."

He blinked at that, but it took him only a moment to recover, and he mumbled the usual empty condolence. "I'm sorry for your loss, ma'am."

"You needn't be," I said bluntly. "One can only lose things of value. But I did not come to talk to you about Charlie. I came here for work."

A new light came into his eyes. It gave me hope. "Any children?" he asked.

"No."

"Other family?"

"Parents, once," I said. "We are no longer close."

"Did they disapprove of your marriage?"

"Quite the opposite. I did."

He laughed, a throaty rasp that made the room feel even warmer, though I was sure he understood that I hadn't spoken in jest. He put his ruddy hands down flat on the broad desk. "So now, with no husband and no children and no parents, alone in the world, you've taken it into your head to become the first lady detective."

"You make it sound like a whim, sir. Do I strike you as whimsical?"

"No, ma'am."

It was time to play all my cards. I'd given the matter extensive thought, ever since the moment the advertisement caught my eye; now was my chance to voice those thoughts to a man who could change my future.

"Sir, here is the crux of it. Women can go places men are not welcome. They can win the trust of other women, the wives and companions to whom the criminals have confided their crimes. They can travel in genteel circles to insinuate themselves with seeming gentlemen. I'm certain the men who work for you have many talents, but there is one thing none of them can do: be a woman."

There was a mix of consternation and admiration in his voice when he said, "All right, then. What do you propose?"

I was ready for the question and seized the opportunity with both hands.

"Give me a trial," I said. "If you have a case in your possession that needs solving, give it to me. If I cannot solve it, I go on my merry way. If I can, you employ me as the first female operative of your agency, and welcome."

He thought it over, still standing behind the desk. He tented his thick fingers together, fixing his gaze on me. I bore it.

After several long moments, he bent down and rummaged in one of the desk's countless drawers. I waited, finding the tension almost unbearable, listening to the soft rustle of paper and a low humming, until he selected something from the sheaf of papers and stood.

"Your first case, then, Mrs. Warne," he said, sliding an envelope across the desk.

CHAPTER THREE
BLUE EYES

The contents of that file had brought me to Joe Mulligan's on a night as hot as Hades, then into this close room with this dangerous blue-eyed man, a man who believed me willing to do the most tawdry and provocative things. Whatever the reasons, good or bad or both, I was trapped. A lamp on the desk cast a dim half-light. There was nothing else in the room but a chair, a bed, and us.

"How much will it take?" he asked, reaching into his trousers and producing a wad of cash from a pocket, staring at me expectantly.

I tried my best to brazen it out, letting my body remain still while my mind skipped and worked and fluttered. "That all depends, sir."

"On what? Get on with it!"

"Goodness," I said. A real prostitute would have used an oath. If I got out of here alive, I'd learn some. I forced a sauciness I didn't feel. "Most men in your position aren't in a rush."

I began to move, ever so slightly, to get between him and the door. If I needed to, I realized, I could run.

Unless he could run faster.

"I'm not most men," he said.

At that moment, I realized he was acting like a man who wanted me out of his company, not out of my clothes. I forced myself to reassess. He was standing as far from me as possible, his body rigid, counting bills out onto the wooden chair. After each bill, he glanced up appraisingly; seeing my lack of reaction, he sighed and added one more bill, then repeated the pattern.

I dropped my coy pretense and asked what was on my mind. "Exactly what do you want to pay me for?"

"I want you to go away. Take the cash and go away. Don't come back to this tavern tonight."

I was flooded with relief but more confused than ever. "Why?"

"Sweet Lord!" he shouted, and I jumped at the booming curse in the small room. Whatever his purpose with me, whoever he was, he was still frightening. "Will you take the money and go?"

"No!" I said. "I have business downstairs."

"Chicago is full of taverns. Do your filthy business elsewhere."

"It's not filthy," I said. "You don't understand. It's…noble, really."

"Oh, you certainly look noble." The voice dripped with sarcasm.

"You're part of Heck's gang," I snapped back. "How noble are you?"

"Shows what you know. I'm not a criminal. I'm…"

"Yes?"

He'd clammed up. So I looked at him intently again. Appraised him. Remembered. He'd stood out among the men in the bar below, and not just for his height and coldness. Only he was clean-shaven among the six. Also, he stood straighter than the rest, like a military man. My questions grew.

"Are you police?"

"No," he said, but with a bit of a lilt to it, and then it was all clear.

"You're a Pinkerton agent!" I shouted in disbelief.

He closed the distance between us with three long strides and clapped his hand over my mouth. I thought about biting him. If he'd really been a criminal, I would have. But in the circumstances, if we were going to be colleagues, sinking my teeth into his flesh wouldn't earn me a warm welcome.

I mumbled something into his hand instead. He put his finger to his lips to indicate silence, and at my vehement nod, he took the hand away.

"I'm a Pinkerton too," I said. "Well, almost."

"That's ridiculous. There are no female Pinkerton operatives. Who are you really?"

Rather than putting his mind at ease, I'd apparently made him even more suspicious. My story was implausible, of course, despite being true.

"I met with Pinkerton three days ago at the office on Washington," I said. "He showed me the file on Heck. I know about First Eagle. Five thousand dollars. We need to find it. Happy?"

He gave me a grim nod, clearly reluctant.

"Look," he said, "I need to get back downstairs. You've distracted me long enough."

"Why'd you grab me in the first place?"

"Why do you think? I was trying to stick close to him, and if he went off with you, I'd lose him. Which by now, I've probably done. You screwed this up big time."

"Me? It was you!"

We stared at each other for a moment in a standoff. I knew I'd have to be the one to break it, and I knew how. An idea had begun to form in my head. I wanted to see if it would withstand sharing.

"Let's work together," I said. "We both want the intelligence, right? Let me tell you my plan." A few minor adjustments to my original plan would accommodate his presence and even boost my—our?—chance of success.

In a few sentences, with a minimum of fanfare, I sketched out the best way to proceed. My role, his role, all of it. He listened, motionless.

After hearing me out, he nodded once and said, "All right."

A compliment for my quick thinking wouldn't have gone amiss, but I wasn't going to quibble. We were in it together now.

❧

Downstairs at Joe Mulligan's, walking straight up to Heck's table, we were greeted with raucous cheers.

"Back so quick, eh?" said Mustache.

"Wasn't for that," said Blue Eyes. "We're acquainted."

"I wanted my friend to introduce me to his friend," I said, shooting a not-so-shy glance Heck's way. Up close, he was almost good-looking, but there was a simpering edge to him that I didn't like, and I was glad he seemed already half in the bag. Things would go much faster.

"Well, how do you do, my dear," Heck said, patting the cushion next to him. I slipped in and laid my fingertips lightly on his arm.

"I'm quite well, thank you," I said, "but nearly dying of thirst."

"Tim," he said to Blue Eyes, "two more."

"Yes, Boss," he replied and was off to the bar. My thoughts trailed after him—Was Tim his real name? Our conversation upstairs hadn't included names—but I forced myself back to the task at hand. It was time for me to resume the role of slattern, and I remembered again just how much depended on my ability to inhabit the woman I was pretending to be. Whether or not I was ready, this was my chance.

I leaned and preened and teased. I inched and edged over the red leather banquette until the full length of my thigh pressed against Heck's, so close I could feel the heat of his skin. When I shut my eyes for a moment, I could see the exact pattern of the crosshatched scars on the back of his left hand. Most importantly, I giggled operatically at his jokes, most of which weren't terribly funny to start with and became less so.

Blue Eyes returned with a round of drinks, then another. This was an essential part of the gambit, but also a dangerous one. I tried to sip slowly. I spilled one drink on purpose. Once, I switched my nearly full glass for Heck's nearly empty one. Even with such tricks, I could still feel the effects of the drink. I began to sense a vague tickle behind my eyes, almost a vibration in the bone, an interesting but distracting sensation. If our moment to strike didn't come soon, I'd be too dizzy to seize it. I wanted to look up and warn my accomplice but couldn't risk it. He knew what he had to do, and so did I. And we knew what would happen if we failed. At this point, no signals or glances would change any of that.

I listened for his voice, though, and could hear him remarking time and again how late it was getting and how any man in search of serious fun tonight would have to look somewhere else than this joint full of priests and princesses. Bit by bit, I could tell, his nudges were having the desired effect. The other members of the gang were slipping away. At last, another hour in, only we three remained.

"And that's why they called him the North Pole," slurred Heck, now utterly tight, and it was time to put the next part of my plan into action.

Blue Eyes knew it too. I saw him lean across the table and tap his glass against the wood, saying, "Heck, I'd like to do you a favor."

The smaller man perked up slightly, and the moment his attention was on my coconspirator, I snaked my hand into his coat pocket and eased out his wallet. I didn't have the lightest touch, but he was too far gone to be wary.

Still wearing an empty smile, I let the wallet fall to the floor next to my foot and guided it gently underneath the booth. I kept my eyes on Heck and saw no reaction, no awareness. Blue Eyes was saying, "I'd like to lend you my hotel room for…your entertainment."

The smaller man turned to me then, placed his hand confidently where my hip became thigh, and said, "Shaaall we?"

This was it. This was the moment. I had to play it, without getting distracted by the terrifying prospect of what happened if I played it wrong. His wallet wasn't the only thing he wore under his coat: on the far side of his body, there was no mistaking the shape of a holstered gun.

"One small matter first," I said.

"Oh?"

"Payment."

"My dear friend's attentions don't come cheap," Blue Eyes said, "but I assure you, every penny will be well spent."

"Oh, I got plenty of pennies," Heck slurred, patting his pocket. It took a tense five count for him to realize he was patting nothing. He swore, but there was little energy in it. "Aw, I'm sorry, honey."

"Don't have to be sorry," I said, leaning close, trailing my finger along his collar.

"Another night, I'd…"

"Tonight," I said. "Don't you want it to be tonight?"

"Aw, of course, but…"

"Smart man like you," I said. "I'm sure you've got more than you carry. Right?"

"Yeah."

"So all you need to do is get to where that is."

"Yeah."

His liquor-soaked mind was a mule that wouldn't get moving. But I was afraid to push any harder than I already had. Especially given that gun.

"I know it's a hassle," I said, "but I'd sure make it worth your while. If you could scare up the funds. Do you think you can do that for me?"

He considered it. We waited.

At long last, he said, "I sure do."

We pretended we hadn't been holding our breath. It was all

I could do to keep my eyes down, but I didn't want to give the game away.

"You come with me." He gestured to Blue Eyes. "And you," he said to me, "stay there."

"I'll be right here waiting," I said with a broad wink.

They made their way out, slowly. Heck stumbled twice on only eight stairs. The second time, Blue Eyes tilted his shoulder into just the right place for the shorter man to lean on, making himself indispensable. The sight filled me with hope. I watched them until they were gone. I waited ten minutes and then went home.

All according to plan.

Well after midnight, I peeled off my shirtwaist, my corset, and the thoroughly damp chemise underneath, which clung to my skin as if pasted there. With a half-filled basin of water lugged up from the kitchen, I scrubbed myself with a rough, wet cloth over and over again. Limbs, chest, neck. Whether it was the smell or the feeling I was trying to scrub off, I couldn't rightly say. Either way, my skin felt raw and ruined, and only exhaustion drove me to stop.

I lay perfectly still on my narrow bed, the only furniture in the cramped, bare room, the cotton sheets unpleasantly warm on my bare back. The windowless room was a boon in winter, I tried to remind myself. But by the time this winter came, unless today's gambit had worked, I'd be on the street. Even Mrs. Borowski's sainted patience would run out sometime. There were no cheaper boardinghouses in Chicago, and I had no stake to move elsewhere. I was a bad cook, an incompetent lady's maid, an impatient shop clerk. I'd already applied to every possible position appropriate for a lady. Only the inappropriate ones remained.

And I wouldn't know until morning whether we had truly been successful. Fatigue and suspense were poor bedfellows. But I had to believe my chances were better with Blue Eyes than without him. Weren't they? And, in any case, wasn't it too late to change the bet I'd made? It seemed we had carried off the plan in style. There was every reason to believe he had executed the last few steps just as capably.

Perhaps I would have been better off continuing my bath, such as it was. I lay awake most of the night anyway.

❧

I had no idea what time Pinkerton would report to his office in the morning, so I went at seven o'clock, figuring I might arrive first. I waited for half an hour in the street, shifting my weight from foot to foot as I rehearsed, before I saw him turning the corner a block away and heading in my direction.

He wasn't alone.

As the two men walked up, the taller one wouldn't meet my eyes. He looked more reputable than he had last night. Out of his criminal's disguise, his near-military bearing was more pronounced, and his ice blue eyes were less forbidding in the bright light of day. When I wasn't terrified of him, he was even handsome. Today, he looked every inch the operative.

He also looked downright cheerful. As did Pinkerton. For the first time in a very long time, I had a feeling that everything was, at last, going to be all right.

Which lasted only until Pinkerton spoke.

"Mrs. Warne! I'm afraid you've gone and missed your chance," said Pinkerton, sounding not at all regretful. "The good Mr. Bellamy here has succeeded already at your task."

"Has he?" I asked frostily.

"Found every penny of Heck Venable's stash. With a right smart plan too," Pinkerton said. "Plenty of drink and a well-timed pick-pocketing."

"Right smart," I agreed. "And did he tell you whose plan it was?"

Now, Bellamy's eyes came up. I could see him calculating, trying to figure out whether he could get away with it. He read my face, and I read his. I saw the moment he surrendered.

"I hadn't gotten to that part of the story yet," Bellamy said.

"Faith, there's more?" Pinkerton asked.

"There's more," I said. "Let's continue this conversation in your office, please, Boss."

Pinkerton looked a bit startled at my forwardness and looked to Bellamy, who nodded with reluctance.

Upstairs, I told the tale from my point of view, giving him the full story of how the evening unfolded, leaving nothing out. I didn't try to minimize Bellamy's role, but I didn't defer to him. I deserved credit, and I took it in full.

As I spoke, Pinkerton listened, his face betraying nothing. I might have been a genius or a chowderhead. I resisted the urge to embellish just to get a rise out of him; the tale was too important.

When I'd concluded at last, he asked, "And is that how it was, Tim?"

"More or less." I could see the tension in the other man's jaw. "I was going to tell you. She helped."

"Helped?" I squeaked. I took a moment to collect myself and spoke more calmly. "The way I see it, it was my plan entirely."

"However you see it," Bellamy responded, "you would have failed without me."

"And you without me."

Pinkerton laughed—a booming, sonorous laugh that bounced off the walls of his office—and slapped his hand against the desk. Relief flooded my body like a drug.

"I don't believe it!" he said. "What a team. I didn't plan to have you try it the same night, but it could hardly have turned out better. Money found, case solved. We've earned our fee from First Eagle. That spells success to me. And I've a promise to deliver on."

Pinkerton thrust his workingman's hand in my direction. Gladly, I shook it.

"Welcome to my agency, Mrs. Warne," he said.

I was grinning from ear to ear. Tim Bellamy wasn't.

CHAPTER FOUR

REAL STORIES ARE SHORT

After my first success—no less sweet for being shared—I began my training as an operative. Pinkerton undertook my education directly. We met in his office, the two of us, day after day. He impressed upon me the importance of writing down everything we could find about a criminal and getting a photograph if at all possible to help in identification. He told me stories, so many stories, of near misses with thieves and vagabonds, demonstrating that there was often only a hairbreadth between success and failure. Some days, I felt honored that he would devote so much time to my training personally; other days, I felt he was so uncertain of me, so worried that I was incompetent, that he didn't trust me to make a single move by myself. If I failed, he'd look a fool, and he didn't strike me as a man who tolerated foolishness.

Some days, he would leave me alone in the room with a stack of case files and the single instruction, "Read." From hours of this, I learned the kind of work that we were doing: hunting bank robbers and exposing counterfeiters, yes, but also interviewing domestics accused of stealing from their owners, gathering evidence for court cases, and once an operative even stood guard at a slaughterhouse after the owner had received an anonymous threat. I felt bad for the man who had drawn that duty. His name was Taylor, and his handwriting was the worst of all the operatives'. Bellamy's case notes were written in a cramped but clear style. Pinkerton's notes,

where they were present, fell into one of two types: a fluid hand
that appeared hastily written, the ink so light on the page some
letters were skipped; and a neater, textbook hand, which I assumed
to be that of a secretary.

The case files were labeled by client, and it wasn't until I had
read a dozen cases in a row labeled *Illinois Central Railroad* that I
realized they must be our biggest client by far. There were ten more
cases with the same label right behind them, with a range of crimes
and conspiracies we had helped investigate or foil. Robberies and
petty thefts, injuries and trespasses, on the trains and in the yards.
DeForest and Paretsky were most often assigned to these, but at
one time or another, it seemed every operative must have served.
I made a note in my mind that, no doubt, my turn would come
as well. Then I flipped to the next case file, labeled *Illinois Southern
Bank*, to read about something new.

I learned the names of fellow operatives from these files, but
Pinkerton only introduced me to the men themselves on the rare
occasion, clearly always by chance. There was never an organized
introduction to the full roster of detectives. One day, I asked why.

"We don't have roll call here," said Pinkerton, clearly suppress-
ing a chuckle at my expense. "We don't have meetings. Most of
us work alone and cooperate when we need to. Besides, some of
these men are deep in with their targets, who think them to be
criminals—wouldn't do to have them spotted leaving the private
dick's building, would it?"

"No," I agreed. "But how will I know other agents when I see
them?" I didn't need to specify that I didn't want a repeat of my
awkward introduction to Tim Bellamy. Nearly a month into my
employment, I hadn't seen him again, and I imagined that pleased
both of us.

"Good question. There's a sign." He rose from his chair and
took the long walk around the desk to my side, then perched on

the desk's edge. He laid his hand on his thigh, palm up. After a moment, he pinched his thumb and forefinger together in a quick motion, then released them and turned the hand palm down. He had me practice until I could do the same, seated or standing, even while carrying on a conversation. It had to look meaningless.

"Now," he said, "the next thing you need to learn."

"Yes, Boss."

"How to lie."

"And how do I do that?"

"Like anything else: practice. So. Lie to me."

"About what?" I asked.

"Doesn't matter," he said. "Tell me where you come from. Tell me what you ate for supper on Wednesday. Tell me the worst thing that's ever happened to you. I just want to see you try."

I folded my hands in my lap, deliberating. His suggestion of the worst thing that had ever happened to me got caught in my mental engine, and I almost opened my mouth to tell him about the child, but I stopped myself. He wanted a lie, I'd give him a lie.

"For my tenth birthday, my mother bought me the most beautiful dress," I said, letting my hand linger on my neck as if remembering a feeling. "It was lilac satin, trimmed with ribbons and lace, and it had a full skirt that swirled when I spun around. I thought it made me look like a princess. I wore it day and night for a week. When she finally made me take it off, I cried."

"What happened to it?" he asked.

"It got too small," I said, "so I gave it to a cousin."

Pinkerton eyed me skeptically. His gaze was penetrating even on an average day, so when he gave you his full attention, it was remarkable. Like two lamps shining straight on you through a pitch-black night. I could feel it in my blood.

"Not a good lie," he said. "Too many words. Real stories are short. Try again."

"When I was ten years old, my mother taught me to read, so when I bothered her, she could hand me a book and be done with me."

The skeptical glare again. "You're leaving something out."

"Yes," I said. "She also did it because a handsome young man had offered to teach me. He played Brutus to my father's Julius Caesar at a theater in Atlanta on a three-month engagement. She didn't want him anywhere near me, so she was compelled to take over the lessons herself."

"And she told you her reasons?"

"No. But I understood."

"You were a child."

I shrugged and met his gaze. "Nonetheless."

"Technicalities," he said. "You're trying to trick me with minor details. That's not the kind of skill you need to develop."

The child was on my mind again, as was Paul. But Pinkerton never would have believed that story, true though it was. I fought the memories down, wrestling with them, packing them away again. "Then tell me what you want to hear," I said.

"Tell me how Charlie died."

Of course he remembered the name. What did the man ever forget?

"Misadventure," I said.

"I'm sure that's true enough," he said. "But tell me more. The truth or a lie, as you choose."

I stood from my chair then, intending to walk about the room. Nothing was riding on this lie, I told myself. Yet I was so tense, I nearly quivered.

Pinkerton grabbed me by the shoulders. "Sit down," he said.

I did, instantly. My heart was galloping. He hadn't been rough with me, but others had, and my body reacted in reflex. This too I would have to train away.

"When a criminal asks you a question, you can't go for a stroll. You need to be able to look someone full in the face and speak a convincing fiction. So tell me, Mrs. Warne. What happened to your husband?"

"He gambled the wrong money with the wrong man," I said bluntly. "The money was someone else's, his cheating was clumsy, and the man was armed. A schoolboy in short pants could have foreseen the outcome."

Pinkerton looked at me for a long moment and said, "I believe you, Mrs. Warne."

"As you should," I said. "It's the truth."

"I know," he said. "Now. When did he die?"

"Six months ago," I said. "The nineteenth of March."

This too was the truth, and Pinkerton nodded that he accepted it as such. "Did you see his dead body?"

"I did."

"Was it your first?"

"It was," I said, "but as a detective, I expect it will not be my last."

"And how did it strike you? Seeing a loved one—at least, someone you'd known so well—with his light gone out?"

I considered my words carefully. The truth wasn't the only option, but it was the easiest. Pinkerton was right. I needed practice.

"What I saw was no longer him. He was gone. The shell he left behind bore him some resemblance, but there was no mistaking what had changed."

"Did you cry?"

"Not then."

"When?"

"Later," I said. "When I was alone."

"How many times?"

"Once."

"There it is," he said, folding his arms. "There's the lie."

"Based on what?"

"On women," said Pinkerton. "Emotional creatures. Even you, Mrs. Warne"—here, he held up a finger, pointed straight at my face—"and I can tell you're about to protest that you're no ordinary woman. In some ways, you are unusual. That does not make you immune."

"And yet," I said, holding his gaze without flinching. "I cried once when he died. That's true." I had cried many times after that, but it was never about Charlie, only the mess he'd left me in.

Pinkerton still looked skeptical.

I went on, "You remember I told you I'd never wanted to marry him in the first place."

"So why did you?"

"My parents insisted." I leaned back in the chair, trying to appear casual, as if none of this bothered me. In my mind, I replaced the real scene with a civil one, a nest of snakes with a simpler story. "They wanted me married off, and he was a charming young man. They thought he had money. He didn't. Or, rather, sometimes he did, but he lost it again."

Pinkerton turned the full force of his attention on me once more.

"Is that all?" he asked. "That can't be all."

"They wanted me married. Charlie was willing to marry me."

"No," he said. He shifted his weight but did not rise. "That story doesn't make sense."

"Everything I said was true."

"Still and all. You're leaving something out."

"Perhaps," I said. "Is that a lie?"

"Omission and commission alike, Mrs. Warne."

I was about to protest that the game of truth or lie didn't allow for the possibility of something in the middle, but before the words got out, the office door opened.

Two men entered. The shorter one was a fashion plate: his frock coat and trousers were clearly expensive, with a smart blue cravat knotted at the neck, and his black mustache was carefully waxed. The second man was of average height, painfully thin, with the palest skin I'd ever seen and close-cropped white-blond hair. He resembled nothing so much as a dead man, halfway between a skeleton and a ghost.

"Boss!" said the fashion plate to Pinkerton, who welcomed him with a smile.

"Mrs. Warne," said Pinkerton, "it's your lucky day. You get to meet two more colleagues. This is Graham DeForest. One of the more experienced operatives here and certainly the most amicable."

"At your service," said the shorter man with a broad smile, bowing low over my hand. Up close, he was devastatingly handsome, possibly the best-looking man I'd ever seen, with a strong scent of cedar cologne. His warm brown eyes caught my gaze and held it.

"Pleasure to meet you," I replied.

"And this is Jack Mortenson. Been with us just a couple of months but sharp as a tack and then some."

The ghost inclined his head to me but didn't speak. I wondered if he could.

DeForest said, "Well, I for one certainly approve of your new hire, Boss. It's delightful to have such a lovely ornament in the office."

I chose my reply carefully. "I hope as we work together you find me more than ornamental."

"I have no doubt of it, ma'am," he said. "Didn't mean to offend." He seemed sincere enough; I heard no sign of irony.

Mortenson spoke up. His voice was higher than I expected, reedy and thin, with a faint drawl I couldn't quite place right away. Tennessee, perhaps, or Arkansas. "Boss, we've got a report for you."

"Report away."

"Information not for…listening ears."

Pinkerton, still perched on the desk edge, looked back and forth between my face and Mortenson's. He didn't consider long before saying, "Mrs. Warne, if you wouldn't mind. We'll start again tomorrow."

"Of course, Boss," I said and refused to let the insult show on my face. "Good day to you, gentlemen."

"I'll live in hope of seeing you soon, Mrs. Warne," DeForest called out as I left.

I marked him down in my mental ledger as a ladies' man, one to be wary of. Even if I were in the mood for romance, I'd be a fool to entangle myself with a fellow operative. Pinkerton had said nothing on the subject, but he didn't need to. I had to choose my time and place to be a woman.

The door closed behind me, and I wondered who'd closed it.

But as I went to set foot on the first step down to the street, I paused. They'd begun talking again already, clearly not waiting to be sure I'd gone. The door was thick enough to muffle their words but not to mask them completely. Curious, I slid back over to the door without lifting my feet and set my ear firmly against the wood, cupping my hands to block out any other sounds.

"…happy to help her in any way needed," DeForest was saying.

"Thank you for that kind offer," said Pinkerton, sounding amused. "I suspected you'd be eager."

"She'll need a lot of help, that's for sure. Will a girl be any use at all?" asked Mortenson's high-pitched whisper.

Pinkerton said, "Absolutely."

"How do we even know?" asked Mortenson. "She helped Bellamy with Heck Venable, but you haven't assigned her to a case since, have you?"

Before then, I wasn't sure I was the subject under discussion; now, there could be no doubt.

"She's in training," said Pinkerton.

"Is that what she's in?"

My fingers tensed, wanting to become fists, but I forced them back into the shape I needed.

"What do you mean by that?"

"Forget I said anything," Mortenson said after a pause.

"No, explain yourself, sir." Pinkerton's brogue became a growl.

"Gentlemen, gentlemen," DeForest said with what sounded like forced cheer. "We have an important report to make, so let's make it, eh?"

"All right. Get on with it," said Pinkerton, and I heard the sharp echo of his shoes against the wood as he strode to the far side of the desk and the groan and squeak as he lowered himself into the chair.

"The gap-toothed bastard said he was chasing runaway slaves, but there's no way Nestor isn't a free man. Been living in Chicago three years now. So we've started gathering the evidence…"

I didn't stay to listen to the rest. I descended the stairs gingerly, placing each foot as near to the wall as possible, toe first and then heel, to avoid making noise. I was an operative now. Listening at doors was part and parcel of the work. Still, I regretted listening at this one.

CHAPTER FIVE
THE PINKERTON CODE

I made my way back to the boardinghouse by the most direct route, along the river. The breeze was welcome. The stench was not. But unfortunately, there was no separating the two. A week had passed without rain, so I could walk close to the river without risking my shoes to mud. I did refrain from breathing in too deeply.

This early in the day, the riverside was not yet bustling, but there was enough activity to occupy my gaze as I walked: a barge stacked with limestone headed to the stone works, a line of Irishmen wending their way toward the railroad office on Madison, hoping for a day's work as track laborers, and a lone man with a rag and a ladder who looked to be scouring the edifices of the shops on Lake Street, one by one.

Chicago had been Charlie's choice, not mine. Marriage had only replaced my parents' edicts with my husband's. But now that my choices were my own, in large part, Chicago seemed as good a place as any. The city was wild and strong. Besides, it would take money to leave.

For Charlie's purposes, when we'd arrived a few years before, fresh off an unsuccessful run in Boston, it had the right balance of law and lawlessness. Midnight games of faro were unlikely to be interrupted by the meager police force, and even the worst disputes, the ones that spilled out into the street, rarely erupted into gunfire. We were neither the Wild West nor the puritanical East but a meeting in the middle. The canal, the railroads—everything came to us here or at least passed through. Wheat, cows, lumber. And criminals, I supposed, thinking of the Pinkerton case files, which named wrongdoers from all over.

Pinkerton. I couldn't forget what I'd heard through the closed door at the top of the stairs. Trained by my parents both with and without intent, I was accustomed to sizing men up in an instant, reading their faces, guessing at their motives. Had I guessed incorrectly at Pinkerton's? Had he hired me only as a prelude to seduction?

The idea seemed ridiculous. In a month of days, he'd given no sign of affection, no indication his feelings for me were anything beyond those of an employer for his newest, untested employee. If he'd wanted to put his hands on me, he'd had a score of chances. Instead, we sat chastely with that enormous desk between us. He barely seemed to register that I was a woman at all, let alone a desirable one. No, that wasn't it.

But I also knew the truth was no defense.

Part of me wanted to turn right around, march back there, and address Mortenson face-to-face, berate him for his crude assumptions. Part of me wanted to crawl into bed and disappear under a blanket, ashamed anyone could think so ill of me. I was uncertain and confused, but as I walked, the emotions settled into a low, simmering anger. At the end of my walk, ascending the boardinghouse steps, I was only angry.

I thought of my father. Making his living as a professional actor and small-time con artist, he was given to broad pronouncements and aphorisms, which he delivered in his most formal, pompous voice. I had followed his rules and codes as a child, but once away from his influence, I realized they'd done me far more harm than good. Yet, like a broken clock, he was right on occasion. *Find your emotion and use it, Kate.* I only had to decide how to use the anger, to turn it to my advantage.

I entered the house and shut the door behind me. Mrs. Borowski was in the back kitchen, an apron over her blue serge skirt and her blond hair pulled back in twin plaits. She bent over the knife-scarred worktable, a pot of potato filling at one hand and a huge wad of white dough at the other. I didn't bother asking if she needed help. I washed my hands at the sink and sat down next to her, brushing my palms with flour, and pitched in.

"You do not need to," she said without looking up, "anymore."

There was never enough money, even when Charlie was alive. For years, I'd been squirreling it away in jars and pockets, and thank goodness. Even that had run out in June. But after her housekeeper quit suddenly, Mrs. Borowski had agreed to let me keep the room a few more months in exchange for my help cleaning and cooking. Since I was barely competent at either, it had truly been a magnificent gesture on her part. I owed her more than money.

"I'll make the ones I eat," I said. "You know how much I love your pierogi."

"You flatter me."

"A bit," I said. "In hopes you'll make them more often."

She made a grunting noise of dismissal, but I knew she enjoyed the compliment. I thought I saw a trace of a smile on her round, warm face.

"So I'll have another check for you tomorrow," I said. I'd signed over my first two paychecks in their entirety as well. After this one, I'd start earning for myself.

"Thank you. Employment is going well?"

I sighed as I pinched dough into a ball and flattened the ball into a circle. She'd made five pierogi in the time it took me to get started on one. "Well enough."

"That is good."

"Although…" I spooned a dab of filling onto the dough and brought the edges together, pinching them to enclose it.

She tapped the back of my hand with a thick finger. "Harder," she said. "And remember the water. Or it will leak."

Dipping my fingertips into a small bowl of water on the table between us, I corrected my technique.

"Is there a problem with the work?"

"Not exactly. There's a..." I searched for the right word. "A rumor."

"About?"

"Someone in the office suspects I'm involved with the boss. In a love affair."

She made a gruff noise. "You are not, of course."

"No."

"Then you shouldn't worry. Truth will out."

"Yes, but it makes me angry." As I gave voice to the emotion, it grew. "If one thinks so, I'm sure many of them think so. It's insulting, and it's wrong. If they think he hired me just to make love to me, they'll never accept me as a detective." To my surprise, I could feel tears prickling behind my eyes. I hadn't realized quite how upsetting it was to be doubted. I'd wanted the job for the money, but now that I had it, there was more. I wanted to do the job and be respected. Besides, if it became too much trouble to keep me, no doubt, Pinkerton would let me go.

"Then prove yourself." Her voice was dispassionate, though I didn't doubt that she cared. She was just calmer. I needed to emulate that still core, I realized. I felt too strongly. Always had, though I'd learned to hide it from the beginning.

"I know. And I will. But Pinkerton hasn't put me on a case."

"Have you asked him to?"

I considered it as I wet my fingertips and sealed the filling inside another dumpling. "Well, no."

"Dear, sweet Kate," said Mrs. Borowski. "Don't you know this? You have to ask for the things you want."

"That's how I got the position!" I said. "I didn't just sit on my hands, did I, and wait to be saved?"

"No. But now you need to do the work. And I think I have some things that might help you."

She stood and dusted the flour off her hands, then rinsed them in the sink, and I followed suit. She motioned for me to follow her, out of the formal dining room and down the narrow hall, to a door I'd never seen opened. She unlocked it with a key from her belt.

We had to duck to enter, but inside was a surprisingly large storeroom. It smelled stale, with a whiff of mouse droppings. One wall was lined with shelves, and the highest shelf held a series of nearly identical boxes. Mrs. Borowski traced her fingers on each box as she walked by, her wide hips swaying. Each box was labeled with a room number and a date. She pointed to one, high up, and said, "That one."

The room was 2B, and the date was three years in the past. I was not tall, but I was the taller of us two, and I understood I should reach up for the box. Loose, light things slid around inside, and I set it down at her feet. We crouched down together, and she lifted the lid.

At first, all I saw were a woman's delicate undergarments, a tangle of clearly expensive silk and lace. There must have been a dozen different pieces or more, each lovelier than the last. My breath caught at the fragility of a gorgeous edge of French lace, a pink so pale it was barely a color. She moved aside the corsets and pantalets, gently but firmly, and retrieved a beautiful pair of wrist-length gloves, an eggshell silk.

"These. I doubt she'll come back for them. Part of a disguise one day?"

She handed them to me. The mother-of-pearl buttons at the wrists were cool against my fingertips.

Were they a dead woman's gloves? A rich woman's, perhaps, carelessly left because there was always money to buy more? It didn't matter. They were mine now. I slid one over my right hand and spread out my fingers, which seemed longer and more elegant already under the veil of smooth silk. A thrill shot through me.

"Yes," I said. "These are wonderful. Thank you."

Armed with the garments of a woman I would never know, accepting the help of the only woman I truly knew and trusted, I was ready to become the woman I wanted to be.

The next day, my training included a direct education on the principles of the Pinkerton Code. A violation of any single one of the principles would be grounds for dismissal, Pinkerton told me. I knew the knowledge was essential, but at the same time, I could barely sit still to listen. *Pinkerton agents accept no bribes*, he said. *We never compromise with criminals. We work with local law enforcement agencies whenever possible, apprising them of our plans in a timely fashion. We do not investigate cases of divorce or other matters that might invite scandal upon the clients who hire us. When there is a reward associated with a case, we do not accept it, either as an agency or individuals. We keep our clients informed on an ongoing basis.*

On the final rule, he elaborated, "Never forget the client. We do not investigate for the thrill of the hunt or to follow a hunch or to impress ourselves with our cleverness. We investigate to solve the question that the client has put before us."

"Yes," I said. "I understand."

"Repeat back all six principles."

I did as he asked, rattling them off one after the other with no omission or hesitation, but I knew that absorbing the information wasn't really the test. The test was whether I knew how to apply any of this when it truly counted. And it was time to find that out.

"Any questions?" he asked.

"One for sure. When are you going to assign me to a case?"

He hesitated. "I've been waiting for the right one to come along."

I thought about what Mrs. Borowski had said. The bold leap I'd taken to get hired was only the beginning. If I was going to make a real success of myself, I would have to be bold again and again.

"Boss, I think I'm ready."

"I see. And your opinion is the one that matters?"

"No, only yours, I know," I said evenly. "But I went into my first case with no training at all. I think a month of preparation will do for my second. Let me start."

I watched him closely as he formed his response. He didn't shift in his seat or twist his hands, but I knew he was uncomfortable. "It may take a while for me to find something."

"I'm certain you'll be able to do so."

"Well, until I know you're able to protect yourself, I just wouldn't feel right about it," he said.

"That can be arranged."

He eyed me coolly. I couldn't tell whether he took my confidence as a point for or against my case. It didn't matter in any event.

"Arrange it," he said.

I knew what I had to do next.

§

His face perfectly still and calm above the knot of his vibrant, striped cravat, Graham DeForest braced himself next to a tall aspen. He raised the gun with both hands and closed one eye. "Steady," he said. "Never rush."

The tip of the pistol hovered in the air. I covered my ears. He fired, and the dangling paper target on the far-off pine seemed to explode.

When I'd asked him for the lesson, I had braced for an attempt at seduction, assuming I'd need to parry one to get what I wanted. I had prepared many things to say, firm words of rejection that would be clear but not hurtful, but I was glad not to need any of them. When he put his hands on me, it was neither untoward nor unpleasant. He really did seem focused on the lesson, and he was a good teacher.

"Like this," he said, folding my hands over the gun, pressing my finger against the trigger. When I fired the pistol and my body rocked back from the recoil, his body absorbed some of the shock, making it easier to remain standing.

It would be hard to say who was more surprised after my very first shot hit the paper target, not in the center, but rather close, considering.

DeForest took the gun to reload. I had brought Charlie's tiny Philadelphia Deringer. On the day he died, he'd left it behind by accident, a mistake a loving wife would have regretted. In any case, I had it now.

"Thank you," I said.

"For what?"

"Helping me learn. Other men in your position might not be so kind."

"Mrs. Warne," he said, not looking at me as he reloaded, "I want you to know that I'm on your side."

"Are there sides?"

"You know there are," he said, shooting me a sharp glance for good measure. "For or against women as operatives generally, and you in particular. Mortenson doesn't like you. Of course, Mortenson doesn't like anyone. And Bellamy thinks women are fragile little china dolls. If you're not taking tea at the Tremont House in a crinoline, he thinks you're doing a disservice to your sex. Taylor doesn't care, though it's a good thing his wife doesn't know, because she would. Dalessandro's been assigned to the paper factory for so long, he probably doesn't even know you exist. I don't think I need to go on."

I said, "But you're on my side?"

"Sure," he said. "I like people who shake things up."

He handed me the loaded gun, and I took aim once more.

Guiding and teaching me in this way, DeForest reminded me of Paul: good with his hands, easy to talk to. Of course, Paul had grown thin at the end, pale and wasted. I'd had to help him move the heavier props and scrims so he could keep his illness secret. A weak stagehand would be instantly dismissed. The two men looked nothing alike, but there was a deeper resemblance.

After I'd emptied the pistol of its bullets, we went back to the office together. I wanted to tell Pinkerton, right away, that I'd removed his objection. I needed to know whether this would satisfy him or whether he would quickly manufacture another one to replace it.

As we entered the office upstairs, DeForest put his hand on my back to usher me through the door. His fingers snaked around the side of my waist. I was sure it looked quite intimate, and I didn't care for it. I shrugged him off, trying not to make a scene. Funny how he'd been nothing but a gentleman when we were alone. I read the room quickly—two operatives I didn't recognize were deep in conversation with Mortenson, who didn't look up, and Bellamy, whose glare confirmed that he'd seen what happened and didn't approve.

The boss himself looked up from his papers, read the set of my jaw, and said, "Let's talk in my office."

Once the three of us were behind the closed door, I said, "You said I could go on a case when I could defend myself. I can do that now. DeForest'll tell you."

"She's a natural," said DeForest, winking at me. "You can send her to the woods with me anytime."

I winced at his suggestiveness and hastened to clarify. "We were shooting targets in the woods; that's what he means."

"She's a dab hand with a gun," said DeForest.

"You can defend yourself?" Pinkerton asked me.

"Yes."

With no delay, he reached out toward my side, where the gun hung in the holster, and I had only a moment to react. So I did. I pulled the gun away before his fingers could close around it, and holding it by the barrel, I swung the grip down against his wrist. He yelped in surprise.

Without looking away from him, I returned the gun to the holster smoothly. Pinkerton rubbed his wrist. I knew it would sting for a few minutes but leave no damage or mark. It had been my mother's favorite punishment for that reason.

I heard DeForest chuckle gently. I very much wanted to answer with a grin, but instead, I turned to the boss, waiting.

Pinkerton looked neither impressed nor angry. If he was surprised that I took the bold step of striking him bodily, despite our very different positions, he was covering it exceptionally well.

He folded his arms. I folded mine. There was no need for me to ask the question aloud; he already knew it. He looked me over with his burning gaze, reading my resolve in my braced stance and raised chin.

"Very well then," he said. "Tomorrow. Look rich."

CHAPTER SIX

THE SNAKE RING

The next day, I approached the office in the early morning, before the heat of the day had settled on the city. I wore the same claret gown I'd worn for my exploits at Joe Mulligan's, with a fichu patterned with small blue flowers to make the neckline more modest. An additional petticoat belled out the skirt, a straw bonnet artfully crowned my neatly bound hair, and the rich silk gloves given me by Mrs. Borowski provided exactly the right finishing touch. I was beginning to suspect that the main difference between rich women and whores lay mostly in the accessories.

I was lost in thought—What case would I be assigned? What would happen if I didn't succeed?—but slowed my steps when I noticed a man with a heavy beard and a cheap, worn sack coat lingering in the entryway.

I could try to ignore him, but he was right at the door, blocking my progress. He seemed enthralled with something in his pocket. I thought about circling the block once to avoid him and see if he'd cleared out by the time I returned, but I didn't want to be late, and I didn't imagine anyone seriously dangerous would linger in the entryway of the best-known detective agency in the United States. Even the most foolish criminals would have better sense.

Striding toward the door, I cleared my throat to suggest he move aside.

The man turned and caught my eye, and I knew him instantly under the disguise.

"On the job, Mr. Bellamy?" I asked.

His icy blue eyes narrowed. "Hello."

"Mrs. Warne," I said, though I knew it was impossible that he didn't recognize me.

"Yes."

When he said nothing more, I added, "You may have heard I'm starting my next case today. I hope to secure the evidence quickly and return in triumph."

He answered me with a derisive laugh.

I decided to address the matter directly. "You have no confidence in me, then?"

"None at all."

"Mr. Pinkerton seems to disagree with you."

"I think he's made a mistake."

"Oh, do you?" I decided not to be riled. "And have you told him so?"

"I have," replied Bellamy coolly. "Women are too delicate to do what our position requires. You might skate by for a while, but there will be a reckoning. When the day comes and you're called to perform an extraordinary task, you'll find yourself unable."

"I will not."

"Oh, I don't doubt you have the desire," he said with something in his tone that approached kindness, making it far more insulting. He lectured me as he would a child.

I thought about what DeForest had said. Well, I would not be taking tea in a crinoline, not for Bellamy's sake or anyone else's. I was here to work.

"Then what do you doubt?"

"Your strength. You imagine you have the wherewithal to act, but our mettle is tested beyond imagination. In our service, a man has to be willing to do many things."

"Ah, there you're wrong!" I said, eager to interrupt.

"Am I?"

"Willingness to do many things will never be enough. We must be willing to do *all* things."

The dark beard and unruly hair surrounding his face made his icy blue eyes stand out even more brightly. He stared me down. I didn't move. "You talk a good game. You convinced him with your talk, I take it. But you don't convince me."

"Perhaps someday, I shall."

He shrugged.

I knew a lost cause when I saw one, and besides, Pinkerton was waiting. I brushed past Bellamy on my way indoors. He even smelled like a genuine criminal, with an undercurrent of dirt and liquor. It was an excellent disguise, truly. I would never give him the satisfaction of telling him so.

Upstairs, Pinkerton perched on the corner of his desk, with Mortenson leaning back in a chair. They fell silent when I came in.

I said to Pinkerton, "Why is Tim Bellamy lurking in the doorway downstairs?"

"He's working, Mrs. Warne."

"Yes, but what is he—"

"Mrs. Warne. Focus. Let us review your case, not his, please."

"Yes, Boss."

Four hours later, I entered a small dry goods shop not far from the Clark Street Bridge. I lifted the hem of my skirt out wide as I stepped over the doorframe, raising my chin over my shoulder. If I had learned nothing else from my mother—and it was possible that

I hadn't—I had learned how to swan about in a full-skirted gown. The woman I had to be on this case was the woman my mother had often pretended to be when press-ganged into cooperating in my father's schemes: glamorous, perhaps a little silly, and rich as Croesus.

There was a single clerk in the room, mustachioed. I heard the bells on the door handle jingle behind me and saw his head turn to watch my fellow operative Jack Mortenson enter the room. I pretended to browse the shelves, ignoring the new arrival, and kept watch on the clerk out of the corner of my eye.

The case file had been thorough. Boris Obanov, thirty years old, emigrated from Russia five years before. Dead broke. Fell in with the criminal element three years ago when he was in a spot of money trouble and had only been getting in deeper since. He moved stolen goods, and a private citizen whose wife's most treasured ring was missing believed Obanov to be in possession of it. He wanted to see Obanov and any accomplices brought to justice. Securing possession of the stolen ring was the first step.

Our intelligence had also told us what we needed to know about the store itself. In order to offer more goods than its competitors, it was packed with shelves that ran nearly the length of the entire room, ceiling to floor. Behind the clerk's counter was an extraordinary cabinet with no fewer than a hundred tiny drawers. The drawers didn't lock, but neither were they marked. Our sources told us this was where Obanov secreted stolen objects. There was no chance of finding something at random within them, especially with the clerk watching. But we had a plan.

While Mortenson spoke with Obanov in low, hushed tones, I pretended to be interested in the more womanly items. I ran my fingers over bolts of cloth stacked high, plaids and stripes and patterns, and noted where the fabric blocked me from the clerk's view. Then, I deliberately interrupted their conversation several times, asking inane questions. Eventually, I paid for three spools of thread, changing my mind on the colors at the last second and fumbling the change I was given so that Obanov had to fetch it from the floor. I asked for double-thick needles and was rewarded with a glimpse at one of the tiny drawers, leaving only ninety-nine more to wonder about. Obanov was annoyed with me, and Mortenson pretended to be irritated as well, the tension between them growing with each minute.

When my final transaction was complete, I went to the door, pushing it open to make the jingling bells ring through the shop but didn't leave. I tied a rag around the bells to muffle them. I circled back quietly to where the men were now arguing and tucked myself behind the bolts of fabric, getting ready. Obanov showed Mortenson the ring. I could barely see it from my hiding place but knew how beautiful it was from the description: a gold ring in the form of a snake, its head a teardrop emerald, very like the queen's ring, so we were told. One of the drawers was open, and I quickly memorized the position. Third from the left, fifth down.

Mortenson handed the ring back to Obanov and asked about something else, gesturing at a barrel ten paces away. The clerk hastily put the ring back in its drawer before following Mortenson to the barrel in question. I got myself into position.

Moments later, Mortenson was arguing in earnest over the contents of the barrel, refusing to pay the agreed-upon price, and the men's voices went up and up.

Then Mortenson shoved Obanov, knocking him to the floor. This was my chance. I reached into the high drawer and palmed the ring, then walked briskly for the door without looking back, the bells making almost no noise as I exited. I tucked the ring into a pocket at my waist as I walked out into the street.

A scant few minutes later, Obanov threw Mortenson from the door into the open street. Mortenson dusted himself off and stalked away, muttering.

Now, I only had to wait for Obanov to discover the ring's absence. We knew he would be alarmed when it disappeared; our hope was that he would immediately dash to his accomplices to let them know what had happened. He was on the lookout for Mortenson, but he wasn't on the lookout for me.

I positioned myself in the prearranged location, across the street behind a cart selling nutmegs. If all went according to plan, Mortenson was halfway down the block near a law office, but we were both on our own from here on out.

It took three-quarters of an hour, but my patience was rewarded. Obanov must have checked his precious drawer and found it empty. He charged out into the street, looking frantic, and turned north.

I followed Obanov through the crowd at a fair distance. At first, I had no trouble tracking him, thanks to his flowing white scarf, but as soon as he joined the surging crowd, that advantage was gone. As we crossed over Kinzie on LaSalle, I had the first inkling that my task might not be within my reach.

An abolitionist rally on the church steps had drawn a crowd, with sympathizers surging down the block in their fervor. *All men are free*, they shouted. *So shall they be.* Someone thumped a drum, marking time, like a public heartbeat. The streets pulsed and teemed. I could barely keep myself oriented to where I was, let alone track a man mostly in black among dozens of others who were almost identical from a distance. The people were so thick on the street, I found myself jostled from the left and the right. Once, I was even struck in the ribs with an elbow at such velocity that it left me breathless. I didn't dare turn to see who had struck me. I couldn't take my eyes off Obanov.

Six blocks later, crossing Erie Street, I felt him slipping away. It was beginning to seem an absurd exercise, thought up by a scholar in a room for the purpose of driving me mad, and the rapid-fire sounds all around me—shouts, laughter, arguments, distant applause—seemed designed to seal the bargain. A fast-moving omnibus nearly ran me clean over on Chicago Avenue. I had no idea what direction Obanov might be headed, so if he winked out of sight for even a moment, there would be no finding him again. I hastened forward to close the distance between us.

As we crossed over Market, everything changed. The commercial traffic of the city thinned, as did the crowd. Instead of being surrounded, we were nearly alone. I began to fall back, but he turned in my direction, and my studied air of nonchalance was not enough to disguise me. It was too late.

He saw me, and he saw me watching him.

Obanov turned back the way we'd come, crossing to the other side of the street and fixing me with his gaze as I passed, then skedaddled. I was left in the street, cursing myself, helpless.

At least I had the ring, I told myself. I hadn't scotched the operation completely. We wouldn't find the gang today as we'd hoped, and I'd have to accept that failure, as much as it pained me. But with the client's stolen property safe, at least we could make a case.

I patted my hip for the ring, hoping to reassure myself by pressing my fingers against its slender shape.

It wasn't there.

With disbelief, hoping against hope I was wrong, I pressed harder and took a closer look. I had not been wrong.

There was a thin cut in the bottom of my pocket, a slice that seemed to have been made with the flick of a knife. A common pickpocket's trick. I'd read about it in the case files not two weeks before, on a long list of techniques a particular petty thief had confessed to. Now, I was on the wrong end of it. No matter how many times I pressed my fingers against and inside the pocket, there was no ring.

I walked slowly, ever so slowly, back to the office. I had never felt so soundly defeated.

Without the ring, no case. Without the case, no success. Without success, my position as an operative would be short-lived. I could only hope for mercy from Pinkerton.

CHAPTER SEVEN
NO TOURIST

Pinkerton was furious. I could see it in the way he leaned over his desk, pressing his weight onto his fists, even before he spoke. He had been distant with me before but never angry. I flinched when he opened his mouth, expecting the worst, and felt his wrath. Even preparing for the worst isn't the same as hearing it.

"Ridiculous! Foolish! Incompetent!"

I held my tongue to start with, hoping his anger might burn bright and burn itself out. All I could do was try my best not to make it worse.

He went on, "Tell me why I shouldn't dismiss you right now."

As clearly and evenly as I could, I said, "Someone stole it from me."

"That could be. Or you might be the one who stole it."

I stuck my finger through the slice in my pocket, wiggling it, the flesh pale against the fabric of my dress. "And this?"

"You could have made that yourself."

"I did not take the ring," I said, anger burning my throat. I was sure that a cluster of operatives stood listening outside the door, enjoying my humiliation. They were smart enough to be silent, but they were there.

"Then who did?"

"I don't know. Someone else."

"Any guesses?" he asked, hissing on the word *guess*.

I had plenty, but it wasn't the right time to share them. "None."

"And what should I do with you now?"

"Believe me."

"Isn't that what guilty people say?"

"It's what innocent people say too." I searched my mind, remembering case files. "The girl who worked for the Chapellets, remember? She didn't do it. The cook accused of stealing copper scoops from the Devigne house. The Irishman they said robbed the mail off the train in Michigan City. You investigated all of them. They were all innocent."

If my powers of recall impressed him, he hid it well. He shook his head, his eyes half-closed. Those meaty fists on the desk stayed clenched. It almost looked like he could push right through the wood with them.

My mind sped forward, searching for an answer, a way out. Someone with inside knowledge might have stolen the ring, but any pickpocket on the street might have taken it too; they'd slice into any old pocket and catch what fell out, with no knowledge in advance. There was no one else to take the blame, but I didn't deserve it either.

I stepped closer to him and leaned hard against the desk, staring him down, holding nothing back.

"Boss. You say you can tell when I'm lying. Look at me now. I'm not lying."

He focused his powerful, punishing gaze on me and stared for a full minute. I heard—or imagined I heard—the eavesdropping operatives breathing in the silence. Quiet settled between us uneasily. I didn't flinch or back down.

After a minute, I repeated, softly but firmly, "Am I lying? You know."

He sat down heavily behind the desk, lifting his hands at last to cross his arms. His gaze did not change.

He said, "I don't think so."

I left his office then, and he did not call out to fetch me back.

The night passed slowly, without sleep. My mind fluttered and zipped, even while I did my best to hold it still, stretched across my narrow bed. My imagination was too good. I thought of everything I could have done differently and how much better things would have turned out, if only.

Had the ring been stolen by someone else from the agency? Mortenson, perhaps? Or Bellamy? Making evidence disappear was a quick way to discredit me. Even DeForest, as kind as he was to my face, might have his reasons for not wanting me around. No one was above suspicion. And regardless of who had done it, the result was clear. My position was at stake.

Unfortunately, as the night's darkness began to give way to the morning's light, I was no closer to figuring out how I might determine who was responsible. The ring was gone, making me look stupid or criminal or both. And though Pinkerton had not dismissed me on the spot, that didn't mean he wouldn't turn to it eventually.

The next day, I could not decide whether my presence or my absence would be more provocative to Pinkerton. Avoiding the office might make me look guilty; appearing there might inspire him to take action, and not in a positive way. At last, I forced myself to dress and walk in that direction midmorning, figuring I could always change my mind.

As I approached the outside door, it swung open, and a familiar, slender figure emerged. Mortenson.

He stopped when he saw me and said, "Just who I was looking for."

"Oh?" I saw no harm in talking with the man, thinking perhaps

I might even be able to win him over to my side, were I charming enough. I assumed he knew about the disappearance of the ring, but we hadn't discussed it. Perhaps he wanted to.

"Come with me a moment," he said, gesturing toward the street.

"For what purpose?"

"An important step in your training."

I grew curious—and a bit suspicious—but I wanted to be cooperative. "At the boss's direction?"

"Oh, I'm sure he'd approve."

I walked out of the office with him, reasoning that nothing would stop me from turning back if I decided I wanted to. We strolled along, down Wells and then Madison. It was an official part of town, with many city buildings, though I noticed it smelled oddly of the stockyards.

He swung a door open for me and, with no warning, we descended into hell.

Lining the walls of the cold stone room were dead bodies, corpse after corpse laid out on metal slabs, like meat on trays at the butcher's.

My hand quickly flew to my mouth. With my free hand, I fumbled for a handkerchief, hoping I could get it up to my nose to block out the terrible smell before I became sick in a dramatic and unwelcome fashion.

If the smell bothered Mortenson, he didn't show it. Instead, he watched me, a bemused look on his ghostly face.

A man in white shirtsleeves and a dark, heavy, indigo apron approached us. There was no sound in the basement room but his footfalls landing one after the other on the cement floor.

"C'mon, Jack," he said, "the morgue is no place for tourists."

"She's no tourist," replied Mortenson. "This is the estimable Mrs. Warne, first female operative of the Pinkerton Agency. As able and manly as you or me, or so we're told."

"Pleased to make your acquaintance," said the man in the apron, a deeply skeptical look on his face. He made no move to shake my hand, for which I was grateful.

Mortenson said, "I thought you might show us around."

What followed was a miserable, terrifying half hour, unlike any other in my life. For the first fifteen minutes, the smell of bloody flesh was overwhelming, and I retained little of what was said. Mortenson continued to look at me, scrutinizing my face over and over, and I made a hero's work of ignoring him. The voice of the man in the apron, who had never given his name, droned on like the buzz of so many flies.

A quarter hour in, things snapped into place. My poor nose became accustomed to the smell. My head cleared. Then, I was able to hear his words, and I actually became interested in what he was saying. Each of the people here had died a suspicious death and been sent to the county for further investigation. He had worked here since the morgue was established, more than ten years before. He knew bodies. Though I knew it was not what Mortenson had intended, I could learn from him.

"Here, you see ligature marks," he said, indicating the neck of a dead unfortunate. Other than the dark, bruised lines on her throat, she looked like she might have been only sleeping. I looked away from her face. I had to.

"How long ago did she pass?" I asked, surprising both the men and myself by speaking up.

"Just a few hours ago," said the man in the apron. "Feel her, and you'll see. Longer than this, and the body stiffens, becomes firm. She still bends."

He lifted the woman's hands, and I was struck by the soft angle of her dangling fingers. Alive, she might have trailed her fingers in the water this way, leaning over the edge of a boat. Now, she would never do so again.

I steeled myself against sentiment. Neither man would appreciate any expression of emotion; that wasn't what we were here for. Now that I understood this for the test it was, I had to show my strength.

I lifted the woman's hand in the same way Apron had, feeling how the flesh responded. The flesh had cooled, becoming waxy. I would not have mistaken her for alive under any circumstances.

"Hmm," I said as if we were only remarking on the weather and nodded in the direction of the next corpse. We moved forward.

Ignoring faces, focusing only on the sites of harm, I saw evidence of many kinds of damage that could be done to the human body. Here, a gunshot; there, a knife wound. Other bodies had no visible signs at all, their limbs as smooth and clean as my own, and Apron told me of internal injuries, damaged hearts, and utter mysteries. By the end, my poor body was still roiling with nerves, but I was fully engaged in conversation, my brain overriding my baser instincts in order to add knowledge to my repertoire.

Afterward, Mortenson returned me to more familiar territory, our heels clacking on the wooden sidewalk in silence the entire journey. Touching the brim of his hat once, he took his leave without a word. I sensed I had disappointed him; he'd been hoping for a womanly, weak reaction. A collapse, perhaps, or at least some sign of fragility.

I'd never been so happy to disappoint someone in my life.

❧

The next day, I did force myself to report to the office, though I avoided Pinkerton's gaze as if everything depended on it—as well it might. While I was able to busy myself around the margins for a few hours, eventually, he said, "Come here, Warne, and let's talk."

I dragged my feet, walking to his office. He stood by the door, ready to shut it as soon as we were both inside. I dreaded the moment when I would pass by him, his intimidating bulk refusing to give quarter, especially since I was afraid he might see me trembling.

I could not linger any longer when a shout came from behind me: "Boss!"

We both turned. Everyone turned. Besides Pinkerton and me, Taylor and Bellamy were also there. Taylor was bending down in front of the office safe, a stack of bills in hand—probably counterfeit—and he was the one who'd spoken.

Pinkerton pushed past me into the outside office, saying, "Yes?"

"Look."

We all witnessed the moment. We all saw Taylor lift the stolen ring from the safe. The gold and gems glinted merrily in the stale air. It was clearly the snake ring from the Obanov case, fitting the description exactly; unless it belonged to Queen Victoria herself, it could be no other.

Pinkerton said, "Well then." His tone gave nothing away

I wanted to feel relief. I did let out a single breath I felt I'd been holding forever. But Taylor's and Bellamy's glares told the story. Whoever had taken the ring had given me respite by returning it, but he'd also made it impossible to prove that I hadn't taken it in the first place. In the absence of proof, I would be both guilty and innocent, always.

Between the morgue and the snake ring debacle, doubt crept in. If the other operatives would be torturing me, staring at me, driving me out, what was the point of it all? I could leave now and not come back. It would be the easiest thing in the world.

But I could make a success of myself as an operative. I knew I could. I'd survived something Mortenson thought I couldn't, and that gave me confidence, but I realized there were reasons far deeper why I needed to remain.

Because I always felt like I was pretending to be someone I

wasn't anyway. Because my complete lack of trust in every new person I met might finally be turned to some positive purpose. And because Charlie would have told me I couldn't, but Charlie was dead, and it was time for me to make my own choices.

I'd already known I had to be twice as good as any of the men on the job. Now, I would have to be twice as good as twice.

Everything depended on it.

CHAPTER EIGHT

SURVEILLANCE

After the unexplained theft and return of the snake ring, I cast a suspicious eye on all my fellow operatives. Even without the formal meetings or introductions that Pinkerton so eschewed, after three months, I'd learned a great deal.

Bellamy specialized in disguises, which was why he had charge of the costume closet, and often gave advice to other operatives on the best way to take on a role. Many times, I found him in the office pasting things onto another man's face with spirit gum or scrutinizing his clothes for telltale signs that he did not belong where he was being sent. He alternated between eyeing me disdainfully and looking right through me, and I still thought him the most likely saboteur.

Graham DeForest, as befitted his stylish and ingratiating aspect, specialized in seductions. Not true seductions—Pinkerton took pains to emphasize to me that neither his male agents nor his female ones would ever be asked to complete a private act for the public good—but DeForest ably handled any case where flirting might get us closer to our goal. I knew firsthand how very charming he could be. Suspicious of him as I was, I still found myself smiling under his flattery.

Mortenson, who by his physical presence was both hard to disguise and not particularly suited for seduction, was an excellent functionary. If the case called for an ersatz inspector, Cincinnati businessman, or government representative, all Mortenson needed to be completely convincing was the right suit of clothes. Sometimes, Bellamy added thin, gold-rimmed eyeglasses as a crowning touch. Mortenson's skill was to blend into the background, and I still had trouble drawing a bead on him.

Even the men I barely knew had their roles, easy to peg. Taylor was the muscle, Dalessandro was the sap, and Paretsky was the gentleman fallen on hard times.

I, of course, didn't need a specialty. I already had one. I was the woman.

I knew I had much to learn, but I also had a natural aptitude for the work. My initial success with Heck hadn't been a fluke. The same things that made me miserable as a child—moving constantly from place to place, never knowing if a new person was friend or foe—made me adaptable.

My parents had taught me, in their way. When I was young and they mostly ignored me, I learned not to offend or disturb them. I was always, always agreeable. We moved from place to place, after a year or only a month, and I had to learn new personalities, new surroundings, over and over again. From Charleston to Atlanta, Houston to Bowling Green, then north to Pittsburgh or Portsmouth, wherever my father found a theater that would pay him what he felt he was worth. Everywhere was so different. Some cities felt like they weren't even in the same country, but I couldn't let that bother me. I learned to be an invisible visitor, congenial, silent.

When I was old enough to be of use in my father's schemes, I learned to play my part—a lost girl, a sad girl, a hungry girl—exactly as I was told. As far as I knew, every child grew up sleeping backstage at theaters while her father declaimed Shakespeare's words as the gravedigger in *Hamlet*, clowned about in *She Stoops to Conquer*, and rattled his chains as Jacob Marley in *A Christmas Carol*. As far as

I knew, everybody fled cities in the middle of the night when some scheme or another angered the wrong mark. As far as I knew, the world was divided into operators and victims, winners and fools. By the time I realized I had options—I didn't always have to be agreeable or go along—I was already eighteen years old, pregnant, and married to a man I didn't know well enough to dislike yet.

I couldn't change those years. But at least I could put everything I'd learned to good use.

To make myself a better agent, I threw myself into learning every skill I could. I read about poisons and found that I could procure no fewer than a dozen deadly compounds from the city's pharmacists and grocers with little difficulty. I taught myself, huddled in a half-dark bedroom, to pick a wide variety of locks with nothing more than a hairpin. Begging DeForest's indulgence, I learned to load and fire a hefty Burnside carbine, a standard rifle, and a Colt Pocket Revolver, as well as improving my aim with the Deringer I now carried whenever I felt the case called for it. I even persuaded Mortenson to take me back to the Cook County morgue for another tour, which he did with obvious disgruntlement and not a whit of grace.

I also knew I needed to perfect surveillance, and after I'd been an operative for six months, I fell into the habit of surveilling targets I could easily locate: my fellow operatives. Knowing that any one of them might have been involved in the disappearance of the snake ring, I had a second motive to investigate each and every one. If some information about their character came into my possession this way, so much the better.

I started with Mortenson, who was highly visible in crowds due to his pale aspect, and successfully followed him three nights in a row without being caught out. The first night, he went to a tavern and stayed for several hours, emerging rumpled but firmly upright. The second night, he went to a church—a shorter stay, but no more revealing. The third night, I lurked in the shadows outside the office and nearly bounced on my toes in curiosity to see which way he would go, left or right. In the end, it was back to the tavern again.

Then I tried following Pinkerton himself, but he never went anywhere other than straight to his home, so there didn't seem to be much to be learned there. Several nights in a row, I shadowed him down the exact same path, right and left and another left and right again, right up to his front door. He never turned or wavered, which seemed right from what I knew of him.

Then, for good or ill or both, I chose to tail Graham DeForest.

Since our shooting lessons, on the occasions that we saw each other in the office, he had always continued to be excessively solicitous. *You look utterly lovely today, Mrs. Warne! I suppose there is no surprise in that.* But he had not made any physical overtures, and I was grateful. He had been a better friend than anyone else in the agency. I began to believe what he had told me, early on, in the woods: he was on my side. Given his flashy dress and suave manner, I expected he had at least one lady friend to occupy his time. Indeed, I would not have put it past him to have half a dozen.

I knew where he lived—he'd mentioned the intersection several times—so I decided to wait a few blocks from there and watch for him. It was different to catch someone in a crowd than it was to track them from the beginning, and I needed the practice. However, the first night was an utter failure. I would have sworn he never passed me, even as it grew dark outside and then pitch-black. Perhaps he'd come from another direction? Or perhaps I had missed him entirely, turning my head at just the wrong time. Clearly, I did need the practice I'd assigned myself. I went home to a scolding from Mrs. Borowski and a cold plate of stuffed cabbage, gobbled down quickly next to the stove.

Three nights later, I tried again, doing a few things differently.

First, I warned Mrs. Borowski I wouldn't be home for dinner, so she wouldn't worry. I dressed in men's breeches and a shirt and hat from Bellamy's disguise closet, with a heavy overcoat to protect me from prying eyes and the weather alike. Walking the streets as a woman alone, late at night, invited comment. I wouldn't be well disguised enough to pass as an actual man in speech or manner. But at a distance, it would discourage curiosity.

I caught DeForest halfway between the office and his home, quickly falling into position well behind him on the opposite side of the street. It was the perfect distance to track his movement with little fear of being discovered. I was already starting to congratulate myself when I realized he was taking a different direction, not headed home at all.

His figure, half a block more distant now, scuttled down an alleyway in the gathering dark. He was peeking furtively behind him—or was it my imagination? Did he suspect being followed? Or was I just on edge, too nervous, reading intent into his actions based on my own fragile state of mind? I hadn't thought about what I would say if I was caught out. I thought about it now. Perhaps, in the end, the truth would do. But how much better it would be if I didn't need it.

A handful of turns later, in a commercial district with few lights and even fewer signs, he ducked into a basement-level doorway and vanished. Afraid that if I delayed, I would lose him, I plunged inside, arriving into almost total darkness.

While my eyes adjusted, I ran my fingers along the wall behind me to steady myself. Having something to touch made darkness less disorienting—a hint I'd learned from DeForest himself. The thought almost made me lose my nerve, but having begun the adventure, I wanted to see it through. Besides, now I wondered— what was this place, and why would he come here?

Once I could see more than shadows, I scanned the room

quickly. First, to find DeForest. All depended on his position; I would need to choose mine accordingly.

I located him at the far end of the bar, sitting alone, signaling for the barman with a single upraised finger. I ducked back to avoid being seen. He didn't look in my direction, but I played it safe. The breeches I'd chosen were the right color to help me blend in with the men around me, but I knew there was more to being a man than the clothes. I tried my best not to cock my hip, not to fold my hands, not to do anything that might give me away as a woman. I leaned back against the wall as casually as I could.

His drink arrived. He curled his fingers around it but did not put it to his lips. I lingered at the edge of a crowd, half a dozen men playing billiards, as if I were awaiting my turn in the rotation. It was an unusually dark room, and the game seemed to take a very long time, with no sense of urgency. I could tell something was afoot, but it was impossible to know what, and all my investigative energies needed to be saved for the more important task. I pulled the brim of my hat down over my eyes and watched.

DeForest sat for a quarter of an hour, sipping only once from his glass. He scanned the room frequently, making me nervous. Perhaps he had figured me out and was killing time here, making me wait, as a punishment. Perhaps he would stride over any minute and inform me the jig was up. I could only watch and wait, without looking like I was doing either. I felt a little frisson of excitement. I'd come to practice surveillance, and that's exactly what I was doing. A long career as an operative would put me in a position like this a thousand times. Rehearsal couldn't hurt.

Finally, a blond man slid onto the stool next to DeForest's. He ordered a drink. They looked at each other but not quite with recognition. A quick glance. I saw something odd in the way the new man positioned his body, not straight ahead but angled slightly toward DeForest's, that made me wonder. Not friends, not strangers. Something else.

A terrible thought crossed my mind. They could be exchanging intelligence. Pinkerton had forbidden working with criminals to support our cases—it was in the Code—but it must be a daily temptation for the operatives infiltrating gangs. Perhaps DeForest had given in to temptation. Worse, he could be tipping off a gang that we were coming. We all knew well that there was far more money in evading justice than delivering it. Had he stolen the gold-and-emerald snake ring, planning to fence it, and changed his mind? Was it only one of many things he'd stolen?

There was a discussion, then a decision, and the two men moved off, leaving their drinks on the bar. Like a shadow, I moved with them. Through the crowd next to the pool table, toward a warren of rooms in the back. I backed off, moving more slowly and lingering with the others, so as not to draw suspicion.

After a decent interval, I edged closer to the hallway where I'd seen DeForest and his companion disappear. There were several rooms in the back, with curtains drawn across each doorway. I peeked through the first, and it took every mote of my self-control not to exclaim in shock.

Two men were there, their faces pressed close together in a kiss.

I'd never seen anything like it. I had heard such gal-boys existed, that there were men who treated each other like women, but I had never imagined I'd see such a thing with my own eyes.

And then I thought about DeForest and realized with a sick feeling in my stomach that his purpose here, while fully illegal, was not criminal in the way I'd thought.

Yet I'd come this far. I needed to know for sure.

I pressed myself close to the wall, remaining as close as I could to invisible, and peeked through the next curtain. I saw a smudge of bare flesh and looked away before I could see more. There had been two hats on the floor, and neither was DeForest's. That was enough.

Behind the third curtain, I saw him. He and the other man were seated side by side on a small couch, facing away from me. They leaned on each other, toward each other, with their heads bent over their laps like schoolboys looking at a turtle.

I couldn't—and didn't—linger. A tiny alarm at the back of my brain began to clang louder and louder. Every moment I stayed put me in danger of being discovered. I had to leave, and finally, feeling my feet and my mind heavier than I could have imagined, I did.

❧

I said nothing. Not to DeForest, not to anyone. Aside from Pinkerton, he was my only ally in the agency. If I exposed him, I would lose a friend. His predilections clearly hadn't impeded his abilities as an operative, so there was nothing to gain from speaking up. I had to be practical.

The first time I saw him after that night, quizzing him at Pinkerton's behest about the habits of train-based pickpockets, I was uncomfortable. I asked him questions, but I couldn't concentrate on his answers. An image of him with the other man, their heads bent together, sprung up unbidden in my mind. His words buzzed in my ears, and I had to ask him to repeat himself. I learned what I needed to, but I was concerned our bond had been irrevocably altered.

The next time I saw him, I only thought words and not the image: *I saw him with a man.* After that, the information faded, day by day, until it was barely a tickle at the back of my brain.

Walking away from what I'd seen that night, I thought it might be hard to keep it hidden from him, knowing something he wasn't aware I knew.

But I could keep secrets, even one as potentially incendiary as this one.

And so I would keep it, for a while.

CHAPTER NINE
A VISIT

I had been a Pinkerton operative for more than a year before someone tried in earnest to kill me.

By then, I was living in a smaller, finer boardinghouse just off Des Plaines Street. My unusual comings and goings at Mrs. Borowski's had started to draw notice from my fellow boarders. I gave a false name at the new house to make things easier. Whoever I was on the inside, as far as this corner of the world was concerned, I was Miss Cora Harris, spinster. That was all they knew and all they needed to know.

My new boardinghouse was comfortable and elegant. I had a good-sized room with a bed and bureau and my own private dressing room. The bedspread was soft under my fingers, and the drapes at the window were new enough not to be faded from the sun. The window overlooked the street at the front of the house, shaded by a pretty, delicate birch tree. I pretended I was fully accustomed to such lush surroundings. Miss Cora Harris had not been raised in theaters and flophouses, terrified of being left behind on purpose or by accident; Miss Harris was a lady.

And while I returned to the boardinghouse nearly every night, all my days were spent on cases. A year of experience had made me wiser and more useful as a Pinkerton operative. I knew nearly every kind of case. Counterfeiting, blackmail, burglaries of all kinds. I had impersonated a fortune-teller to suss out a poisoner, a case that was not just memorable because of its novelty but because the nut juice Tim Bellamy offered me to darken my skin did not fade completely for an entire month. I assumed he'd stained me on purpose, but I didn't complain, either to him or to Pinkerton. I knew that appearances were everything. If I appeared to be a difficult employee, even if I had every reason, I'd lose the ground I'd gained with the boss. And Pinkerton had come to rely on me more and more. Sometimes, he even seemed friendly.

It was only unfortunate that my least favorite kind of case was also the kind Pinkerton found me most essential in solving: the murders.

The Harrington case began with a tapping on my window, just after four o'clock in the morning.

Groggy with sleep, all uncertain, I heard the noise. Was it even there? Was it part of a dream? I opened my eyes to see.

As soon as I knew for sure that the sound was real, and the gentle tapping became a louder series of knocks, I immediately slid across the bed and pulled my Deringer from the nightstand. I thumbed the hammer, stood, and wrapped my robe more tightly around my body as I walked toward the window. I drew aside the curtain with one fingertip, just the narrowest sliver, and looked out. I could not have been more surprised at what I saw.

Tim Bellamy stood under my window, hunched against the nighttime chill and darkness, staring up expectantly with his cold, blue gaze.

After a few long moments, he said in a normal speaking voice, "Let me in, please, Mrs. Warne. I don't think either of us likes me standing here."

I replaced my gun in the drawer and hastened into the hallway, unlocking the front door of the building and holding it open to admit him. He immediately handed me something and stood silently with his heels together on the carpet, waiting, like a messenger boy.

I opened the paper note, hastily folded and not quite square, no envelope. It read:

136 Sedgwick. Fatal case. Come right away. AP.

"He was going to send a messenger," said Bellamy quietly. "I offered to come instead. I didn't think you should go alone this time of night."

It wasn't the time to argue. I could defend myself against his chivalry some other day. I turned back toward my room and said, "Come on."

"Mrs. Warne, I don't think—"

"The hallway's worse than outside. Someone will come along. Think of my reputation."

That got him moving. He stood in my room like a statue, facing the closed door, while I dressed hastily. I would have suspected any other man of peeking over his shoulder while I was *en déshabillé*, but I doubted our white knight would lower himself to something so base. Had the circumstances been otherwise, I would have needled him about it to amuse myself, but had the circumstances been otherwise, he never would have been standing there.

After that, the only question was whether or not to take my gun. But if Pinkerton hadn't suggested it, I likely wouldn't need it. It sounded like the violence was in the past tense. I slid a jackknife into my boot just in case.

Bellamy and I walked together in complete silence, keeping a brisk pace, block after block disappearing behind us. I scrambled a bit to keep up, my breath coming faster, but I had no intention of asking him to slow down. When the boss said *right away*, I knew he meant it.

As I'd expected from the address, the house was impressive. Three steady floors of good brick behind a cheery green front door and bright white shutters. It would not have been stretching the truth to call it a mansion. Walking up to it for any other reason, I would have been jealous, but the word *fatal* loomed large in my mind. If this case was what I feared, I would not have traded places with the mistress of the house for anything.

Pinkerton, in his shirtsleeves and a sober charcoal vest, met us inside the front door.

"Empty?" asked Bellamy, receiving a curt nod as his answer. He then stood by the door, facing outward, his arms folded as if keeping watch.

To me, Pinkerton said, "I know this wasn't the most pleasant way to wake up. But I needed you to see everything before it was disturbed."

"A fatal case, you said."

"Yes."

"How many? When?"

"One. Last night, we think."

I asked the easy next question. "Why aren't the police chasing this?"

"We'll call them shortly," he said.

I chose my next words carefully. I was still sleepy but not too sleepy to understand the gravity of the situation. "How do we know about this if we didn't hear it from the police?"

He looked at me in silence. I quickly realized he was giving me the chance to change my question so I wouldn't get an answer I didn't like.

Still, I needed to know. "Have we been hired to find the truth or to put together the evidence to support a lie?"

"Fair question," he said. "Her husband found her. Cut her down, said he thought she might still be alive. She wasn't."

"So she's a suicide, and he thinks...what?"

"Well, he told me that she appeared at first to be a suicide, but when he looked closer, he saw signs that she might not be."

"Like what?"

"I'll need you to see her yourself. Are you prepared?" He paused with his hand on the closed parlor doors.

"Is anyone?" I asked and pushed past him into the parlor to look at the dead body.

The woman lay on the carpet as if resting, which I supposed she was, only forever. She wore a simple homespun dress with a pattern of small flowers, pink on cream. Had I not been told, I wouldn't have taken her for the lady of the house. I looked up at the nearby balcony, where I could see an overturned chair and the frayed ends of a cut rope. The other part of the rope lay a few feet away as if flung there. Other than the cut, it looked brand-new.

Pinkerton and I both stopped, as if by accord, a few steps away from the body. He pointed to the marks around her neck. They did indeed look like the marks of a noose. But there were other marks too, lighter ones—around her wrists, as if she had been bound. There was no blood, either on the body or around it. The faint scent of verbena lingered near the body, not disguising the unmistakable stink of death. She'd worn a lovely perfume, but she'd died like all of us do, with the undignified loss of bodily control. I raised my handkerchief to my nose and mouth to ward away the worst of the stink, trying to concentrate.

"Who is the husband?" I asked.

"Jay Harrington. President of National Cattle Company."

"Rich?"

He gestured, with one sweep of his arm, to the house around us. It was more sumptuous on the inside than the outside. The Persian carpet upon which the body lay likely cost more than the agency saw in a month. The library walls were lined with rich-looking, leather-jacketed books. The foyer floor, if not marble, was an excellent facsimile thereof. I should have known without asking the question, but it was hard to focus. Good detective work involved a complete view first, then a narrowing. Methodically, I noted everything, then tried to make sense of what I saw.

"I suspect she was tied up," I said, pointing to her wrists. "Then tortured in some way, hoping that she'd give up information."

I looked over her wrists again and her neck and eyes. One eye was partly open, giving her an uneasy look, almost as if she were just starting to wake up from sleep. But the pupil was fixed. There was no red in the white, as I would expect from someone who had died of strangling, either by someone else's hand or her own. I had seen examples of both. There were no burns or open wounds on her pale skin, just the scrapes and bruises, all superficial.

I added grimly, "I don't think they got what they wanted."

"If that's the case, why would they kill her?" Pinkerton asked. "Why not hold her for ransom? The husband would have paid dearly to get her back."

I bent down and knelt on the carpet, looking more and more closely at her mouth. Her lips were slightly swollen. Not bruised but reddened. I used a pencil to open her mouth and peer inside as best I could. There was something behind her teeth that didn't belong. I braced myself for the task and put my fingers inside the dead woman's mouth, pulling out a wad of torn fabric. Stained cotton. I showed it to Pinkerton and said, "I think they intended to hold on to her. I think they killed her by accident."

He nodded soberly, and I realized that he had already guessed the answer. She had died by smothering, not by strangulation, and she certainly hadn't done it herself. The rope, the hanging—it was a clumsy attempt to disguise what had really happened. Not suicide but murder, and not a planned one. Improvisation.

"You agree?"

"Yes."

I said, "So why did you bring me in to look?"

"I figured you could do a more thorough inspection to see if

I'd missed anything." He gestured at the wad of cotton. "I hadn't gotten that far yet. Also, I suppose it was a sort of a test. But the third thing is the most important."

"And that is?"

"I need you to help me figure out what to do next."

I looked down at the dead woman, considering.

Pinkerton added, "No witnesses. No information. Just the dead woman and anything she can tell us."

I stood, stretched, and looked away from the body, trying to clear my mind. The house was lovely. It was a good reminder that having lovely things doesn't save a person from the world. And it might have been the money that brought misfortune to the Harringtons' door.

The door, I thought.

"She didn't do it herself, so someone was here. So how did they get in? And how did they leave?"

"The husband didn't notice anything. Or if he did, he didn't say."

We checked the doors ourselves. No sign of forcing, either at the front door or the back. Thinking out loud, I said, "Well, the locks might have been picked, but they weren't forced. What if the perpetrator had a key?"

"You think the husband let someone in?"

"Could be. But I was thinking something different. Maybe it was his key, but someone else got their hands on it."

"How?"

"Where do you keep your spare house key?" I asked him, knowing the answer.

"In my office. In my desk."

I was beginning to get the seedling of an idea. I turned back to the body of Mrs. Harrington. She looked like a doll now, a broken doll. I tried to look at her corpse only as a collection of details. Her hair was several shades darker than mine and her skin several shades more pale. Her eyes were closer together, and she was narrower at the shoulders. But these were all minor details and could be overcome. The key element was present. We looked to be about the same size.

"I have an idea," I said. "The husband is our client?"

"Yes."

"How is he?"

"What do you mean?"

I searched for the right words. "Mad with grief? Sobbing, screaming? Or can he keep himself together?"

"Stunned, I think, but coherent. What do we need him to do?"

"What time does he go to work?"

"I can ask."

"Does his wife ever visit him at his office?"

He was only a heartbeat behind. "Let's find out."

❧

Three hours later, at Jay Harrington's downtown office building, I walked in through the front door with my head held high. Only I wasn't myself. I was Sarah Harrington, in a square-necked, sprigged dress and graceful, feathered hat, risen from the dead.

I'd carefully chosen the dress from Mrs. Harrington's wardrobe that was most like the one she wore when she died. I drew the line at removing the actual garment from her body, but the greater the resemblance I bore to her, the better my plan would work. We would only get one chance.

Bellamy had remained back at the house. Pinkerton had already arrived here before me, pretending to be a customer, speaking with Mr. Harrington himself. He'd originally asked to be paired with another man in the office, giving him a better vantage point, but a jolted, nervous Mr. Harrington admitted that he couldn't think of a single man in his office who he fully trusted, who would be one hundred percent beyond suspicion. I couldn't blame him.

Poor man. He was admirable for even trying this gambit. We were all doing our best, but we'd never known the dead woman. Everything truly depended upon his successful charade.

I hoisted the lunch bucket. It was not empty, because we might need to play the scene all the way to the end if no suspect gave himself away at my first appearance. Cold chicken with rolls and butter awaited us if we needed to extend operations. I knew they would taste like dust; food eaten on a case always did. Readying myself for my performance, I neared Mr. Harrington's desk.

"Oh, Jay!" I called in a voice we'd rehearsed together to be as little like mine and as much like hers as possible.

"Sarah, dear," he called back and held his arms out toward me.

My knees nearly buckled under me at the naked longing on his face. No one had ever looked at me with such passion, but it wasn't me he was really looking at. I was only his pretend wife coming toward him. The real one would never do so again.

I let my eyes scan the room lightly as I walked, though Pinkerton was the one in charge of watching the reactions of the other men in the office. When it came, the reaction was so obvious not even Jay Harrington, caught up in playacting a normal life, could miss it.

Two desks over from Mr. Harrington stood a short man, thick in the waist under his neat, pin-striped vest. The placard on his desk named him: Gordon Wilder, vice president.

We all heard his audible gasp and saw his head turn. On seeing me approaching and hearing Jay call out Sarah's name, the round little man went white.

His desk was only a few steps away. I would need to pass him to get to Harrington. This gave me the opportunity to be sure, and I took it.

I stepped toward him, saying, "Surprised to see me?"

He staggered backward a full step. If we'd had any doubt of his involvement, it vanished.

As I closed the gap between us, still advancing, a second wave of recognition dawned on his face. There was relief—and much more.

"You're not her," he said.

I was considering my answer when he launched himself at me. I only had half a moment to react, and I got my hand halfway down my thigh toward my knife, but I didn't have nearly enough time to draw it, let alone defend myself. He tackled me around the waist like a dummy, squeezing out my breath and propelling us both to the ground. If Pinkerton or Harrington tried to step in, they were too late; my head thumped hard against the wood of the desk. I felt his hands on my throat, the thumbs pressing down and down and down.

After that, I saw nothing but sparks in blackness, and then even the sparks winked out, one by one.

Only sound reached me then, a man's sobs and hiccups, very close by. The soft weight of a body, breathing, was on me. The hands on my throat were hot and merciless.

Then the pressure vanished. A small, sweet miracle. The world came back. I sucked in air, and it hissed between my teeth. My forehead felt wet. I tried to rise or speak up. My body wouldn't obey.

A hand, gentle and insistent, settled on my shoulder. "Rest," came a voice—Jay Harrington's—and I wondered whether he was speaking to me or to Sarah or to both of us.

CHAPTER TEN
TRUTH

By the time two policemen in uniform arrived, I felt well enough to stand, though the right side of my head was still bleeding, and Pinkerton kept telling me to sit down. I refused and insisted on hearing Wilder's confession.

He quickly named his three accomplices and detailed their wrongdoing. As we thought, they had only meant to find out from her where her husband's money was hidden or to hold her for ransom if she would not tell. He had simply crammed the fabric meant to muffle her cries too far down her throat. He had no experience in this, after all. Once she went silent and he removed the gag to check her, it was already too late, and there was no saving her. At least he had the decency to cry while he told us how they'd killed her from sheer stupidity. I knew it wouldn't help Jay Harrington to know the details, nor did it help me. But at least justice would be done. He had pretended to hang her to cover the crime; now, he would hang in earnest.

Three days later, my head still buzzing from time to time, I went to Sarah Harrington's funeral. She had been a much-loved woman, and there was a large crowd of crows to lose myself in. She had sisters, cousins, friends, all there to lament her untimely passing, seeking comfort in the mourning crowd. Tears and howls abounded. I didn't cry, but the melancholy that had descended upon me when I saw her dead body only deepened as I saw her laid to rest.

Having stepped into Sarah's life, however briefly, I felt a kinship with her. I knew it wasn't possible that she could know that we had gotten justice for her, but I hoped for it anyway. Her killer had been found. He would pay with his life for hers. I wondered whether his death would balance the scales in some way. I didn't feel bad about the part I'd played in leading to Wilder's death; he deserved the punishment, and I had no doubt he would have killed me too, if he'd had the chance, if it would have saved him.

After the service, as the dead woman's real friends and family sought comfort in one another's familiar company, I could no longer pretend I belonged. I wasn't sure where to go, so I headed back to the office. It was a long walk, but I had nowhere else to be.

When I climbed the stairs and opened the door to the inner office, Pinkerton sat there in a small puddle of light from the desk lamp, bent over his ever-present ledger.

"Welcome," he said. "Talk a while?"

"Sure."

My bones seemed to hum with fatigue, and my mind wouldn't stop racing. When Pinkerton brought out the bottle of whiskey, I didn't protest. I'd never liked the taste of whiskey to start with, and I hadn't gotten used to it. The burn didn't agree with me. But I liked the sleepy feeling in my limbs afterward, and the burn I dealt with. It felt like a kind of penance. Perhaps, I told myself, I should feel penitent.

Pinkerton poured me a glass.

"One for yourself too," I said.

"Don't care for the stuff. But you need it. Drink up."

We sat in silence a while. I wasn't wearing the dead woman's dress anymore, but a grateful Jay Harrington had donated several of her gowns to our costume closet, not wanting anything in the house to remind him of her. I could see them from where I sat. I had nothing to say really. But I enjoyed being in the company of one of the few people in the world who understood how I was feeling in that moment and why. Often, that had to be enough.

I wasn't surprised when he eventually broke the silence, only by how he chose to do it.

"Lie to me," said Pinkerton.

So we were to play a game. I wasted no time beating around the bush or questioning his motives. I said, swallowing hard, "I have no regrets."

"Lie. So, then, what is your biggest regret?"

"Charlie."

"In what way?"

"I never should have married him. My parents forced me to."

"Aren't you innocent, then? Since you were forced?"

"I could have found a way," I said. "There are always choices. I could have run away. Spat in his face. Starved myself. Jumped in the river. Anything."

"Given up the baby?"

A lead weight plunged from my throat to my belly.

"Baby?"

"Oh, Warne," he said with not a little sadness. "I knew from the beginning you were leaving something out. Didn't take a genius. There are many reasons a woman might want a husband but only one reason she might *need* one."

"There was no baby."

"Lie."

"There wasn't," I said, "in the end."

I tilted the liquid in the glass, trying to center myself, trying to focus. My voice was softer as I confessed, "Not a live one, anyhow."

"I'm sorry for your loss," he said.

"Me too," I said simply.

"Not Charlie's, then?"

"No," I said. "A young man named Paul. A good friend."

Even after all this time, I could see Paul's face clearly in my mind. A wry smile, a noble nose, eyes that danced with warmth. I'd trusted him and no one before or since. Six months we'd known each other, at the theater in St. Louis. A stagehand and an actor's daughter. Six months, and that was all.

"You don't strike me as the type to get carried away in the moment, even at a young age."

"He was consumptive," I said. "A lunger."

He nodded. "So you knew you'd lose him."

"Yes. He knew he'd die of it. I wanted him to be happy for a moment. He was. We both were."

He lowered his head as he spoke, and I couldn't read the emotion. Disapproval? Wry humor? Titillation? "So your favor to him was to surrender your womanly virtue?"

"As I told you when you hired me," I said, "someone has to be first."

I smiled, then, to let him know it was all right. That part of it, I'd made my peace with. That part, I didn't regret.

And he smiled back, patted my hand, and tipped a heavy pour of whiskey halfway up the glass. I reached for it with silent gratitude.

I told him the rest briefly. Weakened and fading fast, Paul died a month later. Two months after that, my family traveled to Boston so my father could appear in *The School for Scandal* at the Newbury. When my traveling sickness didn't subside after the journey was over, I began to suspect I was with child. After that, it was only a matter of weeks until my parents found out, cursing me as a whore and a burden and threatening at last what I'd always feared in secret: utter abandonment, casting me out into the world alone. Perhaps that wouldn't have been as bad as what actually happened. Only days later, my father shoved me toward Charlie Warne with a sum of money to sweeten the pot. I found out much later they'd only met twice, over cards. The rest was inevitable.

Perhaps I should not have spoken of it. That night, I dreamt terrible dreams. The gore that streaked the bed. The animal sound of my own screams. The child, who I never saw, not more than a glimpse of a blue elbow smeared with red blood. Perhaps a midwife could have helped, but there was no one to call her; I was alone. The doctor afterward had said there was no way of knowing what could have made the difference. Charlie had been on a riverboat bender and didn't return until two days later, or so I was told. I was mad with fever by that time. The infection nearly killed me, the doctor said, and no other child would ever take root in my womb. I had no memory of the week. Only its first hours, which I would have given anything to forget.

The night of Sarah Harrington's funeral, I awoke from the nightmare of my memories, my bedclothes soaked with whiskey sweat. It was not even midnight.

It was a strange end to a strange day, one of the longest of my life.

But strange days were becoming more and more common in my life after choosing the path of the Pinkerton operative.

℘

The first year of my employment flew by, and before I knew it, the second chased after it. Sad President Pierce left office, replaced by the bachelor Buchanan. Both the North and the South hoped that his presidency would bring them something they wanted, though in the end, we could not both be right.

I grew more confident in my work but could not shake the feeling that the other operatives regarded me as a mere curiosity. I confided in Mrs. Borowski, who was my best confidante though she was no longer my landlord. As we lounged in a beer garden on a warm afternoon, I told her everything.

"And Bellamy! That one. He still looks at me as if I were a dog riding a bicycle."

"And how do you look at him?"

I wasn't sure what she was getting at. The suds swirled in my empty mug. "What do you mean?"

"As an obstacle?"

"Yes, I suppose."

"Not a person?"

"Of course he's a person."

"But do you credit him that way? With thoughts and feelings, the same as you? Everyone is just doing what he thinks best, Kate."

"But they're wrong."

"And likely, they think the same of you. They think you're mistaken, and you think they are. What's the difference? You need to treat them with respect, no matter what. Eventually, they will do the same."

"That could take a long time."

"What's your rush?" she asked and took a long drink of her lager.

She made a good argument. Who cared what they thought? I was able to do what I needed to do. And every time we brought a criminal to justice, I felt the flood of excitement course through my body, and there was no better feeling. I had found a good place in a bad world, and there was nothing else to be done but stay in that place as long as I could and do my work as well as I could do it.

In the fall, it seemed only a curiosity, if a tragedy, that a hurricane off the coast of the Carolinas brought down a ship with four hundred souls aboard. But then the news spread that there had been an unearthly amount of gold—two million dollars!—aboard as well. The Ship of Gold went down in September. The Panic began shortly after.

The month the banks closed was the worst. Once-comfortable people who'd lost their savings in bad investments became desperate, quick to turn to crime. And the enterprising criminals of the Midwest were quick to take advantage, setting up snow jobs and long cons that made the victims of the crash believe they could make a quick buck and get back to where they'd been. But there was no going back; there never was. We kept busy, to say the least.

But we had reason to fear for our future. The Panic was a disaster for the railroads, and our fate was utterly entwined with theirs. Ohio Life's collapse, plunging grain prices, declining settlement in the West—it all added up to less for our friends at Illinois Central.

And I found that the more I worked with the Pinkerton Agency, the less I found myself thinking about anything else. By the end of the year, Mrs. Borowski nearly had to drag me away from the office to socialize. I canceled plans with her on short notice twice in a row, so when she proposed tickets to an Olive Oatman lecture, I agreed and promised I would not renege. I was glad she persisted, as I didn't want to lose her friendship. Still, even as we sat in the audience looking up at the woman at the podium, I found myself thinking like a detective.

Mrs. Borowski had devoured *Life Among the Indians* and couldn't wait to hear the woman's firsthand tale, and she sat in rapture. But I found Miss Oatman unnerving, with the blue tattoo covering her chin that made her look like some kind of talking skull. She seemed weary, defensive. No one else seemed to find her tone amiss. I wondered if even an evening's harmless entertainment was beyond me.

I was deeply suspicious. Was her tale true? Abducted and held prisoner by Indians from the tender age of fourteen but unmolested for all those years? Had her sister, also a prisoner, died of starvation as she claimed? There were countless other ways to die, many of them more excruciating, many of them someone's fault. I was always looking for angles now, always wondering if people were what they seemed.

Certainly, these days, I never was.

CHAPTER ELEVEN
SEDUCTION

I knew the howl of an unhappy child when I heard one. Halfway across the park, I halted at the sound and immediately scanned the horizon for its source. Was it a girl or a boy? How old? And where? I followed as the scream shifted from a long cry to a series of shorter, breathless bursts.

Near the base of a tree, I spotted her. A small, curly-haired girl with a reddened face, her mouth open and trembling. She clutched her leg, and while I saw no blood, her awkward position on the grass made me suspect she had fallen from a low branch above.

"There, there," I said as I approached. "Everything will be quite all right."

The girl glared poison at me. I very nearly walked away. I'd never had a good manner with children, having no sisters or brothers nor children of my own who'd lived.

Nonetheless, the girl appeared to be alone, so I continued to draw closer and knelt down alongside her to make sure she wasn't badly wounded. "Let's take a closer look at that leg, shall we? Can you tell me if it hurts?"

She shook her head vehemently, but whether she was saying no to my first question or my second, I couldn't tell.

"Oh goodness! There you are! Violet, what's happened?"

I didn't even have time to turn to look in the direction of the woman's voice before the little girl's body was swept up into the air, the broad fabric of her striped skirt swinging wide. I brushed the dirt from my own dress and rose to meet the new arrival.

The dark-haired woman cradled the child, her head bent over the smaller one, whispering soft and comforting words directly into her tiny ear. I felt like an intruder standing this close. The girl's heaving shoulders began to settle. Her crying began to slow.

The woman seemed to notice me then and looked at me over her daughter's head.

"Oh, what you must think of me," she said. "What kind of mother am I?"

I didn't know what kind of mother she might be, but I did know whose wife she was. There had been a very good likeness in the case file. She was Catherine Maroney, the suspect's wife, the woman I'd come to Philadelphia to find.

"Could you use some help managing?" I asked, not missing a beat. "I'd be glad to see you two home."

I'd been assigned to the Adams Express case in the early summer of 1858, only days after one congressman beat another nearly to death with a cane on the very floor of the United States Congress, proving how mad our world had become. The transport company Adams Express, our client, had lost a stunning $40,000 in gold from a locked pouch between Birmingham and Mobile. Pinkerton and I deduced that if the pouch hadn't been unlocked in transit, perhaps it had been tampered with even before it was loaded on the train, and suspicion fell squarely on the shoulders of Nathan Maroney, the Birmingham stationmaster. He'd already been arrested, but the company was hesitant to bring suit without solid evidence. Maroney was Southern, the company Northern. The case was a pure tinderbox.

"They've called for a man half horse and half alligator," said Pinkerton. "Instead, I shall send them you."

Dispatched to Birmingham to befriend Maroney's wife, Catherine, I was hastily rerouted along the way to Philadelphia, where she had fled scrutiny. Upon arrival in the new city, I was caught with no plan, no residence, no easy way to find Catherine and her daughter, Violet. Had this been my first case, I might have panicked, but with several years of experience behind me, I simply set to the task.

With careful inquiries and a few timely tears at the station, everything expressed in my well-honed drawl, I found the Society Hill boardinghouse most hospitable to Southern women and secured a room. Then I made a habit of lingering in the places my fellow guests frequented. One of these places was a lovely park along Sixth Street just past Independence Hall, and that was where the sound of Violet Maroney's cries had reached me, bringing me the luck I needed to break the case wide open.

Mrs. Maroney and I became fast friends. She was a socially gregarious woman, and her isolation in Philadelphia had been a great trial to her. Having found my willing ear, she bent it at every opportunity. She had a habit of complimenting her listener effusively, even when nothing was being said. *Oh, you'll understand. You always understand. I'm so glad you're here, and isn't it wonderful to sit like this? No one else is as much a comfort to me as you are.* When she began saying these things, I knew they weren't true—she'd only known me for three days; how could I be a comfort?—but saying them made them true somehow, and I came to expect and depend on her confidences, drinking them up like the roots of a parched plant.

It was hard for me to reconcile our easy friendship with my unfriendly intentions. In a way, I meant this woman harm. If her husband were never convicted, she would be able to enjoy his ill-gotten gains. The money would flow. Her life would be better. My sole purpose was to take that away. And in pursuit of that goal, I would misrepresent myself to her, claim to be someone I wasn't.

But I found a way to make my peace with misrepresentation. We were all misrepresenting ourselves to each other after all. To live in this world daily was to traffic in the business of leading other people astray. Thanks to my upbringing, I'd had more experience with that than most. Now, it was my profession.

After a week, I had heard Cath Maroney complain countless times of how lonesome she was in this Northern town, how resentful she was to be exiled. I had tried a number of times to shift her subject, wondering aloud why her husband was not with her, asking the reason for her stay in Philadelphia. But she lied smoothly, claiming her husband had sailed to England for a time to resolve an issue with a family inheritance, and she never even mentioned his Christian name.

When the breakthrough came, it took all I had not to reveal my shock.

"Oh, Mrs. Wofford," she said.

"Kate."

"Of course, Kate. You know I've been so lonely for female companionship."

"I do know it! I'm so glad we found each other."

She reached out to squeeze my hand, and I smiled.

"There's nothing like the comfort of a bosom friend. However—"

"Oh!" I said, uncertain where the conversation might lead. "Am I failing in that regard? Please do tell me if there's another way I can be a better friend to you."

She made an odd face and sighed. "It's certainly nothing of yours I need, my dear. Female companionship is a great joy to me. But there's another type of companionship I'm also quite eager for, and as of yet, I've not found it in this city."

Still unsure of her message, I said, "I'm sure this city has a great many things."

"But does it have the satisfaction only a man can provide?"

I couldn't suppress my reaction. "Cath!"

She laughed, peals of laughter rippling through the air like bells upon bells. "I do believe I've shocked you."

"You have!" I knew she trusted me, but to speak so openly about such things, especially as a married woman whose husband was known to be absent, was utter madness. No matter who I seemed to be, shock was apt.

She said, "We must claim what we want, Kate. Do you hide your desires and thoughts?"

I had to answer carefully. "We all hide something."

"Not me," she said with a laugh. "And I'm all the happier for it."

Running my fingertip along the table and recognizing my luck at last, I said, "I do believe I know a man who can provide…what you're looking for. He'll just be passing through the city, but I imagine—I suppose—well, a man staying only a short while in Philadelphia would suit your purposes, wouldn't he?"

She beamed and clutched my hand. "I knew I could trust you."

"Completely."

I sent my missive from the telegraph office on a Monday. On Wednesday, my answer came in the person of Graham DeForest, looking more handsome than ever, bearing tidings from home and the name Graham Kelley.

Both professionally and personally, I was overjoyed. I had asked for him to be assigned, of course, but there was no guarantee Pinkerton wouldn't send someone else. There was no one more suited to the task than DeForest. It would only be a matter of time.

I met him in his boardinghouse and not mine, just to be safe. His was far from Society Hill. After pleasantries, he stretched like a cat and said, "So help me get my bearings. You didn't say much."

"I hate to bankrupt the client with long telegrams."

"I'm needed, you said. For what?"

"To be a very good friend to Mrs. Maroney."

"Aren't you already that?"

"Not in the way she seeks," I said and explained.

He nodded, following perfectly. He didn't seem nearly as shocked as I'd been, but he knew more of the world, I supposed. "Her husband isn't dead yet, but she's already acting the merry widow."

"She'll be merrier with you as her very good friend."

"I understand. You'll introduce us, yes? Have you primed the pump?"

"I told her she'd adore you. And she will."

He put up his feet. "So I get into her good graces, take her around the town."

"Yes."

"All the while, you'll be the angel on her shoulder."

"Devil, more like."

"Both, as the situation warrants. You can urge her to trust me, to run away with me. If she's going to do that, she'll need money. If she has any idea at all where her husband's stolen money is, she'll retrieve it in an instant. We'll have our evidence and be done."

It sounded more mercenary in his words than it had inside my mind. I couldn't deny the other outcome of a successful plan. "And her heart will be broken."

"Kate," he said, setting his feet on the floor and taking a more serious tone. "Do you think I revel in that? I don't. But the money is stolen. It's not her husband's, and it's not hers. Our client demands its return. That's what I'm here to do, whatever it takes."

"Whatever it takes? You'll do absolutely anything?"

"Of course."

I wanted to be perfectly clear, and for once—inspired, perhaps, by Cath herself—I spoke the truth flat out. "You'll seduce her?"

"If it's required."

"But how could you even..." I began.

He eyed me suspiciously, pulling himself back a little bit into his chair as I trailed off. We sat in silence for a tense moment.

I didn't need to tell him, but I wanted to. I couldn't be myself with anyone else, certainly not with Cath, but I could with him. His secret was between us, and I knew it, but he didn't. The time had come to strike it.

All in a rush, I said, "Look, DeForest, I know about you."

His demeanor remained cool. "Ha ha. If you're trying to get me to confess something, it won't work. We're both better operatives than that, aren't we?"

"I wasn't trying to find it out, I swear. I was just practicing my surveillance skills. But..."

"Kate," he said, more serious, his dark brows as low as I'd ever seen them. "Enough. It's not funny. I've come a long way to help out."

I said, "I saw you once. The bar off LaSalle. With the blond man." I named the address and saw recognition dawn on his face.

In that moment, the man I knew dropped away. The sleek, jovial face became instantly pale, almost haunted. In his eyes, I saw true fear. He made sense to me then. He wore the mask of a ladies' man to conceal what kind of man he truly was. He'd had a fellow feeling for me from the beginning because he knew, so perfectly, what it was to be different from everyone else.

"Oh God," he said and reached for me with both hands. He pinned my arms to the table, his hands on my wrists, clutching tightly. "I can't—you can't tell anyone. How much do you want? Anything, you can have it. Anything."

"DeForest," I said. "No."

"Please."

"You're my friend," I told him. I had to tug on my hands

twice, the second time with some force, to get him to release me. "I won't betray you. You've been too good to me, whatever else you are."

A smile tried to work its way onto his face, but the fear didn't leave his eyes. In some way, I couldn't possibly fathom him, his unnatural interests, his decision to be like he was. But the undertow of his terror I understood.

I said, "So you understand why I asked about what you plan to do with Cath."

He said grimly, "I plan to do what the work requires."

"Good, then."

The introduction went as well as I'd hoped, and the two of them got on like a house on fire.

That very first evening, the three of us dined in an ale house off Second Street, near the water. DeForest made a sly joke about the salubrious effects of oysters. Cath giggled merrily, putting her hand on his arm. I pretended I didn't understand, because it didn't feel right either to laugh along with them or to act shocked by their instant intimacy. They would do what they would do. I could encourage or discourage it, whichever I thought made it more likely for Cath to desert her husband and turn over everything she knew about the stolen money to us.

I sat there a divided woman, both that night and the week of nights that followed, whether I was with the two of them or alone with Cath. As she swooned in raptures about her good friend Mr. Kelley's attentions, the operative in me gloated. We'd soon have what we needed; everything was going according to plan. But another part of me cringed and shrank away. I wanted to warn her not to get too attached, and on occasion, I did. The woman I was pretending to be would have done the same. It was safe. I could say, *Now don't forget you're a married woman to the eyes of the world.* I could say, *I know love overwhelms all reason.* I could not say, *The man you love will never love you, will never love a woman at all, doesn't have any esteem for you, is tricking you every minute of every day, and so am I. Run, run, run.*

But who wouldn't love DeForest? His careful attention, his suave manner, his devastating grin. She stood no chance.

I told myself we could only catch her doing wrong if she did wrong. If she were truly innocent, there was no evidence we could manufacture that would entrap her. That was how I slept that night and many others. The guilty were the ones who ensnared themselves, imprisoned themselves, surrendered themselves. We were only collecting on a debt.

G

After a week, I went to visit her one morning, and I could tell immediately from the pink in her cheeks that a corner had been turned. Cath and I had breakfast together at the boardinghouse table, and she couldn't stay still, poking the legs of the table with her toes, tapping her fingers merrily on the saucer under her teacup. She only made idle chitchat while we ate, but I knew far more was to come and proposed we go out for a walk together. It was raining, but she readily agreed.

We raised our umbrellas and stood close together, keeping the rain off our shoulders and giving us some small measure of privacy. We were barely even off the porch, but she wasted no time in clutching my hand and whispering her news.

"He wants me to run away with him."

"A scandal!" I said. "Delicious! Will you?"

"I want to. Oh, how I want to."

"You two do seem to…get on."

"We do!" She laughed in delight, but her face quickly grew serious. "But oh, I don't know. Nathan is counting on me…"

It was the first time she'd ever used his name with me. I chose my words carefully. They needed to pertain to the story she'd told me as well as the story that was true. "Nathan abandoned you."

"Yes and no. He told me he depends on me. I'm the only one who can save him."

I steered us toward the park. The rain made a soothing sort of patter on our umbrellas over our heads. "A lot of men say things like that. Doesn't make them true. What do you have to save him from anyway?"

"I can't tell you."

I pretended to pout. "Oh, but you tell me everything!"

"I want to. It's only that—well, I haven't been completely honest."

"I'm sure you had good reason. And you can, you know. Be honest."

"You may judge me."

"Would you judge me," I asked, taking a confessional tone, "knowing I was once married to a gambler? A man with no control, no restraint, who lost all our money time and again?"

"Of course not. That's not your fault."

"We never know the men we marry," I intoned, "until well after we've married them. And by then, it's too late."

She nodded fiercely. "It's so."

"So if this—Nathan, was it?—has done wrong by you, I say you owe him precious little."

"But he hasn't deserted me. Not exactly."

I sensed her starting to push back, falling into the position of defending her husband against me, even though I was only echoing the worst of what she herself had thought and said. I needed to change tactics. I took her hand and paused.

"I suppose you're right. Married for better or for worse, isn't that what they say? Though it's been far more of the worse lately."

She clutched her umbrella a bit more tightly. "It has."

"But if he's kept his promises to you—well, has he kept them?"

"He's tried." She looked unsure.

"In that spirit, I guess you need to keep your promise to him. Forgoing any chance of your own happiness, of course. It'll be hard to break that to poor Mr. Kelley. He really is such a fine man. So…appealing."

"He is, isn't he?"

"And he certainly seems to dote on little Violet."

"He does."

My words felt like weapons, but there was no going back. I stabbed and twisted. "She deserves to be happy too, I think. I don't know how that can happen if this husband of yours leaves you high and dry. Unless you have the reserves to run away and start a new life somewhere."

I saw the light go on in her head. The choice of words had been right. She gazed out at the rainy park, the tension in her face relaxing, melting away. "I might be able to find reserves like that."

"I don't just mean strength. I know you're strong. I also mean money. Do you need that kind of help from me? I'll do my best."

A smile came over her face. "No, dear, sweet one. I have money."

"Whyever aren't you using it now, then?" I exclaimed. "Cath, you could be so much happier! Either use a little to make your life better or a lot to start a new life outright! Whatever you do, if you have the chance at freedom, I'd take it. I wish I had such a chance."

"Oh, my dear Kate, I wish you did too," she said, and then I knew I had her.

She made her plans and her choice. Her paramour Mr. Kelley gave her the time and date to meet at the station, claiming he had bought train tickets for all three of them. Disguised, I tailed her. She swept into the bank on Market and out again, and it took no time at all for me to discover the alias she'd used there. Immediately after, I reported the wrongdoing to the local authorities, as Pinkerton had advised me. After that, our part was done.

Cath would be intercepted on her way to the station. That way, neither I nor DeForest had to break the news of our deception to her, though our feelings were not the reason for the procedure. It was simply better practice never to reveal a cover identity unless it was absolutely necessary. DeForest might have occasion to become Mr. Kelley again, or I might find myself in Philadelphia in the future as Mrs. Wofford. Hidden things had value, if we could keep them that way.

The logical part of me thought our betrayal of Cath Maroney no more remarkable than any other case, but there was a growing cloud on my soul that had nothing to do with logic. She had been my friend—or as close as I could get to one, given the deceit on both sides. And I knew her feelings for the mythical Mr. Kelley were as true as they could be. She'd fallen in love with the man, even if he wasn't the man she thought, and I'd fed that fire. She'd trusted us, and we were her downfall.

We'd even used her little daughter against her. Was there any forgiving that?

I left Philadelphia the day after the arrest, and the ride home to Chicago was long and lonely. Procedure dictated that DeForest and I take separate trains, and truth be told, I wasn't sure it would be a good idea to discuss it with him. I was still reeling from what I knew he'd done.

The boss had told us many times that he did not expect his operatives, male or female, to perform amoral acts of intimacy with our targets. But regardless of what he expected, I realized at last, these things happened. A woman like Cath Maroney would hardly run away with a man who merely pressed his lips gently against the back of her outstretched hand. She had appetites, and I had no doubt he'd done what was necessary to sate them. I knew she was a criminal, and I didn't admire that, but I did admire how she'd known what she wanted and pursued it without qualms, without hesitation.

I had appetites too but no one to sate them for me, and I lived like a sacred sister. I hadn't even attempted a romance in years. Who would I pursue, or who would pursue me? Everyone I met was either a colleague or a suspect. It wasn't that my fellow agents weren't fine examples of men, some of them very much so—I caught myself more often than I liked noticing a gentle hand, a firm jaw, the muscles of a strong back I might like to feel under my fingertips—but entangling myself with one would allow the others to discount me. They'd say they'd always known I was hunting a husband, not justice. I wouldn't take the risk.

After two and a half years in the same boardinghouse, I still didn't know the name of a single person who lived there other than the landlady, Mrs. Morris, nor did I know even her Christian name. The only man who'd been in my bedroom since Charlie's death was Tim Bellamy, the night Sarah Harrington died. I grinned to myself, thinking how he would react if I told him of the honor, how he would bristle and bluster. I could still picture the outline of his rigid back as he stood, facing away from me, eyes on the door.

There were days that I loved my life, and I couldn't imagine anything that suited me better than the work of a Pinkerton operative. I would not have traded it. But riding the train back to Chicago, free of artifice for the moment, with no one to deceive or impress, I realized how lonely I was.

I stared out the window at the empty dark. The invisible countryside sped by me. I told myself to stop fixating on such things. After all, I doubted the other operatives thought of themselves this way. I couldn't imagine someone like Jack Mortenson, grim and resolute, letting even a trace of remorse for the things he'd done cloud his mind. But I was not Jack Mortenson, nor was I meant to be.

I wondered, not for the first time, whether my experience as an investigator had changed me or whether this was the woman I truly was. All my life, I'd done what my parents told me to do, up to and including my disastrous marriage. I'd thought myself a good girl then, quiet and dutiful, always ready to obey. Perhaps I was disguised even from myself.

The woman I'd become since Pinkerton hired me—excited by subterfuge, capable of any and all lies, slipping into and out of identities like dresses—was she the real me?

Had I been her all along, and the good girl I thought myself the real disguise?

CHAPTER TWELVE
A LITTLE LIFE

Mere hours after I returned from Chicago, I found my position so changed, I felt I was in a dream. From my solo ride of anguish and confusion, I went to the most extraordinary spectacle: a Christmas party at Allan Pinkerton's house.

I had only ever seen the outside of the boss's house, and that only a few times. He was not a man who advocated mixing pleasure and business, for obvious reasons. I remembered, years ago now, tailing him home while I practiced my surveillance skills. He had returned all three nights to this tidy clapboard house on Randolph. Now, I suspected he had known of the surveillance and simply refrained from mentioning it to me out of politeness. I wondered what he thought of me, then and now. He was not a man given to great displays in my experience.

When I entered, the party was in full swing. I took the measure of the room quickly and located the boss surrounded by smaller figures. Two boys and two girls.

His children. There was one girl in her teens, looking somber but excited, and two slightly younger boys, who seemed antsy and uninterested in the goings-on. Then there was a much smaller girl, pink-cheeked to match her pink dress, flounced and ruffled within an inch of her life.

I had never thought of Pinkerton as a father, though I knew he had a family. I knew also, from office gossip, that there had been a handful of tragedies and not all of his children had survived to the present day. But there was never any reason for him to talk about them, either the living ones or the dead. After all, I was the one who was tested when we played truth or lie; he never told me stories in return, and so I knew next to nothing about him. Strange, considering he was probably the person who knew me best in all the world.

Then the music began. It was inexpressibly odd to hear a reel being played while looking at the faces of men I'd only seen acting criminal, not to mention the petite women and round-cheeked children scampering about among them. The fiddle soared, the man with the bow sawing away with great vigor, and for a while, I only watched his face. The music faded away. His expression told the tale. Perhaps that was another skill I could add to my repertoire, this silent pantomime, this kind of energy.

Then I let my gaze slide away from the fiddle player, surveying the room, and what I saw astounded me.

Allan Pinkerton had grasped the hands of his smallest daughter, the pink one, and was scampering in circles in an uneven, galloping gait. You could have knocked me down with a feather.

It put a smile on my face. So he was a man after all and not a machine for solving crimes. Perhaps we could all be like that: intellects in real bodies, living our lives as full people. Perhaps there was hope for me after all.

A familiar voice behind me said, "He'll always be theirs, you know."

Familiar—and unwelcome. I knew who it was without turning. "I don't know what you mean, Mortenson."

"You know it very well, *Kate*," he said. He stood at my left shoulder, and when I didn't turn to look at him, he took two steps to face me, head-on.

Not moving, I corrected him. "Mrs. Warne."

"Was there ever really a Mr. Warne? Can it be proven? Or is it a fig leaf to conceal your lifelong solitude?"

There was a small reddish stain on his starched white collar, just to the left of center, and I fixed my gaze on it. Angry and exhausted, I wanted so badly to tell him the entire truth about Charlie, about how our marriage started and how it ended. A tale of blood and wrongdoing. Maybe that would silence his taunts. But I did my best to emulate Mrs. Borowski, her even temperament, and the calmer soul within me prevailed. If I told, the truth would only become a cudgel he could use against me. The best I could do was give him nothing.

Instead, I said, "I assure you, I'm a true and happy widow."

He was dogged. "And were you a happy wife?"

"Happier than yours, I'm sure," I said. In truth, I knew he was not married, nor had he ever been. But the silence that greeted my rejoinder suggested I'd struck home.

At that moment, Graham DeForest swept to my rescue in a festive moss-green frock coat and contrasting burgundy vest, a cup of punch borne high through the air in each hand. He bowed and handed mine over, smiling broadly under his impeccable mustache.

"Welcome back!" he cried. "Just in?"

"Just."

"Wouldn't be a shindy without you."

I inclined my head royally. "My pleasure, kind sir."

He stepped back and inspected me, nodding in approval. I was wearing the only dress in my closet that wasn't wrinkled and musty from disuse, a striped mint-green taffeta with pagoda sleeves.

Then he looked at our cups and at Mortenson—just seeming to notice him now, though of course, he wasn't—and said, "Sorry, Jack, didn't think to get you one."

"I don't drink spirits."

"And therefore have you none," he said. "But I jest!" He clinked his cup against my cup and gestured to the dancing, bending his head close to mine, effectively shutting Mortenson out of the conversation.

The neglected man slipped away. I couldn't help feeling sorry for him for just a moment—never comfortable in conversation, not anyone's favorite, always the odd man out. But his absence did help me breathe a bit easier, and I took a grateful sip from my cup. I watched him without turning my head; our detecting skills always came in handy, even in an atmosphere like this one, which might not seem to call for them.

After a few minutes, Mortenson joined a circle of conversation that included Tim Bellamy, who had an unusually dainty young lady decorating his arm. I couldn't help but stare at her. Her gown was made of a deep pink silk with five flounces, lovely and clearly expensive. Ribbons ornamented her sleeves. The waves of her jet-black hair, parted in the center and beautifully styled into broad loops, gleamed in the light above her silver, bell-shaped earbobs. Most remarkably, she looked up into Bellamy's face with an open, rapt gaze. I nudged DeForest.

"Is Bellamy married?"

He glanced over with a subtle motion. "Affianced, I believe."

"Good for him, then."

"Won't last. They never do."

The idea of upright, stony Bellamy as a serial fiancé struck me as slightly ludicrous. "He's been engaged to be married before?"

DeForest laughed. "Not him in particular. It's the work. Late nights, too many secrets, never able to talk about anything or build a life in private. We belong to the work first and foremost. Everything else comes second or not at all. The other person never understands."

"Seems like Pinkerton's wife does."

"The exception to the rule. And he's the boss—he's not out on cases day and night. It's different for us. When an operative is involved, marriages don't last."

Softly, I said, "Even if you were interested in such things."

"Actually, I'm strongly considering it."

It was the last response I expected to hear from him, given his situation, which he now knew I was aware of. I dropped my voice but kept my tone casual, in case anyone was listening. We both looked straight ahead, watching the dancers. It made the seriousness of our conversation feel less ponderous.

"But why?"

"People ask fewer questions. Wife at home, nobody wonders. You understand?"

"In a sense."

"As a matter of fact," he said, still looking at the dancers and not at me, "I've thought about proposing to one woman in particular."

"She was still married."

"Good God, Kate, not Cath Maroney, that hotfooted harlot. I'm not a fool."

"Aren't you?" I teased.

His mouth turned up at the corner. "Perhaps."

"So who's the mystery lady? A wealthy widow?"

"A widow, yes. Not so wealthy but very intelligent. Perhaps the most level-headed woman I've ever known."

"She sounds like a peach." I was staring at Bellamy's fiancée, just a slip of a girl with a worshipful smile on her rosy pink lips, and wondering if Graham's intended was as lovely.

He continued, "But I wasn't sure whether you might consider getting married again."

Realization took a long moment. I heard what he said, but I didn't understand it. Then it dawned on me, what he was asking.

A proposal. A backward, strange, left-handed proposal of marriage. From a man I knew had no love for me as a woman and could never have.

I burst out laughing.

There was a hysterical edge to it, an uncontrolled note, and I quickly brought my hand up to my mouth to muffle the sound. I couldn't react like this, in a room full of our coworkers, none of whom knew his secret. I'd just been too surprised.

Moments later, I had smothered the sound. A few people seemed to have noticed—Bellamy and his pretty fiancée both appeared to be looking in my direction—but after a heartbeat, they looked away again, returning to their conversations.

My eyes sought DeForest. He still faced the dancers, so I could only see his profile. The sharp features, the set jaw, so handsome. I couldn't read his expression. I knew my reaction had been unexpected, but he betrayed no discomfort, no disappointment. He was a good man.

I said in a calmer tone, "Graham, what an utterly ridiculous idea."

"Is it? We're both alone in the world, aren't we?"

I couldn't disagree. "Yes."

"We enjoy each other's company very much. I respect your mind, and I think you respect mine. I hope?"

"Yes," I said again.

"Plenty of marriages don't even have that." His tone was level, sincere. "If you get married to a real man, he'll expect to stuff you full of babies and take you off Pinkerton's payroll straightaway. Husbands want to be fathers. You'll go from operative to drudge, trailing after your squalling charges instead of bringing criminals to justice. Is that what you want from life?"

After a pause, I said, "Not when you put it that way."

"I think the old man might not like it though," he said, gesturing to where Pinkerton and his daughter danced, their cheeks both flushed. "He wouldn't understand it was just for show. We couldn't tell him, of course. I don't think he could keep my secret as well as you have. As you will."

I stood, speechless again.

"But that can be managed. Consider it for a few days," he said. "No need for us to rush."

He tapped my cup with his again, then turned his attention back to the song.

My head was still spinning from the idea that Graham DeForest might marry a woman he didn't love just to hide in plain sight. Or perhaps it was the punch. I'd drained my cup, and there was no telling how much of the liquid there had been spirits instead of juice. I felt light-headed but not with joy. As if I might faint.

The fiddle sawed a vibrant refrain, the triumphant end to a reel, and then fell silent. Bursts of applause flowed through the room. Bellamy's fiancée freed her hand from his arm long enough to clap three times, then tucked it back into its intimate resting place. Pinkerton released his tiny daughter's hands, and she tumbled, coming to rest in a giggling heap. He beamed at her. She reached her arms up to be lifted.

Next, a petite woman with dark hair stepped to the front of the room. I could have guessed her identity but didn't need to. Under his breath, DeForest said, "Ah. It's the wife."

This, then, was the boss's wife, Joan. She was not the most handsome of women, but there was something commanding about her despite her small size. Her dress was the plainest in the room, a watered brown silk with only a short fringe of the same color around the sleeves for decoration, with no ruffles or frippery. Her hair was tied back in a neat chignon, without even a ribbon to decorate it. Her hands were folded neatly at her waist.

Silently, she raised her hand and made a single gesture to the man at the piano. He set his fingers on the keys and played three slow, lingering notes. Without a word of introduction, Mrs. Pinkerton opened her mouth, and the most beautiful voice I'd ever heard began to pour forth, singing a lilting, mournful ballad. I was absolutely transfixed.

Oh my bonnie love, I dream you
Far from home tossed on the sea
Sail ye far and sail ye fair now
Long as ye sail home to me
Long as ye sail home to me

Oh my bonnie love, why go you
Leaving me to cry alone
Sail ye far and sail ye fair now
Long as ye come sailing home
Long as ye come sailing home

Oh my love, I want to tell you
Of our child you'll meet one day
Wish my words could ever reach you
But ye've sailed so far away
But ye've sailed so far away

Her pure, sweet, soprano voice sounded clear as a trumpet in the large room, and no other noise competed with it. I was not the only member of the audience who couldn't move a muscle for fear we'd disrupt the spell of Joan's song. Next to me, DeForest was absolutely motionless. I saw no one move except for the little children, who stared up at their mother as she sang, looks of rapture on their tiny faces. Her husband also gazed at Joan with absolute adoration, a love I would never have thought him capable of but now so plain on his face, it could have been written there in ink.

Oh my bonnie one, I loved you
But you've gone across the sea
In her arms you sleep forever

Never will ye sail to me
Never will ye sail to me

Her voice broke on the last few words, as if the emotion of the song was too much to be borne. Whether her sentiment was truth or show, I couldn't say. I only knew that mine rose up and overwhelmed me.

The terrible truth hit me like a fist between the eyes.

The children and husband gazing with wonder upon the woman who belonged to them. The smile she gave them in return, part proud, part shy. This was a true, honest, full family, and I would never have anything like it.

DeForest was right. A real marriage was beyond me. Even if I could find someone to love me—and who would do that?—there would be no children. The doctor had made that clear. Any family I might have would be a cover identity at best. An assigned husband, ersatz children, fabricated as a snare. No one real. No one true.

To my horror, I began to cry.

I stepped back, intending to make my escape.

DeForest laid a hand gently on my elbow. "Kate?"

I shook my head, not trusting my voice, and stepped away. I retired from the room and hoped no one would follow.

Down the hall, I found myself in a smaller room, a dark parlor. I seated myself at the far end of it, trusting the dark to obscure me at least in part. I didn't want to roam farther into the house for fear I'd be an intruder, and that would raise more questions than even my foolish tears would do.

After a few minutes, I was able to get myself under control. I wiped the rising tears away forcefully with the corner of my handkerchief and slapped my cheeks so that the pain would give me something to focus on. It worked for half a minute. I was pinching the web of flesh between my thumb and forefinger for a new distraction when I heard faint footsteps, growing louder.

The footsteps were a woman's, soft and light, leather against a wooden floor. My eyes were dry now. I looked up to face whoever was coming.

Joan Pinkerton entered the room. Even though she was no longer singing, she still retained the aura of power that had flowed from her along with the music. I found myself shrinking even as she approached, before she said a word.

"I'm sorry," I said. "I was a bit dizzy from the heat and just needed a moment. I'm better now."

She walked up to where I sat. There was an empty chair next to me, but rather than seating herself in it, she stared from above. Close up, I could see the pattern in her dress, tiny squares on squares within the silk. Hidden nested boxes.

"You're the famous Mrs. Warne, then," she said in a thicker brogue than her husband's. Her tone too was unlike his. She made it sound like there might be something wrong with being famous—not that I even was—and most definitely something wrong with being Mrs. Warne.

"It's a pleasure to meet you at last," I replied, extending a hand, hoping I could keep my composure.

She gazed at me coolly and did not take the hand.

"Ma'am?"

"Listen once and listen well, Mrs. Warne," she said, not loudly. "You keep your grubby mitts off my husband. Don't think I don't know what you're up to with your late nights and your cases and your *work*."

"Ma'am, you're mistaken, I swear." I was flabbergasted.

"Swear nothing. You lie for a living, like he does. Save us both the trouble."

I opened my mouth to answer back, and she hissed at me, flat out hissed. The tears pricked at my eyes again. If my work was carving out a little life, without a husband and children, was even that little life to be judged so harshly?

All I could do was meet fire with fire or crumble under her scrutiny. When I stood, I was a half head taller than her, and I tried to use that.

"What a lovely little song you sing," I said frostily. "It's so nice that you have something." Then I swept past her and walked back to join the party, wanting to vomit, and not because of the punch.

I sought and found DeForest a handful of minutes later, holding court in the corner with half a dozen other operatives, telling a story of a woman who wouldn't stop pursuing him, which no one else in the room seemed to suspect for the grand fiction I knew it must be.

For a while, I watched him, considering. He was a good and kind man. He would not judge me for the woman I was, because he knew what I did, and it was no worse than what he did. He even respected me for it.

I knew also that my face was not the kind of face that inspired instant devotion. Charlie had made sure I'd known it, and though his opinion was only that of a fool and a sot, it had sunk in with repetition. Men were hardly lining up to lend me a new last name. I hadn't been born a Warne, but without a miracle, it seemed I might die that way.

And there was more to consider. If I were married to DeForest—he would make a striking groom, wouldn't he?—would that keep me safe from the jealousy of women like Joan Pinkerton? Could it be my safeguard against the men in the office who assumed I'd been having an affair of the heart with Pinkerton for years now, simply because they couldn't imagine my skills and capabilities were enough to earn my success?

I knew I would be safety for him, that no one would suspect his secret if he were squared away with a wife. He would have to be careful with his activities, of course, but he'd managed to keep them quiet so far. We could protect each other. Keep each other safe from what we both feared.

I stared at his profile for a long time.

His story came to an end, and his laughter was echoed by the laughter of the men around him, and he caught my eye.

I beckoned him away and spoke quietly and quickly, hoping not to draw attention. Our conversation was short.

"I can't," I said to him.

He searched my face with those warm brown eyes, eyes that made other women melt. "Are you certain?"

"Absolutely."

"You can think about it a while longer, you know."

"Not necessary. It makes no sense for me. I'm sorry."

I excused myself, smiling a little so no one would remember me upset, and left the party shortly afterward.

It was all lies, in any case. I didn't reject his proposal because it made no sense. I rejected him because it made too much. If I didn't say no right away, some time spent pondering it might be enough to convince me to say yes. I was already far too close to the edge. I might think too much about Joan Pinkerton's jealousy, my own barrenness, the utter lack of love in my life that gave someone the confidence to declare that love wasn't even a possibility. One more log on the fire, one more cup of punch, and I might have given in.

I wasn't ready to do that. Not yet.

CHAPTER THIRTEEN
SPRINGFIELD

L ove makes fools of us all. If I had an inkling of what that meant after Philadelphia, the lesson was hammered home in Springfield.

The railroads had never fully recovered from the Panic, but they had managed to find a new equilibrium, especially our friends at the Illinois Central Railroad. I rarely worked with the railroad—DeForest and Paretsky were our train experts—so I was surprised when Pinkerton summoned me to his office one morning and told me to pack a bag for travel. I was even more surprised that he didn't tell me where we were going or why. But he did tell me that our train would be leaving in just over an hour.

Waiting for him at the station as directed, pacing under the high arches of the grand, curved windows, I felt uneasy. For a lousy reason, but it wouldn't be denied. As masculine as they acted otherwise, the men at the agency gossiped like old biddies at a picnic. Word would quickly spread that the boss and I had gone off somewhere together and stayed overnight. I still couldn't shake the rumors of our love affair, though I was getting very good at ignoring them. I chose not to care. And if it scared me at first how easy it was to make myself feel differently about something by simply deciding it, I decided I could ignore that too.

When Pinkerton hailed me, though, there was nothing in his manner beyond the usual friendly, businesslike air. We stepped aboard the train and seated ourselves on the red cushions of the banquette. Pinkerton waved off the porter and stowed our bags on the rack above our heads himself. Quickly, we were underway.

As we rode, he briefed me on the situation. I knew the parties involved or at least the parties we would be meeting with: the vice president of the Illinois Central Railroad and a lawyer who worked with them, mostly on tax matters. Money was missing from the company's account, and they suspected embezzlement, Pinkerton told me.

"How did they find it out?"

"I want you to hear the story firsthand. The lawyer will tell you."

"Which one's the lawyer?"

"The scarecrow. Lincoln. Acts the country bumpkin but sharper than ten tacks."

"And why is he involved?"

"They want someone from outside the company. He has access to the books easily, and he understands them. All the vice president, McClellan, has is a hunch."

"So what are we to do?"

"Not we. You. I haven't got the time. You'll be working directly with the lawyer on this."

"Oh." It was the first time I had heard him make such a declaration. Generally, we stayed in close contact throughout a case. "Just the lawyer?"

"As I said, they need someone outside the company. The two of you will keep it very hush-hush."

"All right."

"And I shouldn't have to say this, but—no feminine wiles. Don't flirt or simper. They won't work on him."

"Is he—" I thought of DeForest.

"Happily married."

"God bless their everlasting happiness," I said.

"Splendid. Now, lie to me."

If I weren't so accustomed to surprise, I would have flinched. As it was, I raised an eyebrow pointedly. It had been quite some time since Pinkerton had demanded I play our old game.

I said evenly, "On a chosen subject?"

"Your choice."

Marriage was on my mind, so I said, "I was three years old when I first remember my mother telling my father she would leave him."

Pinkerton eyed me steadily as the train gently rocked. At length, he said, "I do not believe a child of three years has such memories."

No one had ever heard this story from me, not even Paul. In a way, it was a relief to speak the truth out loud. "I didn't know all the words she said, but I knew some. I remember *worthless* and *fool* and *mistake.* I knew all those words, because she'd said them to me too."

For the first time in our years of staring each other down to test the truth, he was the first one to look away. He directed his gaze out the window, though there was little to see.

"You are an unusual woman, Kate Warne," he said.

If he had wanted further details, I could have provided them easily. Over the years, my mother had told my father she would leave him countless times. Only his response changed. In the beginning, it was *Please don't.* Then *I doubt that.* Later, it became *What would you do then?* And once when he'd been out late drinking with a Greek chorus, *Then go ahead and leave already.* His response never mattered. The next day always dawned with my mother still in place, maybe muttering or maybe apologizing but never gone.

It was good to know, these years later, this behavior was unusual. At the time, I thought it was how all families behaved.

We sped toward our destination.

❧

The room we were shown to in the law office was plain. One of the men matched the surroundings, and the other did not. The plain one was Lincoln, who wore a plain black suit and thin tie at the neck. He was clean-shaven, with hollow-looking cheeks and dark, bushy hair above a high, wide forehead. The other, McClellan, was showier. He had a bushy mustache and quite possibly the shiniest pair of shoes I'd ever seen.

I nodded my greeting to the lawyer first. "Mr. Lincoln."

"Mrs. Warne. I've heard a lot about you."

"I could say the same, of course."

He leaned over—with his height, he had quite a reach—and whispered conspiratorially, "Let's agree not to believe all the things they say about us, shall we?"

"Agreed."

McClellan shook Pinkerton's hand and welcomed him gruffly but seemed not to perceive that I was in the room at all. For only a moment, I was disconcerted. Clients were often surprised to meet me but rarely openly rude. I decided my best response was to ignore that I'd been ignored.

Pinkerton was the first to seat himself. After the rest of us had followed suit, he turned to me and gave a slight nod. I understood his meaning: *it's your show now.*

"Can you tell me how the suspicion came to light?"

"These books," said Lincoln, sliding them across to me.

I searched the men's faces, keeping my own expression level. It seemed clear I was being put to a test.

So I looked over the books. Three ledgers, incoming and outgoing funds, with the name of the company on the cover and the month and year at the top of each page.

Lincoln, possibly taking pity on me, said, "The first page of every month, working backward."

I opened the top ledger, with the most recent entries, to the beginning of August's figures.

There was an odd pattern I noticed right away—a coincidence, likely, but odd enough to jump out. The first four figures in the month ended in 73¢, then 37¢, then 77, then 33.

"These are correct?" I asked. "These four?"

Lincoln nodded, seemingly impressed. I knew I had to be on the right track.

I flipped to the beginning of July, then June. The same four figures: 73, 37, 77, 33.

"They remain the same."

Lincoln pointed to another ledger, and I looked at the previous year's figures. The first was lower, and so was the second. The third and fourth too, and all by the same amount. 63, 27, 67, 23.

"Ten cents," I said.

"All on regular, recurring bills," said McClellan, speaking for the first time since our introductions.

"Your suppliers' prices hadn't changed?"

"Not these."

"Forty cents a month. Doesn't seem like much."

"Other numbers changed too. These were just the easiest to notice."

"How much overall?"

McClellan confirmed the figure Pinkerton had given me on the train.

"So all this extra money isn't being received by the people the books say it's going to. Where is it going?"

The look on the lawyer's face wasn't quite a smile, but it seemed I had passed his test, if no one else's. "That's what you're here to find out, Mrs. Warne."

McClellan said, "There are two men most likely. Our accountant, Mr. Vincent, or the assistant secretary, Mr. Martin. We need someone to prove where the money is going and bring the guilty party to justice. And we need complete discretion. This kind of thing could cause a terrible scandal."

Pinkerton said, "You will have the finest assistance available in Mrs. Warne. She will not fail to bring in your man."

McClellan looked uncomfortable.

Pinkerton left to go back to Chicago, and I remained in Springfield. I wondered what pressing business was taking him home and had a few theories. First, that he was testing me to see how I did without his direct supervision. Second, that he was testing something about the railroad men instead. Third, that he really did have more pressing business besides a highly confidential investigation on behalf of our biggest, most important client. That seemed the least likely explanation.

Lincoln had a list of options for me to delve into, and I annoyed him by dismissing most of them right off.

"He's not going to buy land," I said, pointing at the list. "Too traceable. He'd have to buy it in his own name, and it's not portable."

"Cattle, then."

"No. Still too much paper."

"Gold."

"Maybe. But you have to go to a bank to get it. And a man buying ounce after ounce of gold is going to be remembered."

"Fine," said Lincoln, folding his arms and exposing an extra inch of bony wrist beyond his too-short cuffs. "Tell me where you think it is."

"Gems."

I saw the switch flip in his head. He wouldn't have thought of it himself—I could tell he was the kind of man who rarely indulged his wife in baubles—but he saw the sense in it right away.

From there, we quickly discovered that there was only one jewelry store of any consequence in Springfield. I asked to take a position there as a clerk, and the lawyer quickly succeeded in arranging it, telling the proprietor that I was a country cousin, a bit of fiction that I think amused us both.

Dressed neatly in a white blouse and a sensible skirt of muted plaid, introducing myself with the name Miss Lincoln, I stood ready to assist any ladies looking to make purchases. The proprietor, Mr. Corwin, was younger than I expected, with a long nose, fine eyebrows he often raised in amusement, and thick, dark, wavy hair. He familiarized me with the stock, from the smallest silver pin to the most ornate, gem-studded necklace and everything in between.

As the days proceeded, Mr. Corwin and I spent a good deal of time in conversation, passing minutes and hours as we waited for customers. He instructed me in good principles of service, and I made him laugh, acting the part of a terrible customer, demanding all sorts of fine manners. He had a crooked, warm smile, and I enjoyed seeing it.

Lincoln and I had decided that I would report once a week. The first week, I had very little to say. Some of the wives of men on the railroad's payroll had come in—I had a list—but their purchases had not been untoward. My confidence began to waver, though I didn't show it, knowing he would only believe in me as long as I appeared to believe in myself.

The second week broke things wide open.

Two women made major purchases. First, a dark-haired woman in middle age whose broad, high bosom made her resemble a pigeon selected the store's showpiece necklace, a ruby affair with branching silver leaves. It looked well enough on her, and both Mr. Corwin and I encouraged the purchase, each for our own reasons. She dithered a long time. When she finally decided to take the necklace, she laughed and clapped, and I saw a peek of the schoolgirl she had once been. When she indicated to Mr. Corwin that the purchase should be placed on the Vincent house account, I was sorely tempted to burst into applause my own self. This, then, was Mrs. Vincent, the accountant's wife.

I asked Mr. Corwin whether this was her first extravagant piece, and he mentioned a brooch she'd purchased six months before, a large cushion-cut sapphire surrounded by diamonds. I felt I couldn't ask for more specifics without arousing his suspicions, but I filed away the information, feeling on the cusp of discovery.

Two days later, a much younger woman with auburn hair purchased a stack of gold-plated bracelets, enough to cuff her arm nearly to the elbow. I wrapped them in pretty paper while she discussed the financial details with Mr. Corwin, so I did not hear what name she gave. After she left, I said, "My goodness! Whoever sponsors her purchases must be quite well-off. Whose account does she use?"

"Bronson," said Mr. Corwin without elaborating.

Something about his manner struck me as odd, as he had never been terse with me, not in the least. I drew close to him and asked in a conspiratorial whisper, "Bronson? I don't believe I've heard that name here before."

He laughed then, his charming, boisterous laugh. "Oh, so be it. I was never a good liar. There is no Mr. Bronson; it is a *nom de guerre* of another gentleman of Springfield who doesn't wish his... sponsorship of the young lady to be known."

I said, closer still, "And who might that gentleman be?"

"Tsk tsk, Miss Lincoln," he said, waving a finger. "There are some secrets I can keep."

I thought it would probably not be hard to get the truth from him when the time was right. He was an open and honest man, and I hated to think about how misled he was about my identity and my purpose in Springfield. We enjoyed each other's company so greatly, during those many hours in the store, and I told myself no one was getting hurt. He had no wife; I had no husband. Our flirtation was only that.

Yet I found myself fantasizing, certainly too often, what it would be like for Miss Lincoln to enter into a relationship with Mr. Corwin. How we might sit in front of a fire, drinking warm wine, entertaining each other with outlandish stories. How one of us might reach for the other's empty glass, set it out of the way, and then reach for the person who'd emptied it. I'd been a married woman, and I knew what a man and a woman did in the dark, but what I had not had with either Paul or Charlie was a romance, and I thirsted for one. I reached for Mr. Corwin countless times in my dreams. Some mornings, it was hard to look at him, knowing how his imagined figure and mine had twisted themselves up together while I slept. And one day, when his hand brushed mine as we both reached to close a display case and he turned crimson, stammering an apology, I knew the signs. He'd been imagining a romance with me—or the woman he thought me to be—as well.

My conversations with Mr. Corwin became more substantive, and one night, he insisted on buying my supper so we might continue talking at a nearby restaurant. We talked so long, the food grew cold on our plates. A few days later at the store, a lady with decidedly thick fingers asked Mr. Corwin to slip a particular ring onto my finger to see how it looked, and he did so cautiously, tentatively, and the air seemed so fraught with possibility, I thought I might burst.

In my next meeting with Lincoln, I shared what I knew about the Vincent and Bronson house accounts, and he set his chin against his fist thoughtfully.

"Bronson," he said. "Could it be Mr. Martin, the assistant secretary, in another guise?"

"It could be. We have one way to find out."

"And that is?"

"People tend toward the familiar," I said. "Would you like to try your hand at clandestine operations?"

He cocked his head, curious.

"Find out their mother's names. Vincent and Martin. Can you do it without arousing suspicion?"

"Yes."

We made a plan to meet again in two days, and when the time came, he was so visibly eager, I knew at a glance that he had succeeded.

"Which one?" I said.

"Mr. Vincent. His mother, God rest her soul, was born Emmaline Bronson."

"Good."

"Is it enough to prove guilt?"

"No." I folded my hands in my lap. "But we have a few possible ways forward."

"Enlighten me."

"We could confront Mr. Vincent now."

"Or?"

"We could call in the police. Again, as you might guess, our evidence is slim. Mr. Vincent could claim that the money used to pay for the ladies' gifts came from any old where, and we couldn't prove otherwise."

"So what do you propose?"

"Let me have a conversation or two, and I'm sure we can bring the matter to a head."

"I trust we shall, Mrs. Warne."

The only remaining question was whether to approach the mistress or the wife first and attempt to bring her in as a witness in exchange for a lesser sentence. I decided to start with the accountant's mistress, one Hazel Everette. She was a petite young lady, not very tall at all, but always wearing heeled boots that brought her up to average height. We stood nearly eye to eye, though I had developed a habit of slouching a little in my shopgirl guise. She favored jewelry with a green stone to set off her auburn hair and over time had nearly cleaned the place out of jade and emeralds.

By this point, I had waited on her at the shop already four or five times. After so many weeks, Mr. Corwin had developed enough trust in me to let me watch the shop alone for short periods. On this occasion, he left us two while he walked out to purchase potpies for lunch—especially as I mentioned I was in the mood for the chicken pie from my favorite tearoom, and he'd be such a dear to bring one—so I had the chance to speak freely.

She couldn't decide between three different sets of jade earbobs and, in the end, decided to take all three.

"A pretty penny," I said, reaching under the counter for a few small boxes in which she could carry the jewelry away. "All on Mr. Bronson's account?"

"Of course."

"He certainly funds you generously."

She laughed. "I'm worth it."

"Is he a tycoon?"

"An accountant."

We'd felt quite sure of the identity of the Bronson account's real holder, but with this, the last scrap of doubt vanished. "Goodness, I wouldn't have suspected! An accountant? I can't imagine that his position pays him enough to afford all this."

Matter-of-factly, she said, "No, it doesn't."

"Do you think he's doing something untoward to get the money?"

"I'm sure of it."

Her even, confident tone should have tipped me off, but I went ahead with my planned question. "And don't you think that's wrong?"

"Oh, honey," she said. "Whoever do you think gave him the idea?"

I was speechless. I think she took my shock as the silence of an impressed audience rather than an appalled one.

"He even tried to stop a few months back," she said. "I told him if he did, I'd tell his company and the authorities and the world about what he'd been doing. He's been even more generous since."

So I did not enlist her, as I'd hoped, to testify against him. I reported the conversation to Lincoln and asked if he thought we should try again with the wife. He decided instead to confront Mr. Vincent directly, reasoning that a man guilty enough to yield to blackmail would likely collapse under direct questioning.

He was right. The confession came quickly. The railroad sacked the accountant immediately and claimed his wife's jewelry to recover what they could of what he owed. They chose not to bring criminal charges against him for fear of publicity, and by the time they went looking for Hazel Everette, she and her gems were already gone.

Our failure to bring Hazel to justice—she was more guilty than Vincent in my eyes—weighed on me. I didn't care for the picture of her in my mind's eye—on to her next victim, silk stockings and jade earbobs to help her snare him, footloose and fancy free.

And I had a victim of my own. I reported to my final day of work with Mr. Corwin, and the brilliant smile he turned on me as I walked in the door squeezed like a fist around my heart. Lincoln entered the door right after me, officious and brusque, and Corwin's smile melted away. I could barely look at him as Lincoln explained what had happened, the investigation and its results, and how they would need an official accounting from him of all gems purchased on both the Vincent and Bronson accounts.

When Lincoln gestured to me in passing as he said, "Our fine agent, Mrs. Warne," the look on Mr. Corwin's face turned from surprise to anger, then disgust. I wanted to fling myself into his arms and apologize, tell him everything he thought was between us truly was, even if I'd misrepresented myself, but I kept my composure instead. We'd barely known each other. We had no future—a Pinkerton agent in Chicago and a jewelry store owner in Springfield, a liar and an honest man, worlds apart. As much as I wanted to confess, I couldn't, knowing it would do no one good.

And so I watched his face turn hard, crushing my heart with every passing moment, and finally, I just stopped watching.

CHAPTER FOURTEEN

THE ACTRESS

Allan Pinkerton and I knelt on the floor of Bellamy's costume closet, the cuffs of empty sack coats dangling just above our heads. The agency's new office on Clark Street was a great sign of our increased success, but it hummed with constant activity, and this room was the only place the boss could avoid the never-ending parade of visitors and operatives wanting his attention. We met here for confidential conversations. Only this time, I feared the conversation might be our last.

In the new closet, there was a full rack of gowns, shawls, and other ladies' garments set aside for my use. Bellamy had allowed me the space only grudgingly but didn't interfere with what I chose. A glance around the room told a story that had not changed; men's things and men's things and men's things, and then mine.

By the winter of 1860, the Pinkerton Detective Agency had doubled in size, with two dozen operatives and several clerks on its books. We also had a full-time secretary in the front office and half a dozen men who provided what we called "security": beefy, intimidating men who rarely spoke more than a word or two at a time. I never could tell them apart. They all looked like they might be our sturdy colleague Taylor's cousins or brothers or Taylor himself.

As for me, I was more successful than ever and a victim of

my own success. Requests for female operatives had soared. The world—or at least Chicago—had finally caught on to what Allan Pinkerton and I had known for ages. Women were better suited to certain investigations than men. As a result, there was far more work than I could handle. I was always working at least two cases at a time. Getting less and less sleep.

And now it seemed there would be consequences. The night before, I'd failed to show up for a planned rendezvous with some out-of-town visitors we'd been asked to keep an eye on. I'd rarely made such an obvious error, but the boss had noticed this one, and he'd been waiting for me at the top of the stairs, sleeves rolled up. He motioned me toward the small office set aside as the costume closet and closed the door behind us.

"Warne," he said, "we must talk."

"We are talking."

"About your future."

"I sincerely hope to have one," I said. Bravado was my only possible response; fear had settled into my bones almost immediately. I had no idea what might be coming next. I braced myself for a tongue-lashing at best. I didn't even want to think about what the worst might be.

He sat back on his heels and said, "Our company is growing. There are new cases, new needs. While I would like to assign you to all of them, I can't."

I considered apologizing for last night's error; it certainly sounded like he might be gearing up to chastise me for it. Instead, I said, "You can assign me to most of them."

"No. I have to pick and choose. We turn away cases every day. Hundreds of people ask our help every month. They're willing to pay, and most of them have a good story. I can only say yes to a fraction."

"So hire more operatives."

"Which I do and always have." Shifting, he propped his weight on a thick fist. "But I've decided that we need a new…direction in hiring."

"Meaning?"

"I'd like you to hire and head up my bureau of female detectives. There's a need for more women like you."

I hadn't felt such a rush of joy and adrenaline since the first day I'd walked into this office. "That's a lovely thing to say, Boss."

"I don't say it to flatter you. It's a fact." He didn't smile, and I knew he was telling the truth as he saw it. "Women can go places men can't, and now I need a team of women to investigate those places."

"You could hire them yourself."

"Faith, woman, are you trying to talk yourself out of a promotion? That doesn't sound like you."

Finally, I grinned. "No, it doesn't. So you want me to do the hiring, since I know what it takes to make a successful female operative in your employ."

"That's the ticket."

"And when you say 'head up'?"

"Hire them and train them. Supervise them. Dismiss them if necessary, though I warn you it'll look like poor judgment on your part if you fire too many. Looks like you reverse your opinion too quickly. Hire the right ones, and you'll never have to fire any. Hire the wrong ones, and God help you."

"I imagine you might also try to help me a little."

"A little, perhaps. The truth is you don't need help. You're savvy enough to do this single-handed. So go forth. Assuming you want the promotion, of course."

"If it comes with a raise in pay."

"It does."

"Then, yes, I do."

He smiled, a big open grin. "You could thank me, you know."

I returned the grin. "I could! And you could thank me for taking the job."

We shook hands, which we'd rarely done, and my elbow nearly knocked over a stack of hats piled by the window.

"Make me proud," he said.

"I intend to."

And that was how it began. Not just the first woman detective, I would now be the first woman supervisor of detectives. I would tackle the challenge with everything in me. I couldn't wait.

Once I started looking, nearly every woman in the world seemed like a potential operative. I even considered hiring a woman who tried to pick my pocket on the elevated train. As I rode toward Hyde Park, leaving the Van Buren station behind us, a woman in black exclaimed just in front of me, "Oh no! Was that Van Buren? Does anyone know?" I turned back because, of course, I wanted to confirm that was the station we'd left, and in a split second, I realized it was a trick. Pinkerton had been working on a book about how to identify criminals, and I'd read a draft recently. This gambit was on the list.

When her hand went to my pocket, my hand went to her wrist and locked it tight. Then I asked her to come to the office the next day, not telling her it was a detective office, knowing how that might seem to someone who'd been caught in an illegal act. In the end, she did not show up for our appointment, understandably. I decided it was probably for the best. Perhaps my colleagues wouldn't necessarily warm to someone with her history. It was important to me first and foremost that I choose the right women for the job, but it was also important to consider the conditions and give everyone the best chance for success.

I also placed a newspaper ad and interviewed several candidates who answered it. I'd deliberately left the wording vague. Only the most interested women, I thought, would apply. I imagined a series of adventuresses, women who were almost bold enough to traipse out onto the frontier but stayed in Chicago for one reason or another. Unfortunately, truth didn't live up to my imagination.

On the first day I'd named in the advertisement, a parade of women appeared at the office to interview. Five, ten, a dozen. I judged them and found them wanting as soon as they walked in. Some simply wanted to sit at a desk and thought that this work would be clerical or even merely decorative. Other women barely glanced at me when they came in, their eyes still searching for a man in authority.

After lunch, I was exhausted. The fifteenth interviewee, a woman with brown hair gone gray at the temples, strode confidently into my office and asked, "Is the boss here?"

I answered, "I'm the boss."

The look she gave me could only be described as one of distaste. "I don't answer to anyone in a corset."

Immediately, I invited her to leave, and it would be hard to say which of us was more relieved when the door closed behind her.

Much of the afternoon brought more of the same. But finally, a woman walked in who I thought might be promising. She was the twenty-first.

"Your name?"

"Hattie Lawton," she said, extending a hand. It was delicate and birdlike, and so was she. Glossy chestnut hair, small round shoulders. A print dress in tones of copper and rust that somehow called attention to her striking green eyes. Narrow ankles in expensive shoes. Skin like a china doll. She was among the most beautiful women I'd ever seen. This might come in handy as an operative, or it might make her useless. Beautiful women were memorable.

"Current profession?"

"I'm an actress," she said, and something in me soured. I'd met a lot of actresses, and most of them I'd cared little for. In the wings, they'd often say, *Oh, look at you, you're such a good girl*; if my father overheard, he would look them up and down and ask wolfishly, *What kind of girl were you?* Too many of them smiled and simpered in response, and I'd have to look away, knowing what was to come.

Then she added, "Well, I want to be an actress. My parents disapprove."

"I know what that's like."

She smiled, and her smile was a sweet one, not too perfect. She had a crooked tooth. Not in front, but farther back. It only showed with her widest smile. It made me start to like her again.

I sketched the life of an operative for her in a few short strokes. How we helped out on cases that didn't go directly to the police for one reason or another. How we were able to capture dangerous criminals, counterfeiters, murderers, all sorts of untoward types. How we rarely took public credit and had to be satisfied with private knowledge of our success, hush hush.

She replied, a glint in her green eyes, "Sounds perfect."

Then I asked her, "Are you sure you can do what's required?"

"Well, what's required?"

She was sharp. Things were definitely looking up. "A good question, but one I can't fully answer. You have to lie to people's faces. You have to stay out late, get up early, go days without contacting friends and family if needed."

"Oh, don't worry. I have no friends." I wondered if that was perhaps the first time anyone had offered up a lack of friendships as a qualification for a position. Truth be told, it was helpful.

"Well, the fewer people you have to explain yourself to, the better. This isn't a desk job. There are nights you won't be home for dinner. You'll need to travel at the drop of a hat."

"I'm ready," she said.

So far, she'd said all the right things. One key question remained. "Why do you want to be a detective?"

"Because I like to do what no one else is doing. I know of only one female detective in the world—who wouldn't want to be the second? And I need the money."

I shook her hand and nodded without giving anything away, but her reasoning sounded solid to me.

Late in the afternoon, I found Pinkerton, who asked, "How were today's interviews?"

"Good. I have one likely candidate."

"A sure thing?"

"Not quite sure yet."

"Why? What holds her back?"

"She's beautiful," I said. "It's problematic."

"Why?"

I appreciated him not assuming that it was a case of an unattractive woman being jealous of an attractive one. That played no part.

"Beautiful women are memorable."

"Yes. It limits how you can use her."

"So, your advice. Would you hire her anyway?"

"I hired Graham DeForest, didn't I?"

I mulled it over. The parallel was perfect. Even knowing DeForest now as long as I had and even knowing what I knew, I still sometimes lost my breath when he walked in a room and turned his bright smile on me. His face was compelling enough to make a woman forget everything else. His looks commanded, demanded attention. Hattie would be the same.

Pinkerton said, "Physical beauty is the one thing you can't train into them. They have it or they don't, and you might need it. Understand?"

"Perfectly."

"But it's your decision," said Pinkerton. "You're in charge."

There were women who swooned for all sorts of words. *I love you, I want you, you're so beautiful.* I had never heard three words from a man that thrilled me so much, all the way to my very core. Perhaps because when I'd heard the other words—on the rare occasion they'd been spoken to me—I'd never quite believed them.

I believed Pinkerton trusted me completely.

You're in charge.

These words, at last, were right.

After another day of interviews and another chain of disappointments—silly women, shy women, women who seemed more likely victims than saviors—I needed to take some kind of break. My brain was spinning. I was accustomed to operating in the dark, in the corners, on the job. I was not used to thinking about hiring and training and other mundane concerns. Exhilaration had given way to exhaustion. I hoped it would only be temporary.

While I'd moved out of Mrs. Borowski's boardinghouse long before, I still kept in touch with her, and we took a meal together every so often. I thought she might be amused by my tales of hunting for fellow female operatives, so I planned to meet her for dinner. I suggested Calliope's and hastened to add that I'd pay. She agreed.

I could tell as soon as she sat down that something was wrong. I didn't want to pry right away, so I waited until we had enjoyed a tipple and ordered our meals from the waiter. Then I said, "Mrs. Borowski, you seem a bit—tired."

Her story came spilling out. After all this time, she'd thought that the boardinghouse belonged to her, free and clear. Her husband had told her they owned it. But now, someone had shown up with a deed, claiming to be the owners, and she was unable to produce any evidence to the contrary.

My first thought was that we should take her case and prove

these people to be charlatans. My second thought was something else entirely.

I tried to look at her with fresh eyes. It wasn't easy—I'd thought of her in a certain way for a long time, and there was perhaps no one else living who had captured my emotions so strongly—but I was a professional operative, and I did my best. She was a motherly woman. Comfortable and comforting, even without speaking a word. There was something about her unassuming demeanor that made you want to tell her everything. When she ran the boardinghouse, she'd been organized, perceptive, in control. All essential qualities for an operative. I hadn't seen it before, but now, I could see nothing else.

"Mrs. Borowski," I said, "how would you like a position?"

"Does it pay?"

"Handsomely."

I explained the work, and she said, "I don't see that I have any other choice."

"You always have choices. Don't worry about that."

"You're so optimistic? Even you, even after everything?"

"It's not optimism," I said matter-of-factly. "You do have choices. That doesn't mean they're all good ones. For example, you could become a lady of the night."

"On a pretty pitch-black night," she muttered, and the fact that she could joke about that possibility gave me hope for her.

"Or you could move to the Dakota Territory. Or you could take vows as a sacred sister. Or you could hire on as a cook right here at Calliope's. Or I could lend you money to buy the house back."

"No, you couldn't."

"I'm not finished."

The waiter brought our meals—walleye for her, a veal paillard for me—and I waited until he stepped away to continue. "I just mean there are options. And I will have Mr. Pinkerton assign someone to look into these supposed owners with their supposed deed. But I've also been asked to hire women as Pinkerton operatives, and I think you could be very, very good at it."

"Oh, Kate," she said. "What a strange turn of events."

"I've seen stranger."

"Haven't we both," she said and reached out to take my hand.

*

After another frustrating day of all-wrong candidates, I called a halt. My little band of two would have to do for the present. And so we began the business of turning them from ordinary women into operatives.

I was determined to arrange introductions for Hattie and Mrs. Borowski, the way Pinkerton never had for me in my early days. However, they were over almost before they began.

The first three men I introduced to Hattie—Taylor, Paretsky, and Hill—went tongue-tied and foolish at her mere appearance, tripping over their words, flushing like schoolboys. Perhaps if I had started with Graham DeForest, things would have gone differently. But it was too late. Hattie did nothing to encourage them, but the male operatives acted like marks around her. Nothing good would come of it. Introductions could wait.

The page I did take from Pinkerton's book was to train the women thoroughly, in private, before allowing them to participate on a case. I spoke to them at length about the principles of investigation and tested their recall on matters of law. Then we slowly began a series of trials: disguise, surveillance, persuasion—all the arrows in our profession's quiver.

I had planned on a month of this type of education. My plan was derailed.

CHAPTER FIFTEEN
BELLE

After only a week, Pinkerton came to me and pled for Hattie.

"I need her assigned to this case."

"But aren't the assignments up to me?"

He hemmed and hawed a bit and said, "Yes, you direct their activities. As I direct yours."

"Boss, she's too green." I folded my arms. "If you need a female operative, I'm here. Why can't I do it?"

"She'll be more convincing in this role."

"How do you know?"

I both wanted and did not want him to say what I suspected: that Hattie was younger and prettier than me, and that was what suited her for the case. I couldn't dispute him on the merits if that was so.

He said, "This is confidential."

I rolled my eyes at him. "It's all confidential."

He didn't flinch, so I knew he was serious. "This is life or death. No one can know."

"All right. Tell me everything."

"You've heard of Steel Tom O'Leary?"

I had, and the name was enough to send a cold shiver through my blood.

Grimly, Pinkerton said, "We believe he has kidnapped the daughter of a rival gang leader."

"Caruso?"

"That's the one."

"I didn't know he had a daughter."

"He keeps her out of the papers."

I said, "For good reason, clearly. How old?"

"Sixteen."

"Same as Belle O'Leary, then." Steel Tom had a daughter of his own, which made his boldness in stealing Caruso's daughter all the more shocking.

"Yes. But Carlotta Caruso's missing now, and we think we know where she's being held."

"By O'Leary's men."

"Yes. And Hattie bears a resemblance to Belle, a rather strong one. If she can get past the guards, she can confirm the other girl's there. Then we can send the police in."

"You think it's the only way?"

"It's the best way. Too many things can go wrong if the police go in blind. If the gang gets spooked—nervous criminals—well, I don't have to tell you what could happen."

I nodded. They'd kill the girl if they had to. No question.

"If we give them intelligence, they'll know what to do. Maybe they won't even have to shoot."

"If they do shoot, we don't want the girl caught in the crossfire."

"No. Certainly, her father doesn't."

"Criminals are fathers too," I said, not because he didn't know it, but because I needed a moment to think, and empty words are handy for such occasions.

"They've kept it quiet so far. But Carlotta's been missing for three days."

"Any chance she's just run off with someone her father wouldn't approve of?"

"Some chance," he admitted. "Which is why we need to investigate. And why I need Hattie to impersonate Belle."

"I'll get her ready," I said and went to figure out which of the dresses in the costume closet looked most like it might belong to a gangster's daughter.

We settled on a plan. Pinkerton stood and listened, but I was the one who rehearsed Hattie, even while I applied her makeup. The girl she was pretending to be, Belle O'Leary, used a heavy hand with her eyeliner and lip color. While Carlotta Caruso was invisible to the papers, Belle was the opposite—we'd all seen pictures of her and been privy to her comings and goings as a star social butterfly of modern Chicago. I did my best to make Hattie look as much like her image as I could. While I prepared Hattie, I ran her through the plan again and again. I was nervous for her. As a first case, it was a huge weight to put on her delicate shoulders.

"Belle," I said, playing the role of one of the father's goons. "Why are you here?"

"Daddy wanted me to make sure the girl's comfortable," she said.

"More forceful."

She lowered her voice and sat up straighter in her chair. "Daddy asked me to look after the girl's comfort. Wanted to be sure you buffoons were keeping your hands to yourself."

"A little less."

She cocked her head and tried again. "Daddy asked me to look after the girl's comfort. And make sure everyone's behaving. Let's get her a glass of water, shall we?"

"Better."

Our eyes met in the mirror. I took a deep breath, and consciously or not, she echoed it. I wasn't at all sure she was ready. But what choice did we have? It was a slim chance or none at all.

Three of us would go. Pinkerton and I debated endlessly on whether I would be one of them. He insisted it would be too difficult to explain why another woman was there and that we didn't know enough about any of Belle's friends to give me a cover identity that would hold up. I argued the opposite—a girlfriend, even an anonymous one, was far easier to explain than a second bodyguard. The truth was, even if I had to let Hattie take the lead, I couldn't bear the thought of waiting back at the office, not knowing. I had to be there. So in the end, it was me, the ersatz Belle, and a disguised Taylor, looking every inch the enforcer.

As we rode in the carriage toward the warehouse, I saw every possible outcome in my mind. The poor girl Carlotta already dead, Hattie's deceit revealed, a hail of bullets and blood. Or Hattie triumphant, ordering around gangsters as if she'd been born to it, making a map of the room in her mind and neatly reproducing it on a desk at the police station, leading to a flawless rescue. Anything might happen. Nothing might happen. The worst part was that it was out of my control.

We arrived outside the warehouse, and Taylor preceded us, rapping the back of his knuckles against the door and grunting, "Open up."

There was a shuffling, some murmuring, and the unmistakable sound of more than one gun being cocked. A low voice said, "Yeah?"

Hattie took charge, her tone demanding. "Look here. Daddy sent me to check after the girl's welfare. You can let me in, or I can go home and tell him you'd rather he come to see things for himself. All right?"

The bolt slid, and we were inside.

As all operations do, it went perfectly right up to the moment it began to go wrong. The goons let us in, and our Belle checked on the girl, ordering the delivery of a glass of water. Taylor and I kept our mouths shut, scouting the premises with occasional, furtive glances, counting the number of men and noting their positions.

The girl was willowy and dark and worse for wear—the hem of her dress was thick with dirt, and her hair had collapsed into loose, haphazard loops. She stared at us with wild eyes, not sure whether we were saviors, executioners, or just momentary apparitions. Still, she seemed mostly unharmed. I had just let myself relax and be thankful we would be able to report her healthy when I heard Hattie's voice say, "All right, we'll be taking her with us, then."

My head went light, my chest hollow.

A goon stammered, "Miss Belle, I don't think—"

"Daddy doesn't pay you to think. We give her back in this condition, you think her father's going to thank us? He's going to take every missing eyelash out of our hides. Your hides. I'm taking her home for a bath. She can put on one of my dresses afterward. I'll have her back in two hours. That way, she tells a nice story about how well we treated her, and everyone wins."

"Miss Belle—"

"I'm not taking no for an answer," she said, her small fists firmly on her hips, and unbelievably, the one in front of the door stepped aside.

Three of us had gone in. Four came out.

Once we were in the carriage, the girl said, "Listen, I know my father will pay the ransom. It's only a matter of time."

"Oh, don't you trouble yourself about that," Hattie said. "I'm not Belle, even. I'm—"

"Beg pardon, first things first," I interrupted. "Did they hurt you, Carlotta?"

She looked down before answering, and my throat tightened. But she said, "No. They shouted. And they clowned, I guess. Telling each other they'd knock me around a bit if Papa didn't pay up right away."

"But they didn't."

"No."

"You're safe now," I said. "We're with the third precinct.

Matter of fact, we're headed to headquarters right now." I gestured to Taylor. "Can you make sure the driver knows the fastest way?"

He nodded, and I knew he understood me. We couldn't possibly take this girl to the Pinkerton offices. I had to think on my feet, faster than I ever had. Hattie's impulse had put us all in grave danger. I'd only have one chance to get us out.

The girl flung herself onto me, her arms around my neck, with force sufficient to free a grunt from my belly. She draped herself on me and cried, "Thank you, thank you, I'm so glad, thank you."

To her credit, once Hattie heard me assert that we were police officers, she didn't contradict me. Her reckoning would have to wait.

The plan had been for the three of us to report directly to the station if we had news. Pinkerton was waiting for us there. Words could not do justice to the look on his face when we walked in with Carlotta holding Hattie's hand as if they'd gone to finishing school together. We said as little as possible and left the girl there, as we should have done back at the warehouse.

Out in the street, I breathed a sigh of relief, then immediately wheeled on Hattie.

"Well, that went well," she said.

I wanted to slap the smile off her beautiful face. My fist was already clenched, and it took all my force of will to keep it from flying up.

"Hattie," I said. "What in Hades were you thinking?"

"We wanted her out, right?"

"Yes, but bringing her with us, that wasn't the plan. The plan was to report back. That's it. That's all."

She lifted her chin. "I improved on the plan! We had the chance to get her out ourselves, without waiting for the police, who could have botched it anyway. This way, I knew she'd be safe."

"Do you understand what could have happened? If you'd told her we're Pinkertons?"

"I don't know, we might get some credit for a job well done?"

"Not exactly. Her father knows how to keep his mouth shut, but we don't know if she does. If she told anyone the Pinkertons got her out, word would spread. Someone else tells someone else. Eventually, the people who kidnapped her would find out it was us. And what do you think they'd do then? Send a fruit basket?"

"Oh."

"Yes, oh!" I shouted. "And Steel Tom would know there was a Pinkerton agent impersonating his daughter. What happens if he goes looking for that girl?"

She'd gotten paler and paler with every word, and at the end, she was white as vellum. "I'm so sorry, Kate."

"Mrs. Warne."

"I'm so sorry, Mrs. Warne. Chief. I didn't realize."

"And that is why you stick to the plan," I said.

I was beginning to think I'd made a poor choice in hiring her. Besides, her failure reflected on me and my ability to direct female operatives. I could only imagine what Pinkerton would say. It didn't take me long to find out.

The next morning, he addressed the matter immediately.

"Warne," said Pinkerton. "What shall we do about Hattie?"

"We? Hattie is my responsibility. You made that clear."

"And yet. If you can't handle her..."

"I can handle her," I said, unsuccessfully trying to keep my voice from hissing. "Boss, I will handle her."

"I can step in if you need me to. You two seem to clash."

"I've clashed with plenty of operatives before," I admitted, "but that's all turned out all right. This will too."

"You're sure?"

"No," I said.

"Good. I was going to label it a lie if you'd said yes."

"Just give me some time," I said, not at all sure that time would be enough. And I knew not only Hattie's future hung in the balance.

CHAPTER SIXTEEN

THE SECOND CHANCE

An hour and a half past the appointed meeting time, when my hands had gone numb from cold, I finally had to admit something had gone wrong.

The plan had been to meet Hattie and Mortenson on the LaSalle Street Bridge at five o'clock. In case they were being watched, they would stroll across the bridge while I waited at the top of the span, a large open bag hanging over one arm. It was a cold day but neither freezing nor snowing, so a woman lingering in the open air wouldn't be immediately conspicuous. Mortenson would slip the bills into my bag and continue strolling with Hattie, and all would be well. But by six thirty, with no sign of either operative, I couldn't deny the leaden weight of dread in my stomach.

This time, I had told Hattie in no uncertain terms what would happen if she deviated from the plan. This was her second and final chance.

The counterfeiters were expecting a woman and a man to appear at a tavern off Haddock Place at three o'clock in the afternoon. The man, Mortenson, was there as a purportedly disgruntled former Mint employee who would fix errors in counterfeited bills for a price. Hattie was to serve as a distraction, so that Mortenson could swap out their prototype counterfeit bills and bring them away as evidence. If all went well, we'd have two witnesses and the bills—and an airtight case.

The sun was down, and the cool afternoon was turning into cold night. Clearly, not all had gone well. I hated to do it, but I abandoned my post and hot-footed it back to the office. Even knowing something had gone wrong, I was completely unprepared for what I found there.

An unmoving Jack Mortenson lay sprawled across the top of Pinkerton's broad oaken desk, half his right pant leg red with blood. I sucked in my breath. The blood had also spread across the desk blotter and soaked several makeshift bandages, now piled on the floor below him in a small heap. A knot of half a dozen operatives stood near him, gesturing and arguing, in total disarray.

The first to catch my eye was Bellamy. He looked at me grimly and said, "Shot."

"Shot? Is he—"

"I'm alive," Mortenson said in a thin, thready voice. If possible, he was even whiter than he'd been before, pale as paper.

Then I noticed Hattie, standing alone, her dress wet with blood all down one side of the skirt. I went to her, relieved. As far as I could tell, none of the blood was hers.

"Hattie! Are you all right?"

"Yes," Mortenson answered for her through gritted teeth. "I rescued her."

"Rescued her? From what? From whom?"

"He—he touched her."

My relief vanished, and anger surged up in its place. I could hear the other agents arguing about what to do: Who had the steadiest hands? Who had a desk flask to sacrifice? No one was asking the right questions.

I shouted at Mortenson. "Who did? What? This whole operation went south on a *touch*?"

Hattie, her voice unsteady, whispered, "Everything happened so fast."

"Of course it did! That's how real things happen!"

She stammered, unable to get the words out. I resisted the urge to shake them free.

Mortenson said, barely loudly enough to hear over the din, "You weren't there."

I drew near to him and immediately realized two things: he was on the verge of losing consciousness, and his breath stank of whiskey.

Taylor was the only one directly attending to him, pressing more clean cotton into the wound. Of the people in the room, he seemed the most likely to answer my next question. "Did you give him whiskey for the pain? Or did he smell like this when he came in?"

Taylor looked up at me and shook his head. I knew what he meant by it.

"Mortenson!" I resisted the urge to slap him on the cheek to revive him. "How much?"

Even in his depleted state, he turned a glare on me that could have burned a hole in a brick. "Had to keep up."

"Not if it meant turning yourself into an idiot. I can't understand why you'd behave like a—" I stopped short. He was staring past me, toward Hattie, the fingers of one unsteady hand reaching in her direction, though he was too weak to lift it from the desk.

Hattie seemed not to see it, outwardly oblivious to the chaos in the room, to everything. She wrung her bloody hands in the folds of her stained skirt.

Conditions were hardly right for an interrogation, but I had no choice. We were Pinkertons after all. We did not take action without facts.

"Make your case," I said to Hattie. "I'm not inclined to give a third chance."

Her voice caught in her throat, but she said, "I did everything you said. I let him take the lead. I didn't ask him to—"

Mortenson growled, "Leave her alone."

"You shut up," I said, my voice rising to break through the noise. "Simpleton. Fool."

The wounded man moaned, shifting his weight, and tried to raise himself to address me. I saw his fingers curl in a fist.

"Sweet Lord," came an interjection from behind me, and Bellamy stepped directly between us. He grabbed my wrist and pulled me back from the bloody desk. "Not now, Warne," he hissed.

I wrenched my hand out of his grasp.

He didn't flinch. Instead, he said, "Look, no one died."

"A miracle."

"Let's save him first. Blame later."

He was right, of course. "Fine," I said. I beckoned to Hattie to stand off to the side, but I needn't have. She had gone into her shocked silence again. She pressed her back against the wall as if her weight were necessary to hold it up.

Then I huddled with the other agents to solve the more urgent problem. A hospital was out of the question. Dilloway was chosen to conduct the surgery when someone remembered that his mother had been a seamstress, but they were still tussling over whose liquor would be sacrificed to numb the patient. I pointed out that we had enough laudanum in the cabinet to ease him out of consciousness, and finally, things began to move.

While Bellamy fetched and administered the laudanum with sure hands, I stepped away, turning my attention back to Hattie.

"Tell me. What did he do that you didn't ask him to?"

There was a little more color in her cheeks now, though her hands were still twisted in her bloody skirt. "I could have handled it. The suit grabbed me—"

"What suit?"

"The one in charge, the heavy one. Watkins. Demanded we drink with him."

I glanced over at the still form of Mortenson, Dilloway hovering over him. He wiped the back of his hand across his forehead and started to work. The room had fallen silent at last, so Mortenson's unconscious moan when the tongs touched his flesh seemed remarkably loud.

Hattie flinched. I turned her away from the scene with a gentle hand on her shoulder. "Go on."

"Mortenson was matching him glass for glass. When Watkins was good and tight, he said the least I could do was grace his lap, and he yanked me down to sit."

"And what did you do?"

"I sat."

"And what did he do?"

"Put his hand up my dress."

Her voice was no longer trembling, and I saw a spine of steel in her that I hadn't before. It gave me hope.

Dilloway had located the bullet and fished it out, and we heard the sharp clang as he dropped it neatly into a metal dish. He poured Dalessandro's brandy over the wound and helped himself to a swig. Then he brandished his needle and thread, setting to the next gruesome task, beginning to stitch up the unconscious man's flesh.

I looked at Hattie. She gave a tight smile that was more like a grimace. "Then Mortenson grabs me, hauls me off the fat man's lap, and yells, 'Hands off the lady,' and it all went downhill from there."

"I'll say. Who shot first?"

She inclined her head toward Mortenson. Dilloway was still sewing. Dalessandro's purloined flask was now making the rounds among the spectators.

"Good Lord," I said. "You're lucky either of you made it out."

"Don't have to tell me twice," she said. "The fat man might've killed him if I hadn't jostled his elbow."

"That was good thinking."

"Wasn't fast enough," she said.

"No one died," I said, echoing Bellamy, though there was little else to celebrate.

Now that the surgery was complete, I could see that Mortenson's leg wound was just above the knee. A bad place to get shot, but far better than the meaty part of the thigh a few inches higher, which would likely have been fatal. The wound might still fester, and it would be weeks before we knew whether the patient was truly out of the woods. But at least he would make it through the first day with some blood still in him.

Once Mortenson had been lifted off his makeshift surgical table and was resting on a couch in Taylor's office, I let myself breathe for a moment. I heard the men on either side of me, including our erstwhile surgeon, do so as well. But there was no time to feel relief. The fallout of the botched operation had to be dealt with.

"Someone's got to tell the boss," said Dilloway, wiping his hands on what looked like the last clean rag in the office.

Dead silence followed.

Irritated but certain, I spoke up. "I'll do it. Where is he?"

"Home."

"Come on," I said to Hattie, and she followed.

The night was cold, but the fresh air felt like a wonder after the bloody stink of the office. We moved quickly to keep warm. After a few blocks, I said, "It wasn't your fault. Next time, you'll do better."

She looked over with moist eyes.

"Yes, I said next time. But I have to ask you one question, and I need you to be absolutely honest."

"Yes, Chief."

"Did you do anything to encourage Mortenson? Before this happened? Do the two of you have some kind of…special relationship?"

Her footfalls were the only sound for a few moments, but when she spoke, she did so clearly. "No, ma'am. Not at all. Frankly, he always gave me the creeps."

I didn't smile, though in some part, I wanted to, hearing her echo my own sentiments. I realized I had assumed the worst of her, and I was deeply ashamed, knowing how furious I'd been when men were quick to assume the worst of me. I was accustomed to thinking the worst of people and the best of myself. There was value in switching those around from time to time.

We walked in silence the rest of the way.

In front of Pinkerton's house, I paused and said to Hattie, "Off home with you. We'll start early tomorrow. Six o'clock. You'll be ready?"

"I will, Chief." She took her leave quickly, without giving me a chance to change my mind.

I knocked on the door and was surprised when the man himself answered it. I could hear the noise of children running, which gave me a moment's pause.

"Now this is a surprise," he said. "Please, come in."

I did, and I must have looked confused, so he said, "Joan is upstairs with the children. Glad to see you. Tell me, what brings you out this way?"

After that greeting, I was more than sad to tell him. Framed by the brocades and chintzes of a private home, he looked older, gray and white strands having taken root throughout his hair, even his beard. Seeing him here reminded me that he was just a man, a human like any of the rest of us, and not an unearthly hero who could solve all the world's troubles with a sweep of his arm. It also reminded me how much I owed him. He could have dismissed me after the ring went missing, and he hadn't. How different things would have been if he'd thought I was lying. Then he'd trusted me with the Ladies' Bureau. As wrong as things had gone today, I hoped this failure didn't cause him to reconsider.

From upstairs, a little girl squealed, whether in delight or fear, I couldn't tell.

We stood just inside the doorway as I told Pinkerton the story of Mortenson and Hattie's failure to snare the counterfeiters, sketching it in broad strokes as briefly as I could. He looked alarmed at first, then concerned, then resolute.

"But he seems fine?"

"As fine as anyone can be with a hole blasted in his thigh."

"Good to know Dilloway has surgical skills in the crunch."

"I'm not sure that's the key lesson I'd take."

He said, his voice tense, "Warne, I'm trying my best to find anything positive at all in this."

"Understood. Then yes. I was pretty impressed with his stitching."

"And Hattie?"

"It wasn't her fault."

"You're sure."

"That's what she says, and I believe her. Mortenson was drunk, and he let his emotions get the better of him. I hope your punishment for him will be severe."

"I suspect you'll be very happy with it," he said grimly.

He put on his hat, and we both went out into the street. I walked half a block with him toward the office, my feet moving automatically. He stopped.

"Warne," he said, "go home. Hasn't your day been long enough?"

"It has," I agreed.

"I'll see you tomorrow."

"Tomorrow."

So it wasn't until the next morning that I found out what had happened.

When I walked into the outer office, the misadventures of the day before still hung heavy in the air: the wet-iron smell of blood, chairs scattered haphazardly, the empty flask discarded. I also noticed a gash on the side of Pinkerton's desk—had I missed it? Had it always been there? Or had it happened during the makeshift surgery? It seemed unlikely, but the scene had been such a circus, I was sure I'd missed much.

Almost before I could turn my mind to other possibilities, DeForest was at my side with the gossip. "Did you hear?"

I was in no mood for guessing games. "I've heard a great many things in my life, Graham. Be specific."

"About Mortenson."

"I was here for it."

"You were?"

"I saw Dilloway sew him up."

"Not that, although you need to tell me the details in a minute. I mean his dismissal."

"Pinkerton dismissed him?" So that was the punishment. Harsh, but I couldn't argue with it. An operative who stepped in thoughtlessly without regard for the case could be very dangerous, to anyone present and to the whole company. Mortenson's failure was unacceptable. Bellamy had a foolish, dogged chivalry to him, I knew, but he'd never let it jeopardize an operation.

"With half a dozen other agents standing witness. He answered it by pulling a knife and trying to jump the old man."

"Good God! Then what?"

"Pinkerton disarmed him, knocked him down, and called the police to haul him off for assault. Dilloway and Bellamy helped restrain him. He can do a lot of things, but escaping handcuffs isn't one."

"I doubt he could put up much of a fight with that hole in his leg. Lost a lot of blood too."

"You'd be surprised. I've seen men in a fury do things they shouldn't have been able to do."

"So count Pinkerton lucky. Did he seem surprised?"

"Angry, mostly."

We reflected on that. I couldn't cast stones, of course, knowing my own anger had spiraled out of control, and Mortenson wasn't even my responsibility, only Hattie.

"So," I said, "one less colleague for us."

"And one more enemy."

"One among so many. Will we even notice?" But I knew we would. Mortenson was a smart man, and he knew our ways. Should he put his mind to criminality, he would be a formidable foe.

The first few weeks after his departure, I found myself scanning crowds and peering around corners for him, but he was nowhere to be seen. I asked around the office to find out any news, and both Taylor and Waldorf reported having heard that he'd gone back to Kentucky. I breathed a little easier after that.

After Hattie's baptism by blood and fire, I expected a cakewalk from Mrs. Borowski. Alas. Once her training was complete, I assigned her to three cases. A bank job, a domestic accused of stealing, and a grocery clerk skimming at the till.

She failed at all three. It didn't take long to find the common thread.

She brought back tales of the accused bank robber's hard-luck childhood, in painstaking detail, but nothing we could use to predict where his gang might strike next. In the domestic's case, it happened that both women originally hailed from the same area of Poland, and all we could learn was the depth of the servant's homesickness. The grocery clerk was more withholding, and Mrs. Borowski refused to push hard enough to get any information—so we had nothing at all. In short, she was too kind. In any other business, this would be an asset. As an operative, it was the worst of liabilities.

After the third failure, I knew pure honesty was what I owed her—and the only possible path to improvement.

"You're a wonderful person," I said.

She knew exactly why I'd chosen those words. "But not a very good operative."

"No," I said, "not yet."

"If I get the house back," she said, "I'll go."

"If you get the house back, I'll let you go without complaint."

Alas, when the final report came—Taylor and Dalessandro had done a thorough investigation—the news wasn't good. The Finns who had presented her with the deed to the boardinghouse really were the true owners. Her husband might or might not have purchased the property in good faith, but whatever he'd done, the secret of it had died with him.

I got good and soused with her the night we finally got a verdict. She showed me to a hidden Polish dining club on the North Side, through an unmarked door between a funeral parlor and a brewery. We sat across from each other at a small, round table topped with elegant imported tile, and we washed away our sorrows with tiny, doll-size tumblers of bittersweet plum vodka. In the beginning, the liquor burned, and so did our anger; by the time half a dozen tumblers were emptied, both had faded into a hazy warmth, and we were laughing together. Earnestly, I begged her pardon for not being able to do better by her as an operative; I owed her so much. Both betrayed by our husbands, we had a lot to mourn, and not just in the current instance. I don't remember what she said in response.

I woke the next morning with a dizzy ache all over and spent a half hour lying in bed counting the cracks in the ceiling before I was ready to rise. In the meantime, I turned my cobwebbed brain to the problem of Mrs. Borowski's employment. We needed a position that avoided her weaknesses and took advantage of her natural strengths. If she only had to be who she was, she'd be good at it.

When I hit upon the right answer, I sat bolt upright. The

resulting spell put me flat on my back for another ten minutes, but then I made my way to the office, thrilled at my discovery.

Mrs. Borowski could be of little use to us as the kind of wandering, adaptable operative that I prided myself on being. What we needed her to do was operate in place. No traveling, no disguises. Pinkerton agreed to the plan, and I presented it to her myself.

She got a position, an authentic one, as the manager of a boardinghouse on the South Side. We put out subtle whispers and murmurings that it was a good place to lay low, and over time, the city's criminal element began to send new arrivals her way. She heard their stories over breakfast and conveyed what she'd learned to us. The information was often invaluable. She didn't have to betray or persuade anyone. She simply listened to what was said, either to her or around her. When they thought no one was paying attention, criminals let each other's real names slip instead of using their proper aliases. Some used their real backstories when asked where they came from, which was also useful in pinning down who they might be instead of who they said they were. They revealed themselves in their accents, their choice of words, their unguarded moments.

Her powers weren't limited just to observation and information. Once suspects were staying in the house, we'd find ways to lure them away, sometimes for an hour or two, sometimes longer. There were countless ways to do it. In their absence, she efficiently and neatly searched their rooms, finding evidence and clues that could point us in the right direction, always returning everything perfectly to where it had been, as if she'd made chalk marks before moving shoes, bags, sheets. She could fold a shirt with crisp corners or sloppy ones, whatever the original folder had done, and precisely place something as large as a lamp or as small as a watch. She was excellent at this work. Finally, we'd found her place. I liked to think I had finally repaid the debt I owed her.

Unfortunately, I had barely gotten my feet under me as the superintendent of the small force of female detectives when the work changed again. I was pulled into another secret meeting on the floor of the costume closet, hats and shoes and disembodied mustaches piled up around me as I heard news that changed my future.

Pinkerton told me I was needed elsewhere, and what could I ever say to him but yes?

CHAPTER SEVENTEEN

THE RAILS

Miss Kitty Overchurch of Memphis, schoolteacher who feared that Northern progressivism would harm the integrity of age-old Southern tradition. Mrs. Catarine Labreaux of New Orleans, plantation mistress and proud slave owner who thought the Negroes in her employ deserved, like children, to be protected from themselves. Mrs. Kelly O'Reilly, Irish immigrant, whose husband's livelihood depended wholly on the cotton trade that a war with the North threatened to disrupt. Miss Katherine Filgate of Chattanooga, a spitfire who only wanted to know how Yankee infiltrators might be caught, stopped, and, if necessary, dispatched to their Maker.

I played all their parts and more.

We all served the railroad in our own way, in the roles Pinkerton assigned. For me, he chose a grueling schedule, traveling around the slave states, ferreting out intelligence from stationmasters' wives and daughters. With each one, I might need to be coy or charming, brusque or wheedling, brash or shy. I might pose as a local, or a confident, habitual traveler, or a panicked ingenue uncertain of my surroundings. My job was to quickly surmise what each woman knew that was worth knowing and then move on elsewhere to do it all again. Pinkerton's old friend McClellan had expanded the Illinois Central southward and also taken on responsibilities at the Ohio and Mississippi Railroad, and though no one said for sure,

I suspected he was one of the people reading the reports that we gathered, looking for patterns and forms that might be meaningful. I missed working closely with Hattie and Mrs. Borowski, but the importance of our intelligence work could not be denied.

I spent three weeks in Bolingbroke, Arkansas, slowly cooking from the outside in. I took a train from there to Memphis that broke down so many times, I suspected I could have made the trip more quickly on foot. From Memphis, I made a stop in Atlanta, but the stationmaster there had sent his wife to her family's ranch in Texas for the duration, and he looked upon me hungrily, like a hotel meal sent up to satisfy a late-night appetite. The sun did not set on me in Atlanta, and when it rose, I was halfway to Greenville.

It put me in mind of my parents and the theaters that had been a poor excuse for a home in my childhood. I grew up seeing men who drew pistols on one another onstage raising a whiskey to each other in celebration afterward; whores and mistresses on the stage became churchgoing women on Sundays, hands folded primly. Seeing it over and over again never made it feel more natural. I was deeply accustomed to using other women's names now, playing other women's parts, but that didn't mean it felt easy for me. Indeed, I felt I was losing track of myself under all the disguises.

But during the six months I spent away from Chicago, seeking intelligence for the railroads, I was not the only one coming unmoored.

Chicago had lulled me into complacency. We were like-minded people among other like-minded people, and besides the rallies, little of the Southern strife had bubbled up to interrupt our daily lives. But in the cities of the slave states, I couldn't deny the air was sour with resentment and ire. The streets were alive with militia. The headlines screamed rebellion. In my youth, the South had felt like a different country; now, it felt like a different world.

For one thing, no Negroes walked alone on the streets. If I saw them, they were trailing behind their masters, with downcast eyes and slumped shoulders. Not for a minute did I believe they truly thought themselves inferior to the men who walked ahead of them, but I was looking at them through Yankee eyes. In my childhood, I'd never known anyone who owned slaves. The people we associated with didn't even have enough money to own a second pair of shoes.

Or perhaps my memories were all tainted by what I saw once on the street in Murfreesboro. A slave walked behind his master and tripped in the dirt. The white man turned and beat the black man, savagely, silently. Just as silently, the black man wrestled the whip from the white man's hand and beat him with it. He got in two good strokes before someone shot him. Then everyone went about their business. I wanted to help, but what could be done at that point? The man was already dead, and I was beholden to my duty. I could not give myself away. There had been no opportunity, but I knew the more time I spent in these places, the more outrages like this I would see. And I would let them happen, because the woman I was pretending to be would never intervene. It joined the long list of things that troubled my sleep.

Pinkerton called me home in June of 1860, and as soon as I saw the skyline of Chicago again, a wave of gratitude washed over me. I spent a week at home, being myself. I needed it so badly.

For the first time in a long time, I could walk down the street without my neck on a swivel, trying to capture every action of every person in my mental record. For once, I could have a meal without trying to persuade my companion to disclose some kind of secret. It was unfortunate that I didn't get to see DeForest, but I knew he was on an important assignment, and all I could do was pray for his safe return.

I dined out with Hattie, catching up as best we could, and she told me she missed our conversations, which warmed my heart. She asked my advice on her current case, an impersonation of a fortune-teller, which reminded me of the time I'd taken on a similar role. I told her the story of my stained skin, and she laughed so hard, she spat wine onto the table. This sent me into gales of laughter as well, and we both ended by wiping away hysterical tears.

My brief time in the office reminded me why I liked the operatives I liked and why I didn't like the ones I didn't. I fell into our old patterns immediately; it was such a relief to do so. These were the people who knew me, as much as I could be known.

Bellamy stared when I walked in, so outwardly astonished to see me that he stood slack-jawed for several seconds.

"What?" I asked. "Were you hoping I'd died?"

He began to shake his head but then stilled himself, apparently thinking better of responding. He turned his attention to other matters, tucking one case file into a drawer, pulling another one out, and opening it flat on the desk. I thought his cheeks pinked a little, but who knew the cause of that? He always did hate attention, unless it was praise, which he seemed to like just fine. Then again, I supposed the same could be said of me.

The only words he actually spoke to me the whole week were part of a conversation that Taylor started.

"Have you heard, Warne? The Republicans have their nominee for the presidency now."

"Do they?"

"You'll never guess who it is."

"You're right about that," I said, busying myself with papers that didn't necessarily need to be filed right that minute.

"Go on, guess."

"I don't know. Did McClellan jump the fence?" He'd been a vocal Democrat in our dealings with him, and he was really the one and only political animal I knew. He never had warmed to me, not even after I brought in the evidence on Mr. Vincent, so I wasn't inclined to think the best of him.

"Not till pigs fly. C'mon, try again."

"I really don't follow politics."

"You should," chipped in Bellamy.

My best response to him was no response, which I gave.

Tired of waiting for me to play along, Taylor gave the answer. "It's Lincoln."

Now, he had my attention. "Abraham Lincoln? Our Lincoln? The lawyer?" I knew he'd had some political dealings, but I couldn't help but think of him as the scarecrow lawyer I'd met, years ago now, in Springfield. Together, we'd brought the embezzling accountant to justice, though I still remembered the hearts I'd broken to do it, including my own.

"The very same."

"What did he have to go do a fool thing like that for?" I said incredulously.

Bellamy mumbled, "Maybe he wants to be president?"

"It'll never happen," said Taylor, shaking his head.

I had to agree, as much as it pained me. The South would never stand for a president openly against slavery, whether or not he was well-spoken and intelligent. He was the wrong man for the job. We needed someone who could appeal to both sides, though I couldn't be sure that such a man existed. And certainly, I would rather have a man of our cause in the White House, if the alternative was a slaver. Lincoln would never be the kind of compromise that both sides could buy into. But maybe I was fooling myself that compromise was an option for our country. I thought back to Murfreesboro. We were already two countries.

We even spoke different languages. Southerners who agitated for secession were referred to as Secesh, but never south of the

Mason-Dixon Line, where the term was considered an insult. A Northerner who felt the same was a copperhead, but only in the North. I had to be fluent in both languages and remember what to speak to whom, at all moments, in all places. I had no illusions about what would happen if I were discovered in the wrong place at the wrong time.

One misstep was all it would take.

CHAPTER EIGHTEEN
BALTIMORE

All of Richmond's finest hotels were located only a few blocks from the slave market. No matter where I stayed, I would pass within feet of the notorious Lumpkin's Jail, where the howls and cries of those within never fell silent. To keep myself from reacting, I watched the reactions of others, to see if they felt anything. Some did, and some didn't. I had seen men spit and women weep, as well as the other way around, but most seemed to make an effort not to notice. As I passed the rotten structure with a stationmaster's teenage daughter in November 1860, she rolled her eyes. It was all I could do not to cuff her and stamp her bonnet strings in the mud.

Instead, we continued our walk to take tea at the Spotswood, the city's newest hotel and its crown jewel. My room was at the Exchange down the street, a marble palace that was hardly less luxurious, but the Spotswood was more fashionable, and Letty was a creature of fashion.

I was pretending to be a Mrs. Barley, a former resident of the town who had moved away years before, calling on the thinnest of threads to visit with the stationmaster's family. The mother was busy with her sewing circle, but the teenage Letty proved a most willing gossip, and I hoped the tea would yield some results. My favorite trick with young women was to ask where all the handsome young men could be found: it was a good way to keep tabs on the development and movements of any local militia, and it was a topic upon which they could be counted to expand at length.

The front of the Spotswood was tall and imposing, dwarfing everything nearby with its five stories of brick and a woven ornamentation of iron at the ground level. The tearoom itself had all the modern touches: a golden brocade on the walls, generously padded chairs, teacups of porcelain so thin the light shone through them. It was all graceful curves and elegance.

Letty was nattering away, periodically straightening the front of her fashionable navy-blue Zouave jacket in a way calculated to make sure everyone noticed it. I nodded and encouraged her, periodically stirring sugar into my Darjeeling tea, until a disheveled young man suddenly came charging into the room through the far entrance, shouting at the top of his lungs. I couldn't make out what he was saying, but whatever it was, a great grumbling noise like thunder began to fill the room.

In the hubbub, my young companion, a wrinkle of confusion on her pretty brow, reached over to the table next to us and politely asked the man there what the news had been.

"They elected that bastard Lincoln," snarled the man, and now I understood the wave of feeling in the room. It was not excitement but anger. Teacups rattled in their saucers; every once in a while, a profanity soared above the other noises to echo like a gunshot.

Surrounded by fury and disappointment, with a private joy and pride singing in my heart, I had never been so alone. Any one of the people here, told my true identity and loyalties, would tear me apart. The young lady across from me, her eyes wide with surprise at the turn of events, looked innocent enough. But if I told her my high opinion of Lincoln, she would likely have clawed my face with her elegant, long nails hard enough to draw blood.

It was the best possible news and the worst possible news, all at once.

I considered sending a telegram of congratulations to Lincoln, but for two reasons, I refrained. One, I figured my small tidings would be lost in a sea of good wishes. Second and more importantly, no matter how careful we were with identities and codes, there was always a chance my activities would be found out, and I couldn't take the chance, not with the stakes higher and higher every day. It was hard enough to keep track of all my identities as it was.

I submitted my report to Pinkerton, detailing what Letty had told me, and I left Richmond behind for another Southern city to do it all over again.

♌

Train after train near the port of New Orleans had broken down just in time to fail to take assigned cargo northward. While a string of such accidents seemed barely plausible, no one could be completely sure it was sabotage, nor could they identify a saboteur I entered the city with the New Year of 1861 and had not yet left by February. The city itself was lovely, elegant buildings lining every narrow street, the sweet smell of pralines and beignets wafting across the Vieux Carré. But I was uneasy.

All during January, one after another, Southern states had announced their secession from the Union; Texas's declaration on the first day of February had brought the total to seven. With each state, I grew more desperate and more sure we would never be able to turn the tide.

And I was exhausted. All the women to talk to and deceive, all the detailed dispatches to write, all the secrets to keep. I was undercover as Miss Filgate, the role I found most exhausting, as she was so fired up about everything, there was never any rest. She advocated violence against Yankees and darkies alike, and my own stomach turned at some of the things that came out of her—my—mouth.

Miss Filgate celebrated with the other citizens of the Crescent City when it was announced that the seceded states—South Carolina, Mississippi, Florida, Alabama, Georgia, Louisiana, and Texas—had formed a new nation, the Confederate States. She brandished her fists from an iron balcony high above Royal Street, whooping with joy. She shouted her enthusiasm for the new President Jefferson Davis and told anyone who would listen that she prayed for his strength and wisdom to guide us into a new age.

Inside, I wept.

The next day, I stopped by the telegram office, which I had also done on the other thirty-nine days I'd been in New Orleans.

"Anything for Miss Filgate?" I asked as I always did, my mind already on the next conversation I would have back at the St. Charles that afternoon. Should I push Mrs. Jennings harder today? Should I only listen? Should I ask for an introduction to her husband and try to pry information from him directly? Such risk, no matter which way I turned.

But the clerk surprised me. "Here you go."

I took the paper from his hand and sat on a bench to open it, making sure there were no eyes near to see.

The telegram had only two words:

COME HOME

I engaged a hackman for the station and was on the next train.

Hour after hour, we moved smoothly through the night, rolling north. Around midnight, I got the irrational sense that something was going to go terribly wrong. After all, half a dozen Pinkerton agents had been assigned to investigate the possibility of railroad sabotage, including me. The train I was on would make a perfect target. Full of Northerners returning to a stronghold of liberalism. Our deaths would send a clear signal.

I walked the train the rest of the night, passing through every car, looking for suspicious characters. After the third time I passed the engineer, he took me aside and asked what I was up to. Given the choice to reveal my true identity or give up my efforts, I simply told him that I had a nervous stomach, and he offered me a zinc tablet. I thanked him warmly and returned to my seat. I imagined myself revealing the truth, telling him to be on the lookout, but there were too many possibilities—I couldn't be sure, but I thought his voice had a slight softness around the vowels, like the accents I'd heard in western Tennessee. He could be part of any conspiracy just as easily as he could be the savior who would foil it.

The night was long, long, long.

Day found me in Chicago at last, and when I walked in the door of the office, I almost cried at the pleasant familiarity. Men bustling about. Cabinets of case files. The empty garments of the costume closet, the shapes of arms and legs hanging hollow, waiting to be filled. The right kind of flag, posted in the waiting room. Here was home.

And here was the boss, reaching his hand out to shake mine, equally welcome.

"Warne," said Pinkerton warmly.

I shook his hand with all the energy left in my body after the long train ride. "Boss. You said come home."

"I did."

"And here I am."

"It's good to see you, Warne. Even if the occasion..." He sighed heavily. I was already worried about what he might say, and his reticence concerned me even more.

"I assumed it isn't good news."

"Not at all," he said, instantly somber.

I arranged my skirts, tried to ignore the inch-thick coating of coal dust smeared against my sweaty neck, and waited for the story.

"You know we have our ear to the ground for the railroad," he began.

"Of course."

"Well, what we hear isn't always about the tracks themselves. And this time, we've heard something that concerns us a great deal."

"Don't give me the story, Boss," I said. "Give me the facts."

"Lincoln. They plan to kill him."

For once, I wished there had been more story.

He sketched out the plan for me with a bare minimum of fuss. Maryland was against Lincoln and against the North. By a quirk of geography, it was also the best approach to Washington, DC, and Lincoln was slated to pass through it two days before his inauguration. Two rail companies had laid track to Baltimore at different times, so travel through the city required an overland switch. Lincoln couldn't merely pass through and wave from a moving train; he would have to dismount one train and ride via coach to another. That, said Pinkerton, was where they'd surround him and do him in. Rail lines couldn't be laid overnight. There was no way to get him through Baltimore without the overland switch.

"So what are we going to do?"

"That's for you and me to decide."

As terrible as the news was and as unsure as I was that we could actually save a man who half the nation seemed eager to kill, I felt a bolt of energy zing through me. Of all his operatives, the boss had chosen me as fellow mastermind. It was the most important challenge of my life so far.

Time was of the essence. I stayed that night in the office, still smeared with coal dust but intent on every word. We talked all night long to determine the plan. No more than five operatives, we decided, all of us based in Baltimore itself. Naturally, the two of us had to go. Without hesitation, I named Hattie Lawton, who would be more than able to adapt herself to any female persona we needed. It was also natural for me to suggest Graham DeForest. More reluctantly, I had to admit that Tim Bellamy was the best among the remaining men, and he would be the natural choice to round out our team.

We needed a married couple and decided that should be Pinkerton and Hattie. In some recess of my mind, I still felt the sting of Joan Pinkerton's jealousy and still heard operatives jokingly calling me, never to my face, *the other Mrs. Pinkerton*. I would direct everyone's activities, which would necessitate running around at all hours. Bellamy would have the flexibility of a single traveler. DeForest would take a position as a porter at the train station and learn all there was to know about the workings therein. Our intelligence indicated there was an abandoned cabin on the western approach to the city both close enough to reach and remote enough to escape close watch; it would make a fine place to exchange secret communications.

The plan finally determined, Pinkerton dismissed me to rest. I went to Mrs. Borowski's boardinghouse, where she welcomed me warmly and gave me a single room, and after shucking my dress and corset onto the floor without ceremony, I fell onto the bed in my underclothes and slept the sleep of the dead.

The next day, I was on my way to Baltimore. Hattie and Pinkerton would travel together, as befitted their supposedly married state. DeForest and Bellamy would come after, on separate trains. I was the first to go, and I felt it keenly. There would be no one to catch me if I fell.

Upon arrival, I took up residence in the Barnum Hotel, which our intelligence had told us was the most Southern outpost in the city. I laid on a thick Charleston accent and named myself Mrs. Harrington, in honor of the dead woman I had impersonated years before. I still turned when I heard the name and never forgot its associations, so it was perfect for my needs. Sarah Harrington might not have been pleased with the behavior I used in her name—I flirted shamelessly and became known as a bit of a social butterfly—but I thought at least she might be pleased to live on in some way, even such a small one as this.

The Barnum Hotel was a lovely place. Not quite as grand as the Spotswood in Richmond or Willard's Hotel in Washington, it made up for it in cozy charm. The bannisters were polished to a shine, and there was a neatly arrayed stack of logs in every fireplace, always standing ready to be lit. We had fine sherry in the evenings, not too sweet. The front parlor was papered in large magnolia blossoms, making it the perfect place for Southern ladies and gentlemen to repose in comfort. All the women sported a fanned rose of black-and-white ribbons on their hats, called the cockade, to signal their sympathies. My cockade was the same size and style as all the rest. I would spend a great deal of time at the Barnum.

I quickly got to know the other guests. The silver-tongued Sheffields were the life of the party, always lifting a glass to the health of friends, day or night, rain or shine. Captain Danvers was a sinister-looking fellow with a deep groove in his forehead and brows as thick as my thumbs, but a few days' acquaintance revealed him to be a kind, courtly gentleman, lonely for his family back in Norfolk. Two middle-aged sisters, Peggy and Patty Gilchrist, strode about fanning themselves as if someone were paying them to do so and refused to talk politics out of politeness, even if provoked. I kept my ears open and my eyes attuned. I did not have to elicit opinions or tease out personalities. People simply revealed themselves to me by being who they were.

Of all the people in the hotel, the barber in the basement, Ferrandini, was among the most talkative. He had a great deal to say about a great many things. He would not talk to me, a mere woman, of all of them. But from things I overheard, I knew there was a local militia forming, and he was urging every young man he met to join up. So, through coded messages dropped off and picked up without seeing each other face-to-face, I let Tim Bellamy know it was time for a haircut.

The next day, we arranged to sit at neighboring tables at a nearby restaurant. We had a quiet, broken conversation with our backs to each other.

"So there is a militia," I whispered down at my teacup.

"In Perrymansville."

"Called?"

"The National Volunteers."

"Dangerous?"

"Absolutely." Then a minute later, "I need to join."

"Let me ask the boss first."

"No."

"I will ask the boss first," I said more firmly.

There was a longer pause and then, "All right."

"I'll bring word tomorrow at the cabin." I laid my coins on the table and left, knowing there would be no response. We were both professionals. Even more than asking the right questions and sharing the right information, our safety and success depended on knowing when to keep our mouths shut.

While Bellamy and Pinkerton could not be seen together, Hattie and I could stroll in the park without attracting much notice, and so we did. We interspersed our empty chatter with occasional words of import, and as I walked with her back to her hotel, her husband joined us for a short while. That was when I conveyed the information to him. The secessionist militia. Their location and danger. The barber, who needed to be watched. Bellamy's need to learn more. While we knew the plot was unlikely to involve an entire formal group of soldiers, we knew these men were passionate secessionists and couldn't let the opportunity to hear their talk pass. Individual men were not nearly as dangerous as an organized force, and certainly, the most dangerous of them all was an armed one.

Pinkerton agreed with me: Bellamy had to go to Perrymansville, and there was no time like the present.

We met at the abandoned cabin on the outskirts of town the next day. I walked and lurked near the edge of the cabin. Bellamy approached on horseback, and I was surprised at what I saw.

He didn't have access to his costume closet, but he had still managed to transform himself. He wore homespun pants, a shirt that had seen much wear, and a cap pulled low over his eyes. More importantly, he had changed the way he carried himself. He had never seemed a calm man, but now there was something tightly coiled about him, as if his entire body were a spring. He looked like an angry, ready man. He looked like a rebel.

He rode near enough for me to see and hear him, though my shape was obscured by the outer cabin wall, and no one riding by on the nearby road would know that I was there.

"Am I to go?" he asked the air.

"Yes."

"I'll leave word here when I can," he said and began moving away without waiting for an answer.

No one was there to see him go but me. Perhaps because of this, he saluted. Then he wheeled his horse and headed off down the road at a slow, unhurried trot.

Seeing him go, I felt a twinge in the pit of my stomach. Could he possibly convince these men, these potential evildoers, that he was one of them? He was headed straight into the hornet's nest.

I hated the feeling that every time I parted company with someone I knew, it might be the last time we saw each other alive. Bellamy wasn't a friend, but I'd known him a long time, and I respected him deeply. The thought that he might be riding to his death made me ill.

I knew he was the best we had. I just wasn't sure he would be good enough.

CHAPTER NINETEEN
PLOTS AND PLANS

I wanted to introduce Pinkerton to the barber, but I couldn't do so quickly without inviting suspicion, having already introduced him to Tim Bellamy just two days before. Instead, I placed them in each other's path, suggesting Pinkerton appear, with Hattie, at a restaurant called Guy's near the Barnum Hotel. It was very popular with the barber and his ilk. I knew a head-turning young lady like Hattie would draw the barber's attention quickly. Hattie knew how to flirt just enough. A target would bask in the warm sun of her attention without believing her a fickle mistress ready to turn her back on her husband for anyone at all. It was a talent.

Within three days, Pinkerton had made friends with the barber and learned much. The next time I saw him, he was excited and angry in equal measure.

"He is brazen beyond belief!" Pinkerton said without preamble. I had carefully snuck into their room at the Chesapeake Hotel, my room at the Barnum being far too accessible to the Secesh sympathizers.

"How so?"

"Boasts outright about killing Lincoln. For the sake of the country, he says. Man is a tyrant, he says. Says he's willing to die for a cause, as many proud Italians have done before him."

"And the police can't arrest him for that?"

"That's the worst of it. The chief of police is part of the cabal."

"No."

He nodded gravely. "He's ready to step aside when the day comes. He'll send a small force, but only the minimum, to the Calvert Street Station for Lincoln's arrival. There will be some sort of diversion, some noise, that causes them to be drawn off. And then the violence will be done."

"He talks of this in the open? Even though he doesn't know you?"

"In the company of complete strangers. I shouldn't have worried that he would censor himself on my account. I almost believe he would say these vile things in front of the president-elect himself."

I shook my head. "Terrible. But at least we know for sure. No pussyfooting around. There is a plot and no two ways about it."

"Yes. The threat is real. We need to tell Lincoln."

"We do."

"You do, I should say."

"Me?"

"He'll listen to you, Warne," said Pinkerton.

"Will he?"

"He asks after you every time we speak. He was very impressed by what you did in Springfield, says you're the best agent I have. I have to hope he'll listen to you. If he doesn't listen to someone, we'll lose him."

"You've already tried?"

"I have. I sent telegram after telegram."

"But in person, surely—"

"Tried that too. He was polite about it, but he sent me on my way. Said he owed it to the people to keep his path and wouldn't be swayed from it."

"I'll talk to him," I said. Whether or not I succeeded, I'd be a fool and a coward not to try. "What's my cover?"

☙

Ten hours later, I arrived at the Astor Place Hotel in New York. I was sick to death of hotels, truth be told. But our business had to be done where it had to be done. And, I reminded myself, there was no greater business than this.

A large man with a large beard greeted me at the door, and though I hadn't met him before, I knew Mr. Lamon immediately by description. If Pinkerton was a barrel, Lamon was a cask: larger, wider, and rounder in the middle. He was a good friend of Lincoln's, acting as his bodyguard on this journey, whether or not Lincoln wished it so.

Lamon ushered me into the outer chamber of Lincoln's room, which was small but well appointed. I knew Lincoln had been traveling a great deal, and it was our good fortune that he could be intercepted in New York, where a train would bring me right to his doorstep.

When the man himself entered, he looked almost the same; a shock, considering how things had changed since we'd last spoken. The entire world had been rocked on its axis; it seemed incredible that anything could remain as it had been only a few months before. And he, once a local solicitor, now about to be the president—all the more shocking that he, alone among those I knew, would seem like his younger self. He had grown a well-tended beard in the meantime, so his cheeks looked less gaunt, but his eyes, his most memorable feature, still burned with the same intelligence I remembered.

The suite at the Astor contained only us three. I thought to ask Lamon to leave, but as soon as I looked in his direction, Lincoln said, "Anything you can say to me should be said in the presence of Hill here. He is a key advisor."

I nodded at Lamon, and he returned the motion.

Then I said to him, "Do you believe the Baltimore plot is real, Mr. Lamon?"

"I do not want to believe it," he said, shrugging and nestling himself deeper into his chair. "But we are here to listen to your evidence. And so perhaps you will make both of us believe."

It was not what I wanted to hear but no worse than I expected. "And you do understand just how much is at stake here?"

Lincoln said, "My life."

"Respectfully, sir, it's far more than that."

Lamon said, "The future of the nation. Yes, Mr. Pinkerton told us that already."

"Can you be so cavalier?"

"Mrs. Warne," said Lamon, sounding impatient. "Day in and day out, everyone speaks in this rhetoric. Everything is the most or the worst or the highest or the best. Even our friend Lincoln here speaks only in high-flown language."

Lincoln shrugged a bit ruefully. His silence neither confirmed nor denied the charge.

I addressed the silent man. "Sir, you have to understand. We're deadly serious about this."

"I know you are, Mrs. Warne. But you have to understand me. I keep my promises. I need to be in Harrisburg, and I need to be in Baltimore, just as I said I would."

"You made another promise. A bigger promise. You said you would be the president of the United States of America. A free country, of free men. Don't you want to keep that promise?"

He sat back, hands on his knees, too big for his chair. "And you're going to say I can't keep it if I'm dead."

"Yes. But I believe we can compromise," I said. Consulting the copy of his itinerary Lamon had provided, I pointed to a line of text. "I can get you to Harrisburg day after tomorrow for the noon event as scheduled."

"Good."

"Then we leave immediately afterward."

"No."

"Damn it, Lincoln."

"Damn it, Warne," he replied in the same tone without a moment's hesitation.

"What do you want?"

He leaned closer, unfolding and refolding his long, spidery legs. He pointed to a line below where my finger still rested. "I have three speeches and a dinner planned in Harrisburg. I'm going to attend all of them."

"So a dinner is worth dying for."

He said grimly, "I'm not going to die."

"We are absolutely certain that there are men in Baltimore who wish you ill."

"Of course there are men in Baltimore who wish me ill!" He said it as if confirming that the world was round, and for the first time, I believed he did truly understand the danger he was in. There were those who loved him and those who hated him, and he knew it. "But are they really organized enough to do something about it?"

I said, "When you dismount from one train in Baltimore, you take a carriage to the other. Calvert Street to Camden Street. It's a mile between. In the space between the train and the carriage, their plan is to surround you. There will be so many of them, you won't be able to escape. They will swarm you and thrust themselves upon you. They drew lots from a jar to see who would have the honor of murdering you. The lucky man was to be the one with a red mark on his paper."

"And so one of them—if your intelligence is to be believed—will stab me, but we don't know which one? It's whoever drew this red mark?"

"On the contrary," I said. "They all drew red marks. They will all try to stab you."

There was a moment of silence while he let the impact settle on him. Then, making light, he said, "Doesn't that seem excessive?"

"The makers of the plot want to be absolutely sure of your death. The men who will execute the plot stand ready to die in the attempt. Moderation is not their strong suit."

From my pocket, I drew a square of paper. Tim Bellamy had gotten it into our hands, against all odds, in secret. I unfolded it and lay it down on the table in front of us. In the middle was a dark red blot of ink, as rusty and thick as blood.

At last, Lincoln said, "All right. Tell me how we will get through Baltimore."

I said, "You'll leave your dinner in Harrisburg early..." And I told him the rest of the plan, step by step, all we had carefully crafted to save him.

He listened all the way through. At the end, he nodded his assent.

"See you in Philadelphia," I said.

I planned and purchased the costumes myself, Tim Bellamy being unavailable for his usual role as prop master. We had not heard anything definite from him in a week, not since the paper had been deposited at the cabin with a brief note explaining its meaning and import. If anything happened to him, how long would it take for us to find out? Or would we never know? He'd be buried under his alias, if there was even a marked grave. He might be dead already.

I brushed away the morbid thoughts as best I could. I needed to focus on the plan at hand. Perhaps Bellamy was in danger, and perhaps there was nothing I could do to save him. But Abraham Lincoln was indisputably in the biggest danger of his life, and his life depended on the success of this plan.

As planned, Lincoln was interrupted at his dinner in Harrisburg. His private secretary came in to tap his shoulder, and Lincoln excused himself from the dinner party without saying how long he would be gone. By the time a quarter of an hour had passed and people began to wonder at his absence, he would already be on the eastbound train.

Upstairs in the hotel, he changed into a slightly worn brown suit and left his trademark stovepipe hat on the chair. We thought about having him shave to remove his beard, further changing his appearance. But this furtive night trip would be followed hard on its heels by the most public and important moment of his life. He wanted to look like himself for that moment. I only wanted to make sure he got to that moment alive.

I waited in Philadelphia, trusting that the president-elect and his single guard were speeding toward me.

I had arranged for an entire car on the Pennsylvania Railroad sleeper, leaving Philadelphia at seven o'clock in the evening. The train from Harrisburg pulled in at quarter past six, and by prior arrangement, I was to enter the hindmost door as soon as it had pulled to a stop. The two men would be waiting for me just inside that door, one slated to go off in a different direction, and one ready to be spirited onto the Philadelphia train.

I stepped onto the train, and without greeting Lincoln, I flung a shawl about his shoulders and swapped out his hat for a soft mob cap. Then, spinning a finger to indicate he should turn around, I bumped the wheeled chair behind his knees, and he naturally sat down into it.

"Ready to go, Jacky?" I asked.

I saw the mob cap nod, and within the minute, we were off the Harrisburg train and headed toward the next. Lamon left us without fanfare; if all went well, we'd see him upon arrival in Washington.

News of Lincoln's absence from the dinner in Harrisburg would by now be spreading. It would not reach us here, I knew; Pinkerton, a friend of the head of the telegraph company, had had all lines interrupted. There would be no word to or from Baltimore this night, not by telegraph, and nothing else could travel faster than we would. The cutting of the lines also improved our plan, as we knew there would be no communication at all while it was happening. Those plotting against us would not be able to punish us by cutting the lines, since it was already done.

It was time for me to play my part.

Shoving Lincoln ahead of me, my manner entitled and preemptory, I accosted the conductor and thrust our tickets in his direction.

"Where is the rear sleeping car? I have a car reserved. Can you show me where it is? I'm Dolores Mogden, and this is my brother, Jacky. He's not well, you know—his lungs. Taking him down to Baltimore to see the best doctor in the land, thinks he can help him. Well, I don't know if he can, but it's a man's life at stake, so we are gonna try it. By God, we are gonna try it."

I saw the conductor's eyes glaze with annoyance, sending my pulse rocketing. All according to plan.

"I'm Dolores, like I said, but you can call me Dot. Everyone does. Do you need to see our tickets? I have our tickets here. Where should we go? Can you show me there? Maybe tell me about the train?"

He gave the tickets the quickest glance and waved us forward. He did not walk us there, nor did he offer help of any kind, which pleased me no end. The farther away he stayed, the better things would be. The last thing we needed was an attentive man who would look down into the face of the supposed invalid and recognize him for who he really was.

And then we were on the train, and the train was pulling out of the station. We did not speak, but I heard Lincoln give an audible sigh.

The first part of the plan was complete. The second would be even harder.

I watched out the window as we went. Every once in a while, I saw a flash of light, a lantern shining and then extinguished. These were our signals, arranged by Pinkerton to assure us that nothing had gone wrong, not that we had many options if something had. Twenty miles. Forty. Sixty. *All's well. All's well. All's well.*

The train pulled into Baltimore around half past three o'clock in the morning. Now, we had reached the moment of danger. Pitch blackness all around. We were here well ahead of the announced schedule, so the hope was that our enemies would not be ready. But perhaps we had underestimated them. If so, we would only find out once our feet were on the ground and it was too late to run.

The dark of the sleeping city did not jar me, but the silence was deafening. I had never seen a city so large absolutely devoid of people. It was a dead place, full of dead buildings lining dead streets. I did not want to see it spring to life.

It was not a long way between the Calvert Street Station and the Camden Street Station. And yet, it felt like we were crossing an ocean and not just a mile of city streets. The plan was for the sleeping car to be drawn by horse through the dark streets, and it seemed to go well as best I could tell from inside the car itself, jouncing this way and that.

But the train we were intended to join had not arrived yet. We were forced to dismount, and we were in the very last place we wanted to be: exposed, in the street, among the common people. And here at the Camden Street Station, despite the late hour, people milled about, waiting on their own various trains to come or to go. I spotted DeForest at work in his navy uniform, moving things from place to place, but I did not approach him, nor did he approach me. We couldn't even signal to each other. The air was charged, and we couldn't risk sparking it.

When the train finally did come, the news was bad. As I

attempted to direct the joining of the cars, an engineer stepped in. "This car cannot be joined to the others."

"We were assured it could be."

"And I am telling you it cannot."

"I was told so by Mr. Morris."

He sighed. "Morris won't be here until the sun rises, and this train will be long gone by then. You must take passage in the train as it is."

"No, for my brother's health, isolation is absolutely required."

I had chosen not to wear a gun for fear it would show— Dolores Mogden would have no reason to arm herself—but at that moment, I wished I'd chosen differently. Things could quickly go wrong, and once they did, it would be nearly impossible to wrestle them into place again.

A conductor interrupted, "Well, the last car is empty."

The engineer said, "But they don't have tickets for that car."

"Well, what is she supposed to do otherwise?"

"Wait for the next train."

I said, "We can't do that."

The conductor said, "Just wait a minute. I'll try to find someone else who can straighten this out."

I wanted to shout, but everything depended on not shouting. "No," I said firmly. "You're right. We'll take the empty car. We'll go to the back, and we'll go now."

"Ma'am, I don't think…"

"We'll go now," I said and strode forward. As I walked, I breathed, focusing on every breath in, every breath out. Each time I drew breath, I expected to feel something. A firm hand on my shoulder. A man's fingers grabbing my arm. A bullet in my back even. But miraculously, wonderfully, each time I let the breath out, I was still alive and unmolested. Even as I stepped into the car and placed both hands on the handles of Lincoln's wheelchair—*not a word*, I whispered—no one put a hand on me, and we were heading toward an empty car we would claim for our own.

Then, even more wonderfully, we were aboard. A porter handed the luggage up to me through the open door—I saw DeForest's mustache under the uniform cap—and I knew we had done what was needed.

I wheeled my disguised companion far enough into the final sleeping car to know that no one could see us from the outside. I pulled the curtains over the windows.

"Is this it?" he asked.

I held a finger up, and we waited in silence together. The train hummed to life beneath us. And with joy, I felt the train lurch forward on the track, its engine pulsing, the *clickety-clack* sound speeding faster and faster as the train shot into the night, southward toward Washington.

With satisfaction, I told him, "Go ahead and rise."

He did, unfolding, and stretched his long legs. It must have been quite a relief. He sighed, long and low, and I could only think of how hard this had to be for him, how deeply against his nature. He only wanted to be open and straightforward, and all this skulking was the opposite. But we all knew what was at stake if we didn't deliver him safely.

"Sir," I said, but he interrupted me.

"Jacky," he said.

"Jacky," I said, smiling a little for the first time in what felt like weeks, "I think you can rest now. Good night."

He lay down on a lower bunk, a slim pallet far too short for his size, and drew his knees up with another sigh. I knew he wasn't quiet in his heart—who could be, given the danger?—but he also had to be utterly exhausted. I hoped he might have a moment's peace.

For me, there would be none. I closed the door to the

compartment and locked it behind me. I reached under the wheel-chair frame and carefully dislodged the shotgun we had secreted there. Then I set my chair square in front of the locked door, lay the shotgun across my knees, and readied myself to wait out the night.

CHAPTER TWENTY

WE NEVER SLEEP

Whatever my level of tiredness should have been, I felt no exhaustion, no temptation to close my eyes. I had never been so awake in my life. My aim was not as good with a shotgun as with a pistol, but in the close quarters of a railcar corridor, it would hardly matter.

I counted off the minutes in my head as we went, and with every minute that slipped into the past forever, my hope for success grew and grew. I had not imagined we would succeed, but neither had I imagined we could fail. I kept my mind on the next ten-minute interval, and I kept my eyes wide open. The dark world whooshed past outside the curtains of the closed windows. There was no scenery, no sound, nothing to distract my attention. If an assassin appeared, I was dead certain he would find himself no match for me.

We arrived in Washington with the sunrise.

As soon as the motion of the train had stilled, I opened the door to the outside a mere crack and put one open eye against it. We had planned every detail, but this was the last moment where things could go wrong. Would I see Pinkerton? Armed soldiers? No one at all? We only needed to get to Willard's Hotel, and then all would be well.

I scanned the crowd. As one would expect at any train station, there were tears and embraces, nervous-looking couples waiting in silence, children in their Sunday best. There were soldiers galore, but they bustled about without pattern, and none had guns aimed in our direction.

Then I saw two familiar men, and I wanted to sob with relief. Only a surge of pride kept me upright and dry-eyed. I would not collapse in front of Tim Bellamy, not when I knew he had survived his own trials, surrounded by the enemy. The other man was Ward Hill Lamon, grinning brightly under his prodigious brown beard.

"Dolores has brought her brother Jacky home," I said, and Lincoln emerged from the car, already mostly transformed back into himself. Lamon handed him his top hat to complete the picture. Lincoln set his large hand on my shoulder for just a moment, mouthed *Thank you,* and climbed up into the waiting wagon, heading forward.

The men drove off with their new president, and I remained behind to clean up, so weary I could barely stand. After I'd rested, I could let myself feel relief and satisfaction. First, there was work to be done.

❦

Two days later, at the inauguration, we five Pinkertons were reunited. Hattie, Pinkerton, Bellamy, DeForest, and myself, all unscathed. We gathered to watch Lincoln become the president. For the moment, our disguises and roles were all set aside. We were ourselves.

Standing along Pennsylvania Avenue, the scaffolded white dome of the Capitol looming above us in the distance, I couldn't believe our good fortune. If I'd been asked at the beginning of our sojourn whether we five would all make it through the Baltimore adventure, I wouldn't have said yes. Dangers seemed too many, and we seemed too few. But we had this moment, breathing the air and standing together, and I was determined to savor it.

"I'm having new cards made for the agency," said Pinkerton.

I shot him a quizzical look. Now didn't seem the time for housekeeping.

"They'll have our new motto."

"Which is?"

"We Never Sleep," he said and clapped me on the shoulder. He had never beamed at me with such obvious pride. It almost made me blush. A cheer went up from the crowd, which I knew was coincidence, but it still warmed my heart. What we'd done wouldn't be known by the general public for many years, if at all. If a misattributed cheer was the only type I might get, I'd gladly take it.

Pinkerton moved on to whisper something to Bellamy, and I saw him clap the other man on the shoulder much as he'd done with me. If Bellamy was angry that our boss had congratulated a mere woman first, he didn't show it. He smiled and shook Pinkerton's hand with vigor. It was indeed a day for optimism and new beginnings.

I knew Pinkerton was apprehensive because Lincoln had chosen to ride to the inauguration in an open carriage, but once he arrived for his swearing-in, even the boss breathed a bit easier.

Hattie and I clasped hands. On my other side, Bellamy radiated a pure joy I'd never suspected he was capable of; on impulse, I reached out for his hand too. He didn't seem to react, but neither did he pull his fingers away. DeForest and Hattie twined their hands together as well, exchanging smiles. And the five of us watched as Abraham Lincoln—our Lincoln—was sworn in as president of the United States.

Even though we wondered how long the nation could be seen as united, there was an undeniable power in seeing him inaugurated. It felt like a hopeful moment. It felt right.

We heard the end of his speech in utter silence.

In your hands, my dissatisfied fellow-countrymen, and not in mine, is the momentous issue of civil war. The Government will not assail you. You can have no conflict without being yourselves the aggressors. You have no oath registered in heaven to destroy the Government, while I shall have the most solemn one to "preserve, protect, and defend it."

I am loath to close. We are not enemies, but friends. We must not be enemies. Though passion may have strained it must not break our bonds of affection. The mystic chords of memory, stretching from every battlefield and patriot grave to every living heart and hearthstone all over this broad land, will yet swell the chorus of the Union, when again touched, as surely they will be, by the better angels of our nature.

I liked the idea that my nature might have better angels in it. Thinking on the things I'd done, bad things for good reasons, I wanted to believe behavior alone didn't tell a person's story. I looked at Pinkerton's face, Hattie's, Bellamy's, DeForest's, Lincoln's. What had we done so far to get here? Deceived, lied, disguised, misled, threatened, entrapped, captured, hurt. If war came, or even if it didn't, what more would we do? Were we devils, even on the angels' side?

After the Baltimore sojourn, Pinkerton insisted we rest. He suggested some sort of rural retreat, but I only wanted to be in Chicago. I had been away too long. And I knew that despite the successful installation of our man in the presidency, there were still dissenting voices to be heard in many, many different places, and I had no doubt I would be sent out to listen to them again.

So while I could, I stayed. I walked to Humboldt Park, lunched at Calliope's, and spent countless hours simply watching strong men raise the buildings along the river. It was a miracle of modern engineering. The river had always fed the city, but it also posed a threat. Water had never drained properly from buildings on the riverfront, and it was only growing worse over time. A sewer system was the obvious answer, but the buildings were too low, with no space underneath. Chicagoans being who they were, they simply decided the obvious solution was to lift the buildings up. Sewer pipes had been laid atop the ground, and now the ground would be brought up higher than the pipes to bury them. It was the most modern feat I could imagine.

Entire blocks were being raised by means of jackscrews, and there was no better entertainment on a Sunday afternoon than watching people scurry into and out of a shop—open for business, of course—whose door was rising an inch at a time, dozens of men panting away at its foundation. No other city was like Chicago, and a fierce affection for it rose in my chest as I watched it rearrange itself, piece by piece, to make a better place. As we always had, we were taking something raw and refining it, making it more polished, more finished, for the world.

Unfortunately, while we saw our successful operation in Baltimore as a triumph, it was depicted otherwise in the newspapers of the day. Our role wasn't known, but it quickly became public knowledge that Lincoln had been spirited into Washington under cover of night, and that was enough. Cartoons showed Lincoln in a nightshirt, or even his wife's dress, sneaking through the city. I wanted to personally throttle every single reporter, cartoonist, or editor who depicted Lincoln in anything less than a flattering light. We had enough enemies on the other side; we didn't need more among us. And because we needed secrecy above all else, we could not bring the conspirators to justice. We simply had to leave them be. And so even the barber, Ferrandini, was let alone.

Were we merely spitting into the ocean? Would even this great triumph be too little to stave off the coming tide?

On April 12, the Confederates fired on Fort Sumter, and the last thoughts of peace evaporated like summer's morning dew.

I was not there, but it was easy to picture. I had seen Fort Sumter enough times off the coast of Charleston. In my youth, I had found it reassuring. Now, it would always mean something else.

My first action upon hearing the news, of course, was to run to the office on Clark Street. Similarly, other operatives had appeared and were milling about aimlessly. We all knew it was a day of great import. We simply didn't know where the action would take us.

While we gathered in small groups, muttering to ourselves and one another, a telegram arrived for Pinkerton. He opened it in full view of all of us. He fingered the paper and lowered it to the desk slowly, as if it weighed more than paper possibly could.

"What is it?" I asked.

He answered grimly, "It's war."

We'd known it, but at the same time, we couldn't believe it. As terrible as things had gotten, it always seemed something would happen to pull us back from the brink. Nothing had. We were over the brink now and falling.

Pinkerton looked up at the assembled crowd. "And we're needed."

We nodded our heads as one. I had promised myself I would do what was necessary to save the country. The opportunity had arrived much sooner than I'd hoped, but there was no shrinking from it now.

That night, an old friend brought other news, as bad in its way as the news of war had been. I went to visit Mrs. Borowski, desperate for someone familiar to talk to, someone reassuring. There was gray in her blond braids now, and her face was a little less round, but she was still the woman whose words could bring me the most comfort. She offered me fresh warm bread and mint tea, and after we'd eaten and made small talk, she said, "Kate, I must tell you something."

"Oh, I hope it's good news," I said, knowing it wasn't. No one ever prefaced good news with such words.

"I must leave your employ."

First, I put my arms around her wordlessly. Perhaps to comfort her, but mostly to comfort myself. The world was already coming undone. Losing someone I valued so much, someone I relied on, was just one more bit of evidence that things would never be the same again.

"Why? Because of the war?"

"Somewhat."

"You're not"—I searched for the right words—"going to the South?"

"No. West."

"You have a place?"

"To run a boardinghouse in the Dakotas. Near a gold camp. The prospectors, they need somewhere to stay."

"And somewhere to spend their gold. It's a smart choice. Where in the Dakotas?"

"Not far from Yankton." She grinned as she added, "The place is called Bright Hope."

"I wish that for you."

"Kate, you know I will miss you."

"Not as much as I'll miss you."

"Don't put a bet on it," she said, and I saw the beginnings of tears glistening in her eyes. All selfish, I'd only thought of how hard it was for me, but of course, we'd known each other so long now. I knew she didn't have children—we had that in common, despite our many other differences—and perhaps she thought of me as a kind of daughter. The mere thought brought tears to my eyes to match hers.

We hugged again, but I didn't try to keep her from going. I knew it was pointless. And perhaps she would be safe there, in the Dakota Territory, away from the war. There were other threats—disease, Indians—but at least she would never see her home ground become a battlefield.

I could run from it too, I realized. I was determined to run toward it instead.

The next day, I said as much to the boss.

Despite his serious look, I could see that Pinkerton was also preening, and I knew he had something important to say. "I've offered, and President Lincoln has accepted, help in the form of intelligence gathering and security."

"What exactly does that mean?"

"An intelligence service. Our operatives, ensuring the safety of the nation."

"As soldiers?"

"No."

"Then in what capacity?"

"Gathering information."

I was in no mood for coyness. "That tells me nothing. I've been gathering information for you for nigh on five years now and have never been any part of any intelligence service, nor anything by that name."

"You want me to put the plainest word on it? Fine, then. I need spies."

This, I saw, was my chance. "Send me," I said immediately.

"Warne..."

"Where do you need help most? You know I've been every-where in the South."

His self-important air had evaporated, and he looked ill at ease. I could see him searching for the best way to refuse me, and I couldn't stand the thought.

I leaned forward in my chair, intent on making myself heard. "Send me to Montgomery. Little Rock. Atlanta. Wherever you say, I'll go."

He said at last, "Here. Chicago."

"No."

In a firmer tone, he said, "You don't have the privilege to tell me no. You are still in my employ. Or would you prefer not to be?"

"I won't stay," I said. "If you don't send me somewhere closer to the action, that's it. I'll resign and go myself. Watch for my telegrams."

"Warne, Warne, Warne," he said, resting his elbows on the desk. He had rolled up his sleeves. There was more exhaustion than anger in his voice when he said my name. "We can't lose you."

"You've lost me if you don't put me to use."

"Don't you believe I know what's best for you?"

"All due respect, Boss, I don't care what's best for me. You shouldn't be thinking of me. Think of the country."

I could see right away I'd overstepped. It was inappropriate to imply that he was letting his feelings get in the way of his decisions. But all the same, I wasn't sad I'd said it. As much as lies were our business with everyone else, between us, there needed to be nothing but truth.

He said, "I'll think on it."

I bit back what I most wanted to say: *Think fast.*

The waiting seemed interminable, but I knew better than to rush him. If I wanted to be treated as a professional, that was how I had to act. It had been enough so far. So there would be no wheedling or whining, no words of persuasion, no batting of my eyelashes, no gamesmanship. Only waiting for his decision. And if he made the wrong one, then I would react.

Three days later, I had my orders and my new identity.

I was flabbergasted when Pinkerton told me I was right and that I was needed in a place of great danger. He explained that he was sending me where I wanted to go, right up next to the action, but I wasn't going alone.

I was to report to the train station immediately—I already had my bag—and therefore had little time to process the news about my traveling companion until I stepped up into the railcar and sat down next to him.

Tim Bellamy.

He eyed me without surprise—Pinkerton must have prepared him as well—and commented, "Looks like we're equally pigheaded."

"Looks that way."

The train made its lurch into motion, sending us both swaying along with everyone else in the car, and we were underway, bound for Washington.

CHAPTER TWENTY-ONE

INTELLIGENCE

We talked little on the ride, caught up in our own thoughts, reading and memorizing files we knew we'd need to destroy as soon as we reached our destination. Our lives had been built on subterfuge for years, but there had never been quite this much riding on our success at it, and our enemies had never been so thick on the ground.

Even before we got to Washington, I could tell it had changed since my last visit. Miles out from the city, a blossoming of white covered the countryside. Smaller blue figures swarmed about. It was the army, encamped. We glided slowly past their tents, and I searched for the expressions on the faces of the soldiers, but for better or worse, I was not close enough to see.

When we finally arrived, we stepped off the train into hot swamp air. I had spent summers all over the Cotton States and had never felt heat like this before. Beads of perspiration clustered at my hairline as we waited outside the station for our carriage. I desperately wanted to shed layers of clothes and go about with my legs and arms bare. Failing that, I wanted to plunge into a pool or simply turn tail and go north again. But I had already planted my stake in the ground. I couldn't be a passionate patriot only when the whim struck me. I needed to serve, day in and day out. And so I would. Which on this mission, meant Tim Bellamy always by my side.

I knew what it meant, pretending to be husband and wife. Had we been in a different city, pretending to be more well-off citizens, we might have maintained separate bedrooms and not been questioned. Many wives and husbands slept apart. But hotel rooms were not so easy to come by, at least not in the neighborhood we needed to inhabit. Paying for two would have been an extravagance and a visible, dissonant one. So we would share.

Of all the things my job as an operative had asked of me so far, this seemed like it might be the most taxing. I'd feared for my life. I'd lied and cheated, let myself be treated like chattel, been harmed for the good of the case. But all of those things, terrible as they were, were over quickly. This would be weeks, if not months, of work. Even years. From my earliest days at the agency, Pinkerton had avoided assigning us to work together, and now I wished he hadn't. Now, I was facing the hardest assignment of my life, relying completely on the cooperation of a man who still did not seem to trust or respect me.

Then again, I told myself, what man did trust or respect me? Only Pinkerton and DeForest, and neither of them were here. I wished for a moment that the boss had sent DeForest as my partner instead, but I had to trust he had his reasons.

Anyway, we had our orders. We followed them.

With letters of introduction—some forged, some real—we settled into our new roles, and within two weeks, we had the invitation we needed to get underway. Tuesday night, we were to report to General Greene's house on Capitol Hill. The general himself was beyond reproach, as much as any man could be in these wild times. We were there to keep an eye on one of the guests, a Mrs. Rose Greenhow.

We'd been preparing since our arrival, but this was our first big night to debut as our new identities. I readied myself as we stood in the anteroom, waiting for dinner to start. A bell rang out. The man next to me introduced himself, and I swept low in a curtsy, bending and straightening in exactly the manner my mother had taught me ever so long ago.

When I rose, Kate Warne was gone. I was Mrs. Annie Armstrong and none other.

And the man next to me, with the ice-blue eyes, so tall and proud? Mr. Timothy Armstrong, my husband.

How strange. How impossible. I had pretended many things before, but I had never pretended to be truly in love, and how funny that this man should be the one I'd be pretending with. But I would have to tackle it the same way I had any other role. Holding the truth and the lie in my mind together was too difficult. Better to believe the lie with my whole self.

"Shall we, my love?" I asked.

In his eyes, there was only the mildest flicker of shock. No one else would have noticed it. He was a good operative, and I could trust him. I had to.

I tucked my hand through his arm, and together, we went in to dinner.

As we sat down at table, I had my first sight of our target.

Mrs. Greenhow was a robust woman, buxom and round-cheeked, but with nothing of the milkmaid about her. Her hair was dark, bound in a low chignon. I'd read the file a dozen times before feeding it to the flames and could call any of it to mind instantly. Born in Maryland in 1813. Resident in the capital on and off since 1830. Widowed in 1854. Longtime friend to South Carolina Senator John C. Calhoun. Aunt to Stephen Douglas, the senator who had so memorably debated Lincoln in 1858 and lost the presidency to him two years later. They were not related by blood—he had married her sister's daughter, Adele, after his first wife's death—nor did they share much in the way of political leanings. She was well-known as a Southern loyalist, but so far, no one could prove she'd done anything criminal.

We were here for that proof.

⌀

After dinner, we rose and gathered in the parlor. I continued to exchange pleasantries with the young man who had been seated on my right, careful not to sound too enthusiastic. He was quite handsome, with a full mustache and neatly trimmed beard, and he gestured with animated hands that drew and kept my attention. However I would have felt about him under other circumstances, I had to pay respect to my alleged husband first and foremost. I half listened, but my eyes and mind were elsewhere, with Mrs. Greenhow.

She held court at the far end of the parlor, next to a beautiful ebony piano crowned with a colorful spray of flowers in a blue-green China vase. Her full-skirted gown was a bright shade of lapis blue and looked so well with the vase of flowers, I wondered if it had been chosen on purpose.

Artfully, she flirted, and I watched how she flirted. Her hands were deployed like soldiers to any front where they were needed: stroking a man's sleeve to create intimacy, resting on the piano to reinforce her wealth, trailing along the side of her neck to draw attention to her body. She was not a young woman, but she was a beautiful one, no mistake. Her beauty alone was not all she had to offer. She gave off some kind of energy that drew men to her. Her gift, I saw, was attention. There was nothing more intoxicating to these men.

The general next to her bowed his head to listen to her—watching them, I would have bet Union dollars that she spoke in a near whisper, forcing him to bend closer, as a stratagem. I'd used it before. Was I looking at a fellow spy or just a woman who used wiles to get what she wanted? Perhaps I was quick to judge her because I could see how she was well armed with a battery of tools I didn't have at my own disposal: riches, friends, beauty.

"Don't stare," said Tim, leaning in himself, so close I felt his breath on my ear.

"Mrs. Armstrong would," I muttered softly.

"Has my wife no manners, then?" He said it with a chuckle, but I took his point. I turned away from Mrs. Greenhow and began to survey the rest of the room. She was our person of interest, but there was much else to see, and we needed to understand her world.

It was a lovely room, not too ostentatious, every addition thoughtful. The carpet under dozens of feet was brightly patterned with blue and purple flowers on a yellow ground, and golden damask curtains framed the large, clear windows. Someone had paid a pretty penny for this house, and it was impeccably kept up, despite the war shortages. Perhaps that was how we might ensnare her—some of these silks had to have run the blockade.

Pinkerton had given us but little guidance, but we had talked it over again and again, and there were a number of different plans we could put into action. All we knew was that if she were a spy, she needed to be stopped. The weight of our task rested most heavily on me at night, when I heard Bellamy's soft breathing on the other side of our quiet room. The intimacy was almost unbearable. But it was part of the work.

So I flirted with Tim Bellamy, as a wife would with her husband if she loved him: a gentle, teasing interplay, filled with warmth and comfort. And under it all, I spied. I kept an eye on the room and swept it with my gaze, until I alit on something new.

A girl, no more than eight years old, dressed as charmingly as a doll. Her skirt was full, and her dress was an exact copy of her mother's, scaled down for her tiny proportions.

Little Rose.

She was in the file too. Mrs. Greenhow's other daughters were grown, married, gone to Ohio and beyond. Only Little Rose remained. By all accounts, the mother and daughter were mutually devoted, and perhaps that was true, but in this crowd, she looked abandoned, out of place. I thought of all the times I'd been stowed at the edges of ballrooms and backstage at theaters, places no child belonged, never sure I'd be remembered or retrieved. I told myself when I was a mother, I'd take more care with my child. But I'd never gotten the chance.

"My dear," said my unreal husband, "do you want to retire?"

"No reason to, not yet," I said with false gaiety. I could tell by the way he'd said it that he didn't yet think it was time for us to leave. He was reminding me to pay more attention to my demeanor. He was right. This was no place for sentiment. I told myself I was just getting used to the assignment, and that once we'd settled in, I'd be able to regard Mrs. Greenhow and her friends with some dispassionate distance.

One could view these people as people—as I had with Cath Maroney, once upon a time—or as chess pieces, with the queen and the rook and the bishop all playing their parts but with no more will than a painted piece upon a painted board. The chess image was more soothing to my soul.

If they were all chess pieces, then I, a chess piece also, could do no harm. It was simply a game. No one knew whether black or white would win. But we would all play until the game was over, in hope of victory for our side, until the bitter end.

The bridges of western Virginia were burning. If there was a single action that would harm an army, it was to cut off access to the railroad. The Southern army was outnumbered and outgunned and smart enough to know it. Sabotage could turn the tide. I'd heard whispers that our men planned to corner and kill Jefferson Davis or General Jackson, but all those plans seemed like folly. Slaying a leader only gave rise to another leader. They were easily elected and installed. The building of a bridge was a much more complicated act and could have a more lasting impression on the future, all things considered.

There was nothing we could do to stop the burning. We did hear that McClellan, who I remembered well from the railroad embezzlement case, had promised in public that the Union military had no intention of helping slaves rebel and would even put down any such rebellions with our own might. It was a nonsensical thing to say. I could be certain it would infuriate Lincoln, who had enough to handle without his most trusted generals disagreeing with the fundamental operations of his war.

And danger seemed to draw ever closer. Virginia—mere miles away—announced its secession from the Union into the Confederate States, and its capital, Richmond, became the capital of the entire Confederacy. We hadn't moved at all, but we felt an impossible distance from our home in Chicago, and the wolves were at our door.

We shook our heads. What else could we do? We had enough to deal with already. We could only try our best to solve the problem in front of us without worrying what lay beyond.

After establishing the Armstrongs in the city, Tim and I settled in, and I even came to enjoy having him to talk to at night instead of retiring to a solo room. We used the time to discuss plans, to perfect our strategy, and sometimes to jointly compose our bulletins back to Pinkerton. The room had only a single bed in it, and Bellamy, chivalrous to a fault, had set up a bed of sorts for himself on a fainting couch. One night, I absolutely insisted he let me take a turn sleeping on the couch while he had the bed. Whether he believed my argument that we were equal or whether he just wanted to teach me a lesson, he swapped sleeping spaces with me that night. I woke up feeling black and blue in my joints, my muscles, and all over. The next night, I walked to the bed and lay down in it with no protests. He smiled ruefully, said good night, and lay himself down in his nest of blankets again.

One night, we discussed possible new approaches to Mrs. Greenhow, things we hadn't dreamed of trying before.

"I could seduce her," he said.

"Could you now?" My voice was sharper than I intended.

"We need to think of all the possibilities."

"And what would your wife think of that?"

"I don't know. What do you think?"

"I mean your real wife," I said, thinking of the pretty doll on his arm at Pinkerton's party on the night DeForest proposed. It seemed a lifetime ago. I'd been wondering about her since we arrived, but I hadn't ginned up the courage to ask him outright.

"I don't have one. I had a fiancée, but she..."

"Didn't like the work?" I prompted.

He nodded. "She...wanted more attention than I could give. Told me to choose the work or her. And you see what I chose."

"Oh." DeForest had been right after all. How I wished he were here to congratulate.

"Now focus. What's my best angle to get close to Greenhow?"

"I'm not sure it's a good idea. I just—we've taken pains to portray a happy marriage for the Armstrongs, and that would certainly give her other ideas."

"Which might work in our favor."

"I suppose so." I was beginning to see the sense in it, once I brushed off my irrational feelings of ownership. "If you do me wrong, she might turn more to me, feeling sorry."

"Or I suppose it could go the other way. She could freeze you out as a response to her own guilt."

"You've seen her. Do you think guilt plays much of a part in her thoughts?"

Greer Macallister

"We should think it through," he said.

"You're the one who suggested it."

"Please," he said. "It is not my intent to make your life harder, believe it or not. It never has been."

I decided to address the contradiction head-on. "Even on the first night we met, when I solved that case, and you weren't going to tell Pinkerton?"

"I was. Truly. Going to tell him. I meant to, anyway, in my head." He looked down, tugging at a loose thread on his cuff. "I just started telling the story without you—I was so excited we'd pulled it off—and I—well, I'm sorry."

"How can I trust that you're telling the truth?"

"If you don't trust me by now, I can't imagine how much you must be suffering." He smiled, but I could hear his worry underneath the joking words. He was right. We were in this together and no mistake.

He turned down the lamp, and we lay down in our sleeping places, but I was not ready yet for rest. I remembered how cruel I had thought Bellamy when we first met, but spending hours on end with him now, I realized what had given me that impression. He had a way of closing himself off, holding himself back, in public. Those piercing blue eyes were intent, but you couldn't see any of what was behind them, not if he didn't want you to. Either he couldn't keep up the pretense around the clock, or he had made a deliberate decision, but when we were alone in the hotel together, his face was not closed off like that. I could see him feel things deeply. As an operative, he chose to act from a place of intellect, but it wasn't because he lacked the heart to feel. He just knew when it would hold him back instead of moving him forward.

Bellamy was an excellent detective and a powerful ally. Pinkerton had made the right assignment, trusting the two of us to bring down Mrs. Greenhow. Now, all we needed to do was deliver on that promise.

Somehow.

CHAPTER TWENTY-TWO
THE STUDY

In July, we were struck again with terrible news. We had spent the day apart, chasing intelligence from different quarters, and the first thing Tim said to me when I walked in the door of our hotel room was, "We've been defeated at Bull Run."

"Bull Run? I hear Manassas."

"Same thing. The Northern name, the Southern name."

I said, with an attempt at gallows humor, "I supposed I should be used to multiple names of things by now."

"We were winning," he said, "and then reinforcements came. Turned the tide, and we were defeated. Terribly."

"The numbers. You have them?"

"Five hundred dead," he said, his voice tight. "Twice that wounded. The same number missing or captured. More almost than can be imagined."

"Their losses?"

"Far less."

I didn't press him for specifics. Each individual life mattered to the people who knew the light before it went out. But we were already so deep into the war, and this would just press us in deeper. We would have to grow accustomed to losses in the hundreds and thousands. My gut ached, my heart ached, everything ached.

Tim said, "Only one thing I can't figure. Why would they

send reinforcements to that place? They shouldn't have known we were coming."

"But you think they did."

"I think spies got word to the Confederacy of our plans."

"You think it was Mrs. Greenhow?"

"Impossible to say."

I said, with a slight edge of despair I couldn't keep out of my voice, "We have to do something about her."

"If it's her."

I had an overwhelming urge to lay my head against his shoulder. In public, I was so used to doing things like that, as if they were natural. Our cover was complete. We kept making physical contact, running our fingers along each other's arms, clasping hands, gently bumping shoulders, from the moment we left our room in the morning until we returned to it at night. In private, though, we sat at a strict distance from each other. Together alone, we were impeccably proper.

No matter how much I wanted comfort, I wouldn't get it from him. If the news from the front didn't get better, I doubted I'd be able to get comfort from anywhere.

Mrs. Greenhow was getting more comfortable with me or just in general. I knew the members of her social circle, insinuating myself with each over time, and they seemed comfortable as well. She was not the boldest of her peers. That was Mrs. Melanie Chalmers, the wife of a member of the House of Representatives from Kansas.

But even I did not know how far Mrs. Chalmers would go until I heard her say, "That fool Lincoln is forcing the manhood of the Union into service. Another five hundred thousand troops, they say. A million would not be enough to stand against us."

I was shocked that she would be so open in mixed company and watched Mrs. Greenhow closely for a reaction. She gave none.

I said neutrally, "The loss of young men is a tragedy on both sides. Perhaps there will come a day again where there is only one side, and we can all be on it."

"And who will be left by then?" asked Mrs. Greenhow. "Just us, the women. Not much of a nation, then."

"America will always rise."

"Well said, Mrs. Armstrong."

"I believe it," I said and sipped my champagne, wishing I did.

"And why does your husband not serve, Mrs. Armstrong?" asked the pink-cheeked older woman. Her champagne glass was empty every time I looked at her; this might account for her intemperate speech.

I answered smoothly, "He will be called soon. In the meantime, he is here on behalf of his brother's estate, seeking a good price for his horses and other property. The transactions are rather complicated, I understand. We are trying to enjoy our last days together. I try not to think about it, truthfully. I will miss him so."

"You poor dear," said Mrs. Greenhow. "Times like this, it's not so bad to be a widow. A woman without her husband has already lost everything she has to lose."

I nodded silently, with a neutral expression, but inside, I was in turmoil. If that was how she thought, then I suspected her even more strongly of being a spy. If she was a wife only to her country, she might be capable of anything. Though of course, I was a widow too, and the same could be said of me.

❦

While we learned a great deal from watching Mrs. Greenhow during the day, I knew there was more to be learned by watching her at other times too. If she was entangling herself with generals and senators, she wasn't doing it at dinner parties but in more secret places.

So one night, I set myself the task of watching her. I told Tim what I was doing, and he offered to do it instead, but I insisted. If caught, it would be far easier for me to come up with a plausible story than it would be for him. Besides, I was finding the closeness of our hotel room a bit excessive, and spending a few nighttime hours outside on my own would be welcome.

As I suspected, after dark had fully fallen, Mrs. Greenhow slipped out the back door of her house and down the street. I tailed her, calling upon my old tracking techniques, and fetched up only a few blocks away in front of a familiar house that belonged to Senator Wilson.

A door opened, feeding a slice of light into the darkness, and she disappeared inside. I had no idea how long I'd be waiting, but in the meantime, I'd have plenty of time to think as I lurked in the dark.

I thought first of Graham DeForest, who I'd tracked so long ago. Last I'd known, Pinkerton had put him on a long-term assignment in southern Illinois, traveling between the small towns on the railroad to suss out any evidence of sabotage, the region being such an important gateway to Missouri and Kentucky, not to mention Arkansas and Tennessee. Communication hadn't been good, and we weren't encouraged to communicate without a solid purpose in any case. Still, he'd been a good friend, and I hoped against hope he'd make it through this war alive. Doubt flickered in my mind: perhaps he'd make it, and I wouldn't. No one could know.

The breezeless summer evening turned into pitch-dark night, and I watched and watched. The progress of my targets was easily tracked by watching the light and shadows in each room, the movement of curtains, things that were obvious to anyone who was watching. If they assumed no one was paying attention, they were fools. Perhaps he was a fool anyway. If she was seducing him in exchange for military secrets, only one fool was required. She clearly didn't care whether people talked about her; she had the town wrapped around her finger. The society ladies sometimes whispered behind their fans about her reputation, but they always, always went to her parties.

The shadow I knew to be Mrs. Greenhow passed in front of the window and drew near the shadow I believed to be the senator, until one could not be told apart from the other. I thought of Little Rose. Did she wake in the night, wondering where her mother was? Or was there a servant close by who would respond to her cries more quickly and care for her better? I tried to put thoughts of Little Rose out of my mind. More than Mrs. Maroney's daughter Violet, her welfare haunted me. If I succeeded in my mission, her mother would go to prison—or worse. I couldn't let that get in my way.

Dawn was touching the sky when Mrs. Greenhow emerged from the house, drawing her shawl over her head like a hood, to hustle quickly through the semidarkness. I didn't bother to shadow her back home. I already knew what I needed to know and headed back to the hotel to share it with Tim.

He was still asleep when I arrived. I thought he might take the bed in my absence, knowing I'd be out all night, but he was curled in his nest of blankets on the uncomfortable couch. The couch wasn't tall enough for his long body, and he'd drawn up his knees toward his stomach, giving him an odd aspect, half giant, half boy. He'd gripped a handful of the blankets tight in one fist. His other hand dangled, open, off the side of the couch, reaching for nothing.

For long moments, I stood over him, watching. He looked innocent this way, but we'd both left innocence behind long ago. Would he do what was necessary, what Mrs. Greenhow did, in order to obtain secrets? Would he take her in his arms, take possession of her naked body, give her possession of his? I didn't like how that idea made me feel. And yet, I knew I myself would do anything necessary for the sake of our nation. I could not ask less—or more—of him.

I didn't wake him. Instead, I walked soundlessly to the bed and lay my head down on the pillow. Eventually, I sank into a restless sleep, my head and heart full of confusing ideas.

After weeks, Tim and I reached a shared conclusion. We could learn nothing more from mere social contact, but we knew there was a very good chance Mrs. Greenhow had something to hide. Any such evidence would have to be found in her house, and we would have to find it ourselves.

And so, we made a plan. The next time she hosted a gathering at her lovely mansion at Thirteenth and I Street, we would find a way to search the house. Anything we found, we would leave in place, then take our next steps based on what we had discovered. If we found nothing, we would be no worse off than we already were, wondering every day if our mission was a fool's pursuit or if we were only a heartbeat away from making a substantial difference in the future of this terrible war. Could we save lives? Or were we just marking time, following a blind alley? Something bolder had to be done if we were to find out for sure.

We managed to sneak away separately. First I left, pretending to search out water to clean a spot on my skirt, and then he melted away from a conversation and stepped backward through an open door at an opportune moment. Our destination was a small office, unlocked, near the back bedrooms. My heart hammered in my chest.

We didn't speak. He pointed silently to the desk, and I nodded. In my bodice, I carried a small set of lock picks I'd procured in Chicago, and while I didn't consider myself a true expert, I could handle most locks within five minutes. A simple desk lock like this should take no more than three. I drew the packet out, pinched a slender rod between my thumb and forefinger, and bent to the task.

While I worked on the desk, Tim quickly scanned the books on the shelf, tapping and nudging to look for anything out of place. A book either more or less dusty than its neighbors might hold a secret compartment. A shocking number of people went to the trouble of hiding things yet did it poorly. A quick inspection, however hasty, might turn up anything.

After the books, Tim moved on to the wall, lifting each painting to check behind it for a wall safe. He was quick and nearly silent. I was breathing softly, systematically working the lock from a succession of angles, waiting for the click of the tumblers.

So when someone turned the doorknob of the study from the outside, we both heard.

He gestured for me to run toward him, and I did, as fast as I could, but the couch was between us. Without a moment's hesitation, he pulled me over it, and I landed hard on the cushion. He threw his body on top of mine. I didn't know what he planned until I felt his hand tearing pins from my hair and his mouth suddenly on mine, taking my breath away.

He tasted like tobacco and flesh and heat.

My mind was spinning in three different directions at once, but the most important direction was linked to my ears— listening for whoever was coming in the door. I couldn't see, not with Tim covering my entire body with his own. The side I'd landed on throbbed under my corset; I could barely breathe. And even with all of that, I found myself caught up in passion. My body arched against his, pressing closer as he pressed down, and his other hand came up to my waist, even though it wasn't visible from the doorway.

A sliver of light fell across us when the door was opened.

"Pardon!" exclaimed a man's voice.

We looked up, and Tim pulled away from me, leaving my neck and chest suddenly cold. My mouth felt bruised and raw, swollen from his fierce kisses, and the pain was not entirely without pleasure.

"Do you mind?" Tim said with superior frostiness. Even in my current state, I could appreciate what a good actor he was. No one would take him for anything other than a man in lust, interrupted.

Then he raised himself on his elbows, and his weight shifted, and as his hips pressed mine into the soft couch, I could feel the evidence that his lust was not entirely an act.

Mrs. Greenhow's butler stood in the doorway, his silver hair glinting in the half-light. He appeared undeterred. "I'm afraid you can't be in here, sir."

"We are. And we'd appreciate it if you wouldn't stand there gawking."

The butler's expression did not change. He was well trained. "Of course, sir. But I have to ask you and your companion—"

"My wife." Tim's indignant sneer was spot-on.

"I have to insist that you and your wife rejoin the other guests in the drawing room. Mrs. Greenhow does not care for visitors in her study."

Sensing that the man would not relinquish his position, Tim backed down from his. "All right then. We meant no harm."

He swung his legs off the couch and stood in one fluid motion, running one hand through his disarrayed hair to smooth it—I realized that was my work—and then turned to offer me his hand.

At that moment, I realized I had left my lock picks. The entire packet lay under the desk behind me, the short metal bars in their sleeves, and the one I'd been using when we were interrupted likely lay exposed and glinting on the carpet. I couldn't leave them. Even if the servant didn't notice as he escorted us out, someone would, and only a fool could look at the set of tools and not know what they were for. It wouldn't take a spy to realize that we, the couple interrupted in the study, had left them. Then all would be over.

"Not yet," I said.

"Ma'am?"

"Dear?"

"I need a moment, please, needs must—" I looked down at my disarrayed bodice, then up at Tim, through lowered lashes.

"My wife would like some privacy, please," he said firmly.

"Of course. Sir, ma'am. I'll wait for you outside and escort you back."

As soon as the door was closed, I rose from the couch, swept the packet and loose pick from the floor, and tucked them back into my bodice. I then took a half minute to array the bodice flat, tugging and smoothing it into place, so nothing would show. The drawer remained stubbornly closed, and with the butler aware of our presence, it was now too dangerous to attempt to break in. We'd missed our chance.

I did not meet Tim's eyes as we left the room. I knew we were both disappointed that we'd found nothing we could use yet satisfied that our cover identities were still intact. At least not all was lost.

And if we both felt something else—rattled, confused by pleasure, clouded by the discovery of what seemed to be a mutual lust—we did not discuss it. We lay in the same room in separate beds, across a narrow but steady distance, breathing in the dark.

☙

There were a few steps forward, a few steps back. The war felt like war—surging and sinking, grinding on forever. Washington was a city that would not let us forget. Perhaps back in Chicago, things were different, but in Washington, there were troops in the streets and uniforms in every room we entered, large or small. The city was under martial law, and every stroll down the street carried some small risk of erupting into violence, though thank goodness, it happened less often than we feared. We learned the identities of Mrs. Greenhow's frequent visitors and dutifully relayed all we learned in long reports to Pinkerton. But we still had no real evidence, nothing we could use to hasten Mrs. Greenhow's arrest or name her conspirators. All we knew for sure was that she was likely a spy—and a careful one.

There were reasons to despair, but even in this thin soil, hope grew, in an unexpected direction.

In the midst of all this, after the night we'd failed to burgle Mrs. Greenhow's study, I began to recognize what had been growing between myself and Tim. Back in Chicago, I never would have guessed it. But after so many days and nights in each other's company, we'd developed an ease, a rhythm, I'd never known with Charlie. That marriage had been real, according to God and law, and this one was only a fiction. And yet, I was happier in this sham of a union than I'd ever been, even for a day, in the other one.

I learned to dance. Tim was an excellent dancer, a talent I'd had no reason to suspect. I began to look forward to the balls and galas, not just as an opportunity to watch Mrs. Greenhow at work, but also for my own private enjoyment. I became amazingly aware of Tim's hands. How one felt alongside my waist, the other entwined with mine, as we danced a waltz. The strength of his fingers. How it felt when his wedding band pressed against my flesh, warm from his touch. We always did our best to keep up conversation when we danced, since there were so many listening ears nearby.

"Mrs. Armstrong," he said one evening, "I should tell you how fervently I admire you."

"You should," I said with a laugh.

He looked around the room, subtly enough that I doubted

anyone else noticed, and then spoke again, more softly. "I should tell you so…Kate."

I didn't know how to respond. He was clearly making an effort to reach out, a wholly unexpected one. "Shall I thank you? It seems like I should thank you."

"We know each other much better than we did before. I've learned a great deal. My earliest impressions of you were…mistaken."

Our feet continued to move in the same pattern, one-two-three, one-two-three, as I considered what to say. I was glad at what I heard, but at the same time, I was not inclined to let him off easy for how he'd acted toward me in those days. "Once upon a time, you told me I would never be able to do what was needed."

He said softly, "That was a long time ago. I didn't know you then. I know you now."

"You do," I said and squeezed his hand as we made a lazy circle among our enemies.

❧

That night, when we returned to our room, we started off as usual. He put his hand on my shoulder, following me in, and I closed the door behind us. His hand was still there. I closed my eyes, feeling furtive, enjoying his touch, even as I knew he'd pull his fingers away in a moment and walk over to the far side of the room to give me what little privacy he could in our shared space.

But he didn't.

Instead of lifting his fingers from my shoulder, he drew them across my back, toward my neck. I felt his fingertips move upward, teasing the lace at the top of my collar, and then go skittering across the bare skin just under my hairline. I shivered. He placed the whole palm against my skin, enveloping the back of my neck with a gentle pressure.

His touch was like fire.

I said, unable to keep my voice steady, "We're alone now. There's no need to pretend."

He said, "I'm not pretending."

I held my breath.

Into the silence, he added, "I haven't been. Not about you."

There were so many things I wanted to say. They all died in my throat before I could speak them. The air was so heavy, so laden with danger and promise, and I was terrified of losing that feeling. I wanted it to go on and on in perfect balance. But I also wanted what might come after it, the dazzling, dizzying possibility. I wanted it with every part of me. I raised my eyes to look at Tim.

I saw my own torment reflected in his face—fear and longing, too fierce to resist.

His lips came down on mine, and my arms were around his neck before I even registered that he'd moved.

We had kissed before, in the name of subterfuge, but this kiss was only for us and our true selves, and the passion of it was indescribable. Never had there been anything in my life so powerful. I wanted to throw off the shackles of our lives, our responsibilities, anything that didn't involve me and this man right here, pressed against each other, now and for all time.

"Sweet Lord," he said, his voice rich with wonder. In the half-light of our supposed marriage bed, he looked as stunned as I felt.

"Hush," I said and kissed him again.

CHAPTER TWENTY-THREE
MRS. WELLS

And so the world was new. In the midst of such terror, there were still joys, and it helped us redouble our efforts in the spy game. We worked flawlessly as a team, paying visits to house after house, where I would gossip my way into information and he would mentally map every location, every name, every word. Our reports to Pinkerton were written together, as it now seemed one of us could not have a thought without the other. I still went alone on my afternoon social calls, but evening always found us together, and then the nights afterward.

Nights had become sweet torture. Living as husband and wife in the eyes of the world, retiring to a single room with a single bed every night, there was no one to keep us from each other but ourselves. He was stronger than I. I would have given myself to him that first night if he'd asked and every night after. But each night, we fell into each other's arms even in the act of walking in the door, poured our passion into kisses, and then like clockwork, he pulled away, groaning, "God, Kate, we can't," and stumbled away with a grimace that was almost a smile.

Was it a distraction, or a better, more compelling level of deception for our enemies? Who knew? The next time we saw Mrs. Greenhow at a dinner and had to part to take our seats at table, he brushed his lips over my hand and smiled slowly at me before walking away. She leaned over my shoulder and whispered conspiratorially, "How many women can say their husbands still smile at them like that?" I blushed like a schoolgirl.

One night, as we tangled on the bed fully dressed, I began unbuttoning the front of my bodice. Tim put his hand over mine to stop me, and I moved his hand to my breast, pressing against him. He did not move his fingers to caress the flesh there, but neither did he move his hand away.

"How long can we keep on like this?" I asked.

"Don't ask," he said, groaning.

"We're married in the eyes of the world, you know. There'd be nothing wrong with that, to almost everyone."

"But to me—"

"I know, I know," I said, kissing his cheek, his ear, his neck.

He said, "I want to be a true husband to you. Not just as the Armstrongs. I'm sure you know that."

"I know you want to be my husband in bed but you won't let yourself."

"Not just that."

He pulled his hands off me then and took my own hands in his.

"Kate Warne," he said. "I want you to be my wife."

I was truly speechless.

"When the war is over," he said. "We can be together then. The two of us, as ourselves, in front of everyone. We can share a life. Mr. and Mrs. Bellamy. We'll be done with this spying, this skulking around, and we can go back to good, honest casework."

"Was it so different?" I asked. "Deceiving criminals, pretending to be people we're not?"

"You know it was. And will be."

"Yes," I admitted. "And I miss it. Solving things. Having the answer. In this life, there are no answers, are there?"

"Someday, we'll know," he said. "But not today. All I know

today is that I can't imagine living without you. And you'll marry me, won't you?"

He twisted the wedding band that was already on my finger, his eyes as warm and tender as I had ever seen them, promising so much beyond his words.

"I will," I said. "And you'll marry me? Whoever you are?"

He laughed the most beautiful laugh.

I kissed him and entwined my limbs with his. When we woke in the morning, we were still in a tangle on the bed, fully dressed.

❦

At the next night's gathering, I was floating in a pleasant haze. Tim and I kept finding moments to squeeze each other's hands or rest our fingers elsewhere on each other's bodies, tiny moments of connection that never failed to send a zing of pleasure through me.

"You two are simply the loveliest couple," said Mrs. Horrow.

"So kind of you to say so."

"You'll have the most beautiful babies."

"A lot of them, I hope," said Tim, squeezing my waist, and though of course I kept Mrs. Armstrong's sweet smile on my face, I fell to pieces on the inside.

Of course he would want children. He wanted me, sure, but didn't he really want a family? I couldn't give him one. I'd never told him about the child I'd lost or what the doctor had said after. We had never conversed so honestly; there had never been a reason either to intentionally withhold the information or reveal it. He knew about Charlie, about his death, but not how my parents had forced me into the marriage nor how unhappy I'd been in it. I'd been playing a role with him too, without intending to.

He didn't truly know me. He had whispered that to me when we were waltzing—*I know you now*—but it wasn't true. The rush of thoughts that followed made my gut twist. If he didn't truly know me, it was more than possible he didn't truly want me. It was all just another lie. The bottom dropped out of my confidence.

Someone called him away, and he leaned over to kiss my cheek before he went. I almost couldn't look at him. So trusting, so loving, and what was I good for? Only deception and deceit.

The hostess was jabbering away, ignorant of my turmoil. She steered me by the elbow over to the table of sweets and then conducted me into the next room, gabbing all the while.

She stopped and said, "Oh, let me introduce you to another lady from Charleston! This is Mrs. Armstrong."

I curtsied as I had a million times, looking down to the ground and then raising my eyes to my conversation partner, as I'd done over and over. But this time, I got a shock. If she wasn't literally the last person I expected to see at that moment, she was certainly on a very short list.

My mother.

"Mrs. Armstrong, this is Mrs. Wells."

She had aged, as I had, but it was unmistakably her. I had always resembled my father more strongly, but she and I had the same mouth. Hers was agape. Mine was not, but I was far more accustomed to controlling my reactions, or at least I assumed so. Her roles in my father's schemes had never required much in the way of range. In any case, I certainly doubted she'd had as much experience as I had.

Even with my inner life in complete turmoil, I took charge. I was used to it.

"Oh, do let's talk about Charleston!" I said gaily. "I miss King Street so! Have you tried the oyster palace off Anson?"

I tucked her arm through mine and steered her away from the hostess. We arrived in a side parlor, and I strove to maintain an air of calm, as if she were barely just an acquaintance. Which, after all this time, she truly was.

I looked her over more closely. Aged, yes, and possibly come down a touch in life, not that she'd ever been in high society to begin with. Her gown, striped robin's-egg blue and dove gray with a contrasting border circling the skirt just above the floor, was several seasons past fashion. Mine was flashier, a rich shade of purplish-red achieved with beet dye, although of course, that was only the role I played. The true me wasn't meeting the true her. But I might not have survived it if it were really me. The momentum of playacting was all that was keeping me upright.

"Armstrong?" she said. "You've married again, then?"

"Yes."

"Isn't that funny? You used to call yourself Annie Armstrong as a child. How strange you should be an Armstrong at last."

I betrayed no discomfort. Lying was breathing now. "There are many Armstrongs in the world. My husband and I have had a good laugh about it. I promised it wasn't the only reason I loved him."

"Well, you always did like to draw attention to your own cleverness. Where is this man? I'd love to meet him."

"I doubt that will be possible," I said frostily.

"You have more children, I hope?"

"More? No."

She eyed me, but instead of asking the natural question, she chose to needle me once more. "You're hardly young. Be a shame if you missed your chance. A woman's family is her legacy."

"I don't believe that."

"I didn't ask what you believed. I told you how things are."

Her eyes blazed, and I knew we were dangerously close to giving ourselves away. I said nothing in hopes she would collect herself.

Instead, she said, "I suppose, with your choices, you gave up your chance."

My voice strangled, I said, "I didn't choose to have a dead child. That happened to me."

It was her turn to take things in stride. I had never spoken a word to her after the marriage, so it was unlikely she knew what had happened. But she didn't seem to react as if the child's death were news.

In an even, almost scolding tone, she said, "You chose to do the thing that led to the child. I didn't raise you that way."

"You didn't raise me at all," I said.

Her hand flew to her chest, but it looked insincere to me, the most artificial of acts. "Why must you hurt me? I only want what's best for you."

"Do you? Have you ever?"

It was her turn to fall silent, remembering our surroundings. We stayed quiet while a strolling couple passed us, and we all inclined our heads to each other in acknowledgment, behaving as people in our position were expected to behave.

I had so much more to say, but I'd already lingered too long, already allowed myself to be trapped and irritated by her, when I had important work to do.

"I must go," I said. "This conversation is at an end."

"It is not."

"You can't—"

"There you are!" Tim's interruption would have been welcome at any other time, in nearly any conversation, but now, it was a catastrophe. He appeared at my elbow and heartily said, "Wife, at last. I'd been looking everywhere."

There was no way around it. "Mrs. Wells, this is my husband. Mr. Armstrong."

"Oh, is he now?" she replied, extending her hand in a slow, deliberate unfurling, like the movement of a snake.

Tim was looking back and forth from my face to hers. Whether or not he knew the truth at a glance—we did still have that resemblance—he kept his aspect level.

In many situations, we found ourselves perfectly aligned and were able to communicate without words. This was not one of those times. There were no signals, no expressions, for what I was trying to escape.

He said, "Are you fatigued, Annie? Is it time for us to go?"

"Annie?" my mother said, her eyes narrowing.

"Husband, could you excuse us for a moment? I'd love a cup of punch."

"Certainly," he said, his face not showing the suspicion he must have felt. Then he was gone, and I did not know how to escape.

She spoke first, laying her hand on my arm, lightly enough that no one would suspect just from looking at us that our topic was deadly serious. I knew though. She was sending a signal.

"I don't know what you're on about," she said, "and I don't know who you're hiding from. That man, or someone else. Why don't I tell him the truth and see what happens?"

"Go ahead," I said.

She tilted her head and evaluated me. I knew that look of old. "Oh, but maybe he knows, or maybe he doesn't. But I'm certain I can find someone who would be interested to know your real name. Mrs. Greenhow, perhaps?"

Now, my world might come crashing down. I said nothing, showed nothing.

She added, "So if you could see your way clear to smoothing my path with a few dollars, I think I could keep silent."

"That's outrageous! Pay you?"

"I'm destitute. Once your father and I parted ways—"

I was shocked—and almost happy—for a moment. "You finally left him?"

"Yes. More's my shame. Now, I'm a woman alone."

"No shame in being alone."

"Not for you, I suppose. You're proud of yourself? That's why you're hiding under an assumed name, living someone else's life?"

"I'm going," I said, forcing my feet into motion.

She called, "Do give some thought to what I said. You can find me at the Bellingham."

My stomach knotted, because I knew that although I wanted to ignore her entirely, knowing where I could find her was actually quite useful information. I hated that I needed to know anything at all about her, but there it was.

When Tim and I got back to our room, I confessed, telling him who she was and what she wanted. That my parents and I never spoke, and indeed, I had not even been sure she was still alive until I saw her, but that she wanted to extort money from me to keep my identity secret, and I hoped all was not undone. His reaction was swift.

"Let's leave," he said, already standing before the second word was out of his mouth. "Just go. Tonight."

"We can't," I said with a sinking heart. "We spent all this time building our cover identities as the Armstrongs. We'll never get this kind of access again."

"So what else can you do?"

I could only think of one way forward. "Pay her."

"You have the money?"

"Yes."

"Will it be enough?"

I knew he was asking about much more than the actual amount. He was asking about her. I answered as best I could. "For now, it will, I think."

He looked unsure. "Kate," he said. "You're running a very big risk."

"We run a big risk every day. It's worth it."

He drew me close. Usually, my body responded to his like tinder under a match, but today, his embrace felt different. It was warm and reassuring. I wanted to melt into him and never rise.

Two days later, I found her at the Bellingham and counted the bills out into her outstretched hand. We spoke almost no words. I longed to strike her, to shove her, to do something outrageous that would help the anguish on the inside come out. Instead, I did exactly as she asked and walked away. I could not deny her the money, but I could deny her my voice. If she truly had any motherly feelings remaining, that at least might give her pause. But she had never had much in the way of motherly feelings, so I had to take comfort in the fact that however my silence made her feel, it made me feel I had some kind of power remaining, and I needed that.

Three more days passed, then four, and there was no sign of my mother. It seemed she was keeping her word. She'd asked for a large enough sum that I expected it might keep her quiet for a good while. And since she only knew that I had a secret but not what it was, I knew what would happen next: she would come back and ask for more money. She wouldn't reveal the secret before she knew who to sell it to—and for how much.

The real questions were how long that would take and whether we could get our business here completed before time ran out.

CHAPTER TWENTY-FOUR

NEWS

After discussing it at length, Tim and I decided that we needed to let Pinkerton know about the complication. Our only communication with him since our arrival had been our reports, all sent in the same direction, with not a single response to any of them, good or bad. So we sent a report with the detail about her threat and how I'd dealt with it, even though it had no direct bearing on our work with Mrs. Greenhow. And we waited to see what would happen.

Three days later, when there was a calling card from an F. J. Allen waiting at the desk for us, I put two and two together and said to Tim, "Allen? It must be Pinkerton." And indeed it was.

We made arrangements for him to come to our rooms under cover of night, as we could talk most freely that way. He wore no uniform, and when he signed the ledger, he used another name entirely, a Mr. A. P. Egan. We did our best to confuse the issue, not speaking his name at all in the hallway and arriving at separate times. He walked with a cane, which I had not previously seen him do. I wasn't sure whether it was in reaction to an injury he'd suffered since last we saw each other or just part of a disguise.

Once we were all in the room, I sat down on the bed, as there were only a few places to sit, and Tim took his seat next to me. His arm went around my back, whether automatically or not, I did not know. Pinkerton noticed immediately, and after our initial exchange of pleasantries was complete, he spoke up.

"Well," said Pinkerton. "You two are certainly cozier than I would have expected."

I looked at him and shrugged.

"We're husband and wife as far as Washington is concerned," I said. "We play our parts well."

"And as far as real life is concerned?"

"Is there such a thing anymore?"

He looked at me, giving me an intense once-over, a thorough examination. Whatever he saw there, perhaps the firm set of my shoulders, made him grunt in displeasure. He turned to Tim.

"Bellamy," he said. "Tell me the truth."

Inside, I screamed at Tim not to tell. Nothing good could come of it. And somehow, I wanted to keep the secret for just the two of us, protected, sealed off from the world. But my unspoken words were, of course, unheard.

"Kate and I are engaged to be married," said Tim.

At first, there was only a widening of the eyes to betray his feelings. Even that amount of reaction felt unexpected, and I began to fear what might be to come. The seconds slipped by in silence.

With a thin veneer of calm, Pinkerton asked, "I'm sorry, I thought you said—engaged, you say?"

Tim nodded.

With no further warning, Pinkerton stood, snapping, "It is not allowed!" It felt like a cannon had gone off in the room or a clap of thunder. I had seen a great deal from him over the years, and I had never seen him react like this.

"There's no rule—" began Tim.

"I make the rules. And I will not allow it."

"Allow?" I said acidly.

"Keep your tongue," Pinkerton answered back, brandishing a finger in my direction.

"Don't talk to her that way," said Tim, beginning to step forward.

"I'll talk to her how I like. And to you too."

"This isn't right," Tim said. "If it were anyone else, you wouldn't have word one to say."

Pinkerton glared at him. He was far shorter than Tim but more solidly built and gave the impression of being ready to brawl. He gripped his cane. "I don't know what you mean."

"If it were Hattie. Or any other woman. You wouldn't care. It isn't about fraternization."

"Of course it is," said Pinkerton. He sounded convincing enough, but my head was in a whirl, so there was no knowing the truth of it, not in that moment.

"No," said Tim. "It's just Kate. You want her for yourself. You always have."

I lost my breath. Could it be true?

"That is a lie and a slander, and I should cut you loose just for having the gall to say it," said Pinkerton, speaking in a low growl.

"So do," said Tim, not breaking.

"Damn firing you. I should fight you."

I looked back and forth between the men. The two most important men in my life, dead set against each other, threatening violence. How could things have gone so wrong so fast?

"Then let's," Tim said with a snarl.

I didn't know what to do, but I had to wade into the fray as best I could, which meant speaking up.

"Damn you both to hell," I said. "Keep your voices down. What are you thinking? What if we're heard?"

That seemed to rein them both in, if only for the moment.

They scowled at each other, tense, still. I thought about Tim's words. Was he right? Did Pinkerton want me for himself after all, despite his long marriage, despite never laying a hand on me? It seemed impossible, but why else would he react so fiercely? His wife had suspected us, had warned me away. What if she was right?

If that was the case, there was no telling what our punishment might be. Real fear clawed its way up my throat.

With a glance at the closed door, Pinkerton hissed, much more quietly, "You both stay put until I decide what to do with you."

"Whatever you decide," said Tim, his voice velvet over steel, "know this. You can't make me stop loving her. No matter what you do. And more important, you can't make her stop loving me."

"She doesn't love you, you fool."

I was surprised to find myself saying, "Yes, I do."

I had many doubts—whether Tim was really in love with me or just the woman he thought I was, whether our love could survive in peacetime after being forged in the fires of war, whether marriage was the right path for us at all—but I didn't doubt that I loved Tim Bellamy, all the way at my core. Standing next to him, under assault, it seemed to me I could never have felt any other way.

Stopped short, Pinkerton thumped his cane against the bed frame. I flinched at its loud report. Then he turned to go.

As he passed me, he said quietly, "I thought better of you."

As much as I wanted to respond with the same words, I knew snapping back at him would only make things worse. As if things could be worse; as if the world weren't already in tatters.

All I could do was say, "I'm sorry, Boss," as he left the room.

At least he had the presence of mind to shut the door softly behind him instead of slamming it, just in case the wrong ears nearby were listening.

When the boss left, the air went with him. It was deadly silent with just the two of us there. We looked the same from the outside—same people, same day, same clothes—yet everything felt different.

Tim said, "Sorry?"

I took a look at his beloved face. He looked stricken, hollowed out. Did he think I was taking Pinkerton's side over his? The last thing I could bear was anger between us two.

"Sorry it's come to this," I said, turned, and threw myself into his arms.

He resisted for a moment, holding himself still, but then relaxed into me, and we held on for dear life.

❧

Three days later, we received word of our fates. A messenger brought two papers, not just one—a bad sign from the start. The only good news would have been conveyed in a single message to both of us. Different messages meant different orders.

We stared at our twin telegrams from E. J. Allen, both reading in silence, then looking up. I knew whatever happened, my heart would be broken.

My telegram said:

STAY PUT

The extravagance of the extra letters was like a slap in the face. He did not want me to miss his seriousness.

I looked at Tim. His blue eyes had gone cold, resolute. He was holding part of himself back again. Although I didn't know the exact wording of his telegram, I knew the thrust of it.

"When do you leave?" I asked.

He folded the telegram into a tight square and creased it with his fingers. It disappeared into a pocket of his trousers. "Tomorrow morning."

I was unsurprised. "He at least gives us that, then."

"He gives us nothing but what we take. It's only temporary, Kate. He can't keep us apart forever."

Only one question remained. "Where?"

"Richmond."

I felt like a weight had been dropped on my chest. For a moment, I convinced myself I had heard wrong, that there must be some other city that sounded almost the same, but my false hope didn't last long. I could fool others but never myself.

"Good God," I said, tears already wetting my lashes.

He reached out to fold me against his chest, and the last of my resistance was gone. I dropped my telegram to the floor. I closed my eyes tight and surrendered to his embrace.

"Shh, shh," he said. "It's hardly more dangerous than here."

"No! It's far worse! He's not—you don't think he's"—I forced myself to say the worst—"trying to get you killed?"

He shook his head. I could feel it above me. "Maybe. Whatever he wants, it's all the same. We're the best he's got, Kate. He's not going to sacrifice the country for a petty jealousy."

"You really think he's jealous?"

"Unfortunately, I do."

I couldn't agree, but neither could I disagree, not with the thought of Pinkerton's fury so fresh in my mind.

"Though I suppose I'm biased," said Tim. "I don't see how anyone could know you and not love you." He pulled back a moment, cradling my cheek in his hand. He shot me a rueful smile, but I couldn't return it. I couldn't muster the humor.

He went on, "Anyway, right now, I suppose it doesn't matter why. I know how to follow orders."

"You don't have to."

"Don't I? If he says it's what the country needs, whatever his motives, I'd bet money he's not wrong. I'll go to Richmond, as he commands, and meet up with Hattie—he says she's already there— and we'll do everything we can to finish this godforsaken war."

"I need you here."

"You want me here."

"Yes. I want…" Then my words finally failed me, and I pressed my face up to his for a kiss. Even in our sadness, the spark of passion was there. The fire had not gone out.

One last night was ours. This time, we took advantage.

At last, nothing lay between us. Removing our clothes—as we did in a rush, gasping and laughing, flinging each discard aside—was only part of it. I saw him for the first time, from head to toe and with nothing held back, in his gaze or otherwise. He ran his open palms over my shoulders and down to my hips, down and then up and then down again, murmuring so softly I couldn't hear his words, but I gathered that they were complimentary. He gripped me and lifted me against him as if I were weightless, then lowered me to the bed. I thought, mischievously, of suggesting the couch instead, but any thoughts of mischief melted quickly away as his skin met mine. I poured my whole self into loving and being loved.

When I welcomed him into my body, the relief and joy swelled so powerfully within me, I wanted to laugh just as much as I wanted to cry. Instead, I smiled into his neck and whispered his name into his ear, and I said at last, one time, "You're home."

No newlyweds could have had a more glorious honeymoon than we had in that one night, even though we were no more married than we had been the day before. The night would never have been long enough, but it was perfect and would have to do for now.

❧

In the morning, we breakfasted together in our room, a rare indulgence. A steaming pot of coffee with elegant porcelain cups, plates of eggs and biscuits and bacon, hotel silver. It would have been a beautiful domestic scene except for Tim's imminent departure waiting there for us when breakfast was done, looming, undeniable.

And instead of whispering sweet nothings of love, we spent our time between bites and sips getting our stories straight. If questioned—and I knew I would be—I needed something to tell the ladies of our social circle about his departure. Sudden personal business was too vague, so we selected enough details to make the story hang together. We'd say he had been called to report at a base in Mississippi. Our story would be that he would not even tell me where, afraid I'd try to follow. It seemed plausible enough; we'd heard of many wives, both Confederate and Union, putting on men's clothes and enlisting to follow their husbands to the front. If Annie Armstrong had not previously seemed the type to take such drastic action, no one would deny that war made women do strange things. So her husband would protect her by keeping his whereabouts a secret. The irony was not lost on us that even the people we were pretending to be were keeping secrets from each other.

That business completed, I said baldly, "I don't know how I'll live."

"I do. You'll soldier on. Kate, you're the strongest woman I've ever met. If there's anyone who can handle this, it's you."

"Strength has nothing to do with it."

"Doesn't it?"

I tapped my last bite of biscuit against the silver rim of my plate, grinding it into crumbs, then dust. "We're at the mercy of the world. There are people who want to hurt us. I'm afraid our luck will run out."

"And if it runs out, it runs out. We'll be past caring."

"One of us will anyhow."

"Kate, please." He reached across the table to cover my hand with his. "Let's not spend these moments in sadness. I want to tell you how very much I love you. And I'll come back to you. Look forward to that day."

My voice trembling, I said, "You can't promise that."

"We'll be together," he said. "I have no doubt. After the war."

"After the war."

"We need each other. Who else would have us?"

"Who else indeed."

Our plates were clean, and the coffeepot was empty. His train would leave in less than an hour. However much more we could have said, given the chance, there was no reason and no time for him to linger.

He lowered his mouth to mine for one more kiss before leaving, a kiss that lasted until our need to breathe forced us apart, both gasping for air.

I stood in the doorway and watched him go down the hall, and then walked to the window to see him leave the front of the building. He did not turn or wave, which we had agreed upon. I watched him until he was out of sight. I had the same feeling I'd had when he rode off to Perrymansville, what seemed like a lifetime ago—would I ever see him again?

I had to. He was my only chance at happiness. As he'd said of both of us, who else would ever have me?

☙

That night at a ball, I stood as if in a trance, feeling utterly hollow. I feared that anyone who looked at me might know my secret in a glance. I had put on the usual trappings—sprigged gown, silk gloves, golden earbobs, sweet perfume—but they didn't reach all the way inside.

I nodded to the ladies I recognized, and they nodded back, but for a while, no one tried to engage me in conversation. As luck would have it, the first one to do so was Mrs. Greenhow.

Our elusive target looked brighter and smarter than ever, though that might have been my imagination. My melancholy was coloring the world.

She smiled sweetly and said, "Annie, I was hoping I'd see you! And where is that delightful husband of yours? I thought he was ever by your side."

"Duty called," I said.

"Oh no! Where's he off to?"

I gave her the story, parceling it out in small bites only when she asked exactly the right questions, watching her carefully for any sign of doubt or suspicion. She gave none. It was small comfort. I closed by saying, "He only left a few hours ago, and already, I miss him terribly."

"Of course you do. You love him to death."

And beyond, I thought, my eyes filling with tears.

"There, there," she said soothingly, enfolding me in her arms, and though I wanted to resist, there was something compelling and comforting about her embrace. Ironic, that a woman I was now sure was one of my nation's deadliest enemies was the closest thing I had in this town to a friend.

And for the next three weeks, I spent as much time as possible in Mrs. Greenhow's company, for the most complex reasons. Emotionally, she soothed me, and I felt better near her, even though I told her nothing of what truly troubled me. She would have been appalled, to say the least, to know my secrets. I also remained close to her because there was still no absolute proof that she was communicating Union secrets to the Secesh side.

Until there was.

Three weeks after Tim was torn from me and sent to Richmond, I attended yet another party, this one a small affair conducted by the wife of the senator from Kansas. I remembered nothing of the conversation at dinner, which was the usual mix of banal inanities, everyone so scared of saying the wrong thing, they wound up saying nothing at all, myself included.

But afterward, as the women retired to the front parlor for gossip and the men to the rear parlor for cards and cigars, I saw two things. First, a man I didn't recognize appeared next to Mrs. Greenhow. They did not seem to know each other, nor did they speak, but I saw that he held his hand down at his side in a stiff way, without moving it. First, I thought he might be a soldier, but he did not bear the rest of his body in a military style, only the arm. In a motion so slight I almost didn't believe I saw it, Mrs. Greenhow let her arm fall to her side too, pressed it against his, and then lifted it away. They then moved away from each other without speaking.

It looked exactly to me like a way of passing intelligence that I had learned in my early Pinkerton training days. I'd learned it from Paretsky. I'd taught it to Hattie. I was sure no one else in the room had spotted it. They were good. That they had not escaped my notice was more testament to my hawklike attention than it was to their degree of skill.

No more than a minute later, I watched the guest of honor, a Union corporal, draw near to Mrs. Greenhow. She failed to hide the expression of annoyance that flashed across her face at his approach. She recovered quickly and cozied up to him, but she'd drawn my attention once more.

I saw her stroking the arm of the corporal with her delicate fingers, as she'd done a thousand times before. Other arms, other generals, but the same motion. This time, I noticed something new. She kept her thumb firmly against her palm, using only the tips of her four other fingers to stroke.

She was holding something in her hand. Something small.

Something she didn't want the corporal to see.

Now convinced that the unknown man had put a small note

into Mrs. Greenhow's hand, I hovered only feet away from her, watching as closely as I could without giving myself away. She might just tuck the note away in her bosom or do something else to secret it, but I didn't think so. If that were the case, she would have hidden it away before the Union corporal had gotten so close to her. No, she must need to have it readily to hand, which meant she was going to pass it to someone else in the room, which meant I might see who it was.

The senator's wife's maid came into the room and began to clear away empty glasses. It was unusual to have the help intrude in this way; usually, they waited until everyone had gone or at least moved into the next room. So either the senator's wife was showing off the fact that her servants were white, which was a bold statement, or there was another reason the girl appeared.

Sure enough, a minute later, I saw Mrs. Greenhow draw near to her and grasp the girl's wrist. I was close enough that I could tell what she was doing, though it would have been easy to miss. She laid the palm of her hand over the girl's wrist and, with a single, smooth motion of one finger, tucked the note into the sleeve of the servant's dress. And then it was done. The note had been received and then passed, all smoothly, all done by an expert.

Mrs. Greenhow was most certainly a Confederate spy. I'd seen it firsthand.

Now, I had to decide what to do about it.

CHAPTER TWENTY-FIVE

MRS. VAN LEW

A day passed, then another, then another. Three days after I had seen Mrs. Greenhow passing notes at the ball, I still had said nothing to anyone. If it had happened a month before, I wouldn't have hesitated for a moment—I would have put it in a report to Pinkerton, marked urgent, before night fell. Now, I stewed. If Tim were here, I was sure he'd counsel me to disclose everything. But he wasn't here, and that was Pinkerton's fault. I had not forgiven him.

The other part of the equation was Little Rose. If her mother went to prison, what would happen to her? Shuttled around between relatives? Despite the terrible things her mother was doing, it would hurt the girl to be taken from her. I thought of Cath and Violet Maroney, who were likely still separated from one another, years later. Was it my business to tear apart families when the war was already ripping us limb from limb on a nationwide scale?

When I came home from the latest party, I had just vowed to myself that it was time to put aside my fury at Pinkerton, at least temporarily, to report the news. Then the desk clerk signaled to me.

"Telegram for you, Mrs. Armstrong," he said.

The small square of paper gave no clue as to its contents. I climbed the stairs swiftly but did not want to be seen rushing and forced myself to slow down. It could be anything. Perhaps Tim had found a way to communicate with me without revealing himself. Or perhaps Pinkerton was ready to apologize. Or it could be bad news too—I could be fired, if he were still holding his grudge. And now that I was finally sure Mrs. Greenhow was doing the things she was suspected of doing, that would be a shame. If the telegram showed Pinkerton bowing even slightly, I resolved to give him a full report immediately. Perhaps this meant he had calmed down and remembered to focus on the importance of our mission, not his personal feelings about my relationship with Tim.

Up in my room, with a mixture of hope and dread, I unfolded the telegram with trembling fingers.

TWO FRIENDS TAKEN ASIDE STOP SO SORRY

The dread broke over me in a wave, and my throat closed. There could be only one interpretation.

Hattie and Tim had been captured.

What had happened to them, I could only guess and did not want to.

My dread was washed away by fury. Pinkerton probably thought that being vague would drive me to his doorstep. That would have worked with the woman I was pretending to be, and the woman I had been once upon a time, but not the woman I had now become. Now, I trusted no one, and my heart had been wrenched and twisted. It took me only a moment to decide. I would go to Richmond.

It was a fool's errand. I knew that and went anyway. Perhaps I would be sacrificed in the rescue, but that was fine. If Pinkerton thought he could do without me, let him find out what it was truly like. If I could save Tim, I would. If I couldn't, death held no fear for me. For years, I had been sure I would never find a man to love me for the rest of my life. Now that I thought I might have done just that, the length of the life seemed unimportant.

❧

There was so much to do. I needed a horse, I needed a map, and I needed clothes that didn't give away my identity. Keeping my focus on activity made it easier not to cry, not to think about the fact that the man I had finally realized I loved had been taken from me almost as soon as we'd truly found each other.

I lost myself in the procedure, in the checklist. Horse. Map. Two new dresses in an old suitcase. An old cover identity, one I had ready to hand, with a forged pass to deflect any suspicion if I met Secesh barricades on the road. Brief, vague apologies to the desk clerk at the hotel to make sure no one became too interested in my absence. I badly wanted a gun, but I didn't have one, and obtaining one in a hurry would raise far too many questions.

I found what I needed, and within hours, I was on the road south.

Unfortunately, as I rode, there was less for my mind to focus on, and it kept inevitably returning to the same questions: What had happened to him? What would happen? What could I even do when I got there to save him? I concocted dozens of positive scenarios to smother the dozens of negative ones that were already at the top of my mind and spilling out like rich milk from a full jug.

I had never ridden this particular road south before, but I knew it had changed a great deal from a few years before. Everywhere I looked, there were signs of war. Some were obvious, like a scorched field or a torn, stained blue uniform jacket hanging from a fence post. Some were more subtle, like a schoolhouse sitting silent and empty at midday.

I hadn't been able to gather fresh intelligence before I left, for fear someone would realize where I was going and why. I did not stop to rest overnight. My horse put one foot in front of the other, strolling sometimes, cantering sometimes, as the road allowed.

In the beginning, I feared falling asleep in the saddle, but as the journey went on, it became clear that I would not relax into unconsciousness no matter how tired I became. Too much depended on this ride, and I was so consumed by worry, anger, fear. I heard a man's scream from the west, then another, then half a dozen more, and I took a long loop around to the east to avoid the next town on the road, just in case. But mostly, I went straight south, as fast as I could, to reach my destination.

In the end, I got there almost without delay and still arrived too late.

For all of my thinking on the road, I hadn't decided exactly how I would go about gathering intelligence when I arrived. Maybe I was trusting my operative's instincts to carry me through, or maybe my mind was too clouded with thoughts of Tim—what if we'd never admitted our feelings to each other? What if I'd been able to stop him before he told Pinkerton? What would be happening to me at this moment instead of chasing him on a fool's errand into enemy territory? As it turned out, planning would have been moot in any case.

I stopped on the outskirts of town to rest my horse and gather my strength at a roadside tavern before crossing the line into Richmond proper. I had barely found a seat and begun to read the bill of fare when I heard the whispers all around me. It quickly became clear that the whole place was buzzing with gossip. They were thrilled by something bloody. They had been waiting for something like this to happen, and it finally had. A hanging had taken place that day.

I rose immediately and fled outside. I didn't run, because drawing attention was the last thing I needed to do in that hornet's nest, but I went out and forced myself not to collapse. I took the reins off my horse's neck and mounted. Another man was retrieving his horse at the same time, and in the most offhanded tone I could muster, I told him I'd missed the day's excitement and asked if he happened to know where the enemies of the state had been hanged.

"Over there a ways," said the man in a heavy accent, and I followed where he pointed, over a low green hill and a mile down the road beyond.

Had I been on foot, I would have gone slowly, dragging at every step, as I feared the outcome. The horse carried me whether I liked it or not. As soon as I rode over the ridge, I could not look directly at the sight, but the horse kept carrying me forward. I did not have the presence of mind to pull back hard on the reins. The sight was too terrible and too near.

Half a dozen bodies dangled from the makeshift gallows. Six men, no women. Had I not already guessed the identity of one of them, I would have been thrilled to know that Hattie, at least, had escaped.

They would have swung in the breeze had there been one. Signs hung around their necks, too far off to read. I didn't need to get any closer. I knew at least one of the signs read TRAITOR.

And I knew who that body belonged to, the second from the left. Even slumped, I recognized the shape of his body, the long legs, the once-quick fingers. I would never get this image out of my head. Riding closer would only give me more images I couldn't banish.

I rode away then, without any sense of where to go.

I could not let myself feel. There would be time for that later.

❧

At the first likely-looking hotel, I stabled my horse and asked for a room. I steered clear of the fashionable hotels downtown that I'd once stayed in; I knew I would not be able to stand the hoarse cries of the slaves in Lumpkin's Jail, not this time.

When the desk clerk asked how long I'd stay, it took all I had not to burst into tears. Collecting myself, I mumbled something about "three days at least" and was handed my keys. I paid with the

Confederate scrip I'd secured back in Washington, feeling it might burn my fingers. I lay across the bed fully clothed. I think I slept.

In the morning, my eyes flying open with the sunrise, I considered my options, poor as they were. Even if I went back to Washington right that minute, my position was almost certainly forfeit. By now, Pinkerton would have noticed my absence, my lack of communication. But my fury at him knew no limits. Was he the one who betrayed Tim, acting not as our boss but as a jealous rival? It would have been easy for him to do so. And now a good man was dead, and I still didn't know what had happened to Hattie. I couldn't go, and I couldn't stay.

But I could seek out Hattie, and I needed to. I was too late to save the man I loved, but I could at least find a good woman who deserved to live and find a love of her own. If it hadn't been for me, she wouldn't have been a spy in the first place, so I owed it to her.

I didn't know where to find her, but I had an inkling of where to start. The Southern ladies of Washington had been all abuzz about a Northern lady of Richmond, one Elizabeth Van Lew. She was a Richmond girl but educated in Philadelphia, and her family had freed their slaves twenty years before. So naturally, she was suspected of being a Yankee spy. I went to her, hoping the rumors were true.

Naturally, she was suspicious of me and would neither confirm nor deny any of her spying activities. And I was wild-eyed, not my usual subtle and careful self. She was right to keep me at arms' length.

Leaning back in a sumptuously padded chair as high and elegant as a throne, she appeared unruffled. She did confirm that the female spy captured a few days before was being held in Castle Thunder but would not support my visits to her. The most she could do, she said, was to recommend that if I needed to get into Castle Thunder, I should invoke the name of Belle Boyd.

"The partisans in the prisons go bonkers for that girl, like everybody else," she said and excused herself from the room to check on the tea.

This left me alone in the room with Mrs. Van Lew's butler. He lingered in a spot to the left of my chair, which I thought was odd. Lost in thought, I had an awareness that he was there but brushed it aside to wrack my brain. How far should I push Mrs. Van Lew? Should I risk exposing myself by telling her the truth? The gossips said she was on the Yankee side, but what if the gossips were wrong?

There was a blur of motion, just a small one, coming from the butler's direction. It happened again. What was he doing?

Without meeting my eyes, he moved his hand in a strange signal, bringing his fingers together and then apart. There was something familiar about it. He repeated the signal, so I knew it was deliberate, but I couldn't place it.

And then I could. I hadn't seen it in years, but deep in my mind, there was the image of Allan Pinkerton himself making that motion during my very first week of training. It was the signal Pinkerton agents exchanged to identify themselves to each other.

The butler was a Pinkerton agent.

I repeated his signal, carefully, and raised my eyes to his.

In a deep, husky voice, he said, "You must be the great Kate Warne."

"Not so great, I don't think. How did you know?"

"I saw your picture once, in the Chicago office. I trained there, before I was placed here with Mrs. Van Lew, last year."

"Does she know?"

"No. She does much for the Northern cause, but my position is a secret from her and everyone else, for safety."

My next question sprang instantly to mind. "Why didn't you get turned in with Bellamy and Lawton?"

"We never worked together at all. Just the three others."

"Three?"

"There was a third agent."

"Who?"

"Never got his name."

The door rattled, and Elizabeth reentered the room, followed by a young Negress carrying a tea tray. The butler and I pretended we hadn't been talking. In the end, I never learned anything more about him. But between his information and Mrs. Van Lew's, my visit had not been in vain.

❧

Castle Thunder, a warehouse in the Tobacco District hastily converted by the secessionists for their purposes, was located on the north side of town. After finding out from Mrs. Van Lew that Hattie was locked up there, I got what other information I could, but there wasn't much. The proprietress of the lunch counter gleefully informed me that the place was particularly known for ruling its occupants with an iron fist. After that, every hour, I worried about how to get in to see Hattie, and every hour, I worried that I would hear she had already died.

In the end, I entered through a complete, fabricated bluff. I walked straight in the door of Castle Thunder, the black-and-white cockade affixed to my broad-brimmed hat, a soft drawl and a firm confidence my only weapons. I wouldn't attempt a prison break, at least not on the first day. The first order of business was to find out exactly where she was. All I had to do was convince the guard that I was one of the local Daughters of the Confederacy, here to monitor prisoner health and comfort in the name of fine, kind Southern tradition.

"Our Yankee enemies may be heathens, but we are not, suh," I said imperiously.

"Well, we only have the one woman prisoner right now," he said. "Filthy spy."

"She is still a lady."

"She is still a prisoner."

"I'll be brief," I said, and to my great relief, he stepped back.

As he walked me deeper into the prison, I took careful note of my surroundings, drawing a map in my head. There was the door, barred. There were the paths to exits, there was the guard station, and there was where the guard wore his keys on his right hip and his holstered gun on his left.

When he unlocked the cell, I noted the exact position, which key he used, and in which direction he turned it. He motioned for me to step inside, and I did, hesitating briefly for show. Prisons did not deter me, of course, but it would be a useful thing to remind him of my femininity. So I raised my handkerchief to my mouth and breathed delicately through its flowers.

"Much obliged, suh," I whispered.

The bars clanged behind me, and for a moment, I thought this could be a ruse to trap me. What if he knew he had two Union spies in his cell instead of one? It was too late, in any case. I quickly turned back to the matter at hand.

Hattie Lawton sat on a cot in the corner of her cell, her feet on the floor, her elbows on her knees. She'd been taken prisoner on a particularly festive day, it appeared. Her full-skirted dress was printed with a gay pattern of pink roses with green stems and leaves, so artfully done that I could see the thorns from a distance. A pink ribbon at the front, in a bow. Despite her dishevelment, the bow had been tied to a perfect jauntiness and not allowed to unravel.

"Dear lady. I am Sarah Harrington, a good friend of Belle Boyd. I'm here to make sure you're as comfortable as you can be, in the circumstances."

She did not respond. She merely lifted her head long enough to take me in, and her face gave nothing away.

"Are you hurt, young lady? Are you well?"

I worried what they'd done to her. Did she not recognize me? Or was she just being careful, given the circumstances?

"Let me think on it," Hattie said guardedly.

I reached my hands out to hold hers. "We want to do everything we can."

The guard lingered behind me. Just reassuring myself that Hattie was still alive was only part of my purpose here. If I could, I needed to speak honestly to her, as ourselves.

"Might we have some privacy?" I asked. "I need to ask the prisoner some questions about her...female needs."

As I'd hoped, the man winced and hastened to get out of our way. I waited until I heard the gate lock behind him, two dozen yards away, so I knew he was out of earshot.

We lowered our voices. She said it out loud first.

"Kate, I'm so sorry. They hanged him."

"How did they know? Who gave him away?"

"Rose Greenhow," said Hattie. "It must have been."

I shook my head. It didn't add up. "But if she knew about him, she'd know about me."

"Not necessarily. She might have had her suspicions, but she couldn't know for sure you were in it together. Many wives don't know what their husbands do."

"Did the third agent get arrested?"

"What third agent? It was just us two. Me and Tim."

I wanted to ask more, to pry, to seek the truth, but there was so little left in me to fight. I couldn't hold back any longer. "Oh, Hattie."

"Shh," she said.

I needed to collect myself. I knew better.

I wiped my eyes with the back of my hand, then with the sleeve of my butternut homespun dress, much the worse for several days of wear. At least I had the option of changing clothes, a luxury

Hattie would do without during her imprisonment. And both of us had much more important matters than fashion to concern us.

I said softly, "How can I get you out? What's the best way?"

"Nothing. Do nothing at all."

"How am I supposed to leave you here?"

"You can, and you will," she said firmly.

On some level, some part of me—the remote, recessed part that was still alive—was proud of her. I had chosen her well, all those years ago, and even in these crushing circumstances, she was strong. If she survived, she might grow into a better agent than I'd ever been.

If she survived.

"Leave me here," she said. "They've got no real evidence. If they'd had any, they would've hanged me with Tim. They don't hesitate to hang women down here."

"Could they be so awful?"

"What's awful about it?" She shrugged. "Our crimes are as serious as theirs. Our punishment should be too."

"A miserable sort of equality to hope for."

Even in these terrible circumstances, she looked proud. "If we take the good, we also have to take the bad. We don't get to fetch it up piecemeal."

I wanted to hug her, but it would raise too much suspicion. I was only supposed to be asking about her needs. And the guard might be back at any moment.

"We'll try for an exchange."

Then I heard the clinking of keys and knew the guard would be upon us. So I raised myself and said, "It is a terrible story you tell, and I regret that your stay here will last any length of time at all. But my sisters and I will try to come from time to time for conversation and to bring you any items that a lady needs."

"Enough now," said the guard.

Hattie said, "I'm grateful to you, Miss Harrington."

And then we were parted, the heavy bars sliding back into place, with one of us on either side.

❧

Half of me swore to remain in Richmond until I found the person responsible for Tim's death, no matter what; half of me wanted to flee that cursed city immediately. It was a danger to be there, every moment. My cover identity was a tissue; I had no safety net. If I were captured, no one would come to my aid, not even Hattie. Pinkerton would swear ignorance were I fool enough to implicate him, which I was not. Knowing how desperate my situation was made me feel strangely confident. If I was dead already, I risked nothing; there was no life left to lose.

I couldn't stop thinking about Hattie's certainty that only Rose Greenhow could have been responsible for Tim's betrayal. Nor could I get it out of my head that Pinkerton had contributed to his death by sending him here, and I still did not know whether he'd done so to get him away from me. I couldn't risk another interview with Hattie, not so soon. And speaking with Pinkerton was out of the question.

The only way to find out whether Mrs. Greenhow was responsible, I told myself, was to get back to Mrs. Greenhow. I'd been gone only a few days, and I hadn't used my Washington identity in Richmond. I might be able to slip back into Annie Armstrong's life, just for a little while.

I didn't know what they'd done with Tim's body. His family would have liked to have it back, I was sure. Perhaps that would happen. But I was out of designs, out of ideas, out of the kind of energy that drives a person forward. I could not wrestle it back, not that day. It was all I could do not to let myself fall from the banks of the river into the swift current. Indeed, I even stood at the river and looked down for a long time. The day was cloudy, and the river reflected the clouds, all churning white water. The rapids looked strangely soft, like soap bubbles or cotton. Perhaps it wouldn't even hurt.

The only thing that kept me on the bank was the idea that Tim's killer needed to be caught and punished, and I wanted be the one to make that happen. I might be the only one who could. And if Mrs. Greenhow were the one responsible, I saw no reason not to kill her with my own two hands.

CHAPTER TWENTY-SIX
THE ACTOR

Riding back into Washington alone made my whole body ache. It was not the same city it had been when I left. It was the city where I had fallen in love with Tim. To be there without him would be torture. Yet it was also the same pulsing, lively city, the same beating heart of the nation. The same subtle battleground, the same chessboard, where spies like me and spies like Rose Greenhow met and curtsied and lied to each other's faces while we dug furiously for secrets.

The city had not changed. I had. I was in mourning now.

I needed to remember my mission, which, like me, had changed. My mission had been to find the secrets that would help the Union. Now my mission was to find and punish those responsible for Tim's death. Inasmuch as those missions overlapped, I could do both. But if I had a choice to make, I knew which I would choose.

Climbing the steps into the hotel was so terrible, I almost turned and ran. I put one foot in front of the other, and then another, and by the time I crossed in front of the desk, I was fully upright. I wasn't able to pretend that everything was as it should be, but at least I looked normal enough not to set off alarms in every person I saw.

"So good to see you're well!" said the clerk.

"Oh? I just had some urgent business to settle. I'm sorry I didn't let you know."

"There've been messages for you."

He handed me a stack of papers, and I swept them into my other hand without looking. I resisted the urge to pitch them out the nearest window. No doubt Pinkerton was furious with my desertion and commanding me to appear for his pleasure somewhere. I was falling apart, and all he would think about was duty. I had a different duty now. My duty was to Tim.

Upstairs, I set the pile of telegrams on the side table and turned my back on them. I bathed myself and set aside the dress I'd worn in Richmond. I wanted to burn it in the fireplace, but the smoke would have drawn too much attention. I tucked it into an unused suitcase. I was fresh as a daisy on the outside, though a crumbling wreck on the inside, when the clerk called up to announce my visitor.

It was Rose Greenhow.

I had wanted to take my time and think how best to approach her. I needed to carefully plan out what I'd say and how I could bring matters to a head without exposing myself. This was not to be. It would have looked too odd to refuse her, so I accepted, and she swept into the room with a gay, bright voice.

"Mrs. Armstrong! We were so worried about you!"

"Yes, I'm sorry. Unavoidable. My father's health..."

"Where does he live, did you say?"

"I don't think I did say. Western Pennsylvania."

"And you went all the way there and back alone? Is he all right?"

"He's not well," I said, "but he's out of immediate danger. Thank you so much for your concern. But is there anything I've missed in my absence? Did the Tarletons finish those improvements on their house? Is Mrs. Stone feeling better after her flu?"

She did not accommodate my wish for light news but instead steered the conversation in the one direction I was not sure I could comfortably handle. "Did you hear they finally hanged a Yankee spy?"

"No," I said, "I haven't seen the papers. Who was it?"

"It wasn't in the papers. They don't want the Yankees to find out."

"But people talk."

"Officially, there was no such hanging. Because if we hang one of theirs, they'll hang one of ours."

"If they can catch one."

If there was any speck of good in what she said, it was that the hanging was unlikely to be publicized here. If it were in the newspaper, there might be a picture, and someone might remark on the resemblance of the dead man to Mr. Armstrong. It was difficult enough having to talk about him as if he were alive when I knew he wasn't. I would have to be prepared for new levels of lying, new demands on my acting abilities. I wasn't sure I could do it. But I looked into Mrs. Greenhow's eyes and thought, *If you did this, I swear, in a week, you'll be as dead as he is.*

I managed to hold myself together for a half hour of polite conversation, and I sent Mrs. Greenhow off with a promise to call on her the next day. When the door closed behind her, I fell apart immediately. Tim had taken most of his clothes and gear with him, but there was a hastily discarded pair of socks in the corner he had peeled off before climbing into bed with me that last night. I had left them there so my eye could fall upon them, and I could remember him and feel like he was not so far away. Only now, I knew just how far away he was and would always be.

Still, I left them. They were something he had touched while alive. No hands, even mine, had touched them thereafter. There was some good in that, even as the tears stung my eyes and I wanted to fall down weeping, pounding my fists against my skirt. Even if I missed him so much I wasn't sure I could bear it. Even if I cursed myself, moment by moment, for my part in the events that led to his death and listed other names I might curse along with my own.

I searched the room for something else to focus on. My eye fell upon the discarded pile of telegrams that I had not yet opened. Might as well go through them. I could always consign them to the fire if the spirit moved me.

As I went through them, my brow creased, and I took a seat. If they were from Pinkerton, they were his strangest communications ever and not at all like what he usually sent.

I KNOW YOUR SECRET

I looked at the next, dated the following day.

YOU CANNOT HIDE STOP YOU ARE NOT THE WOMAN YOU SAY

Resisting the urge to toss the rest of the pile directly into the fire, I unfolded the next and held it to the light.

MEET ME

There was no name, which surprised me. There was no name on any of them.

The last one said:

I GROW IMPATIENT STOP MEET ME TONIGHT OR BE EXPOSED STOP HOTEL LOBBY 7 O'CLOCK

It was dated that day, and thank goodness. If the ultimatum had come while I was in Richmond, the deadline would have come and gone without me. But now that I was here, I felt I had no choice. I had to find out who this was and what he—or she— wanted from me.

The likelihood was good that it was Pinkerton, using subterfuge to get my attention, since he knew I might not respond to him as an employee to her employer. There was too much unknown about his motives, his guilt. If it were him, though, I could simply walk away. Causing a scene would be as dangerous for him as it was for me, if not more so.

The possibility that the telegrams might have come from my mother also crossed my mind. She might have decided the money wasn't enough. But why would she approach me anonymously, when she could have instantly gotten my attention with her name? She wasn't the one hiding her identity. I doubted she had anything to lose.

I would have to find out firsthand.

So I changed into a plaid dress of muted greens and browns, reknotted my hair, splashed rosewater on my neck, and went down to the lobby at the appointed time.

I edged in carefully, scanning the crowd for familiar faces. Pinkerton was not there, nor was Mrs. Wells. But if not them, who?

When I saw the man next to the grandfather clock, I had my answer.

Age hadn't been unkind to him. He looked about the same. Of course, any gray in his hair would be painted over, and he took pains to dress well, whatever his current level of income. He had always been able to lead people astray, unless they knew him.

"Come upstairs," I said softly, so no one nearby could hear. I was a married woman, at least in this hotel, and I didn't want to raise suspicions by inviting a man to my rooms, but it was much riskier to have this conversation in plain sight of others. I might not be able to contain myself. And if I knew him, or anything about him, after all these years, I suspected he still lacked a sense of moderation.

When he appeared at my door, I opened it long enough to admit him and then shut and locked it quickly. He made a move to embrace me, which I dodged.

"My dear Kate," he said. "So wonderful to see you again after so long."

"I wish I could say the same."

"Don't be that way. A father and his child are always connected, whatever happens."

I saw his eye fall upon the socks in the corner. My anger blazed even more brightly.

"I'll connect my fist to your face," I said boldly.

His affable manner dropped away for a moment. "You didn't learn such behavior from me."

I struck back. "I learned nothing from you. You dragged me around like luggage. And in the end, you sold me off to a gambler. Any success I have is despite you, not because of you."

"Your mother did say you'd grown bitter."

"You've talked to her? She said she'd left you."

"I suggested she say so if she ever met you again," he said. "I guessed you'd be more receptive if you thought I wasn't involved."

My blood ran cold. I gave no sign. I had nothing but my armor, invisible though it was. "You guessed right."

"But you weren't cooperative enough, Kate. And so we're going to need some more...cooperation."

"Go ahead," I said. "Tell the world my real name. I'm not deceiving anyone. My name has changed, because my husband has changed. This one, you haven't met."

"I'd like to."

"You will not." I swallowed the gasp of sadness and fury that came with remembering my husband, who had never been my husband, and the reason why my father would never meet him.

"You can't stop me," he said. "That's what you don't seem to understand. You think you're calling the shots. But I am. Kate, I want you to hear me. I am."

He made a move to grab my shoulders. I stepped back smoothly.

I wished again for my gun, though it was likely better not to have it; I couldn't draw attention to myself with violence, not here. Words would have to do.

"I need time to get the money together. My husband is traveling, I don't have access to the account. I need time."

"Three days," he said.

"I need a week."

"Three days."

"It's impossible!"

"Refuse me again, and it'll be two." He brandished a finger at me, and I almost slapped it away, but I knew he'd make good on his threat if I pushed him any further. I had to take my bad lot and face it. Born to two people who loved nothing so much as themselves, I had grown into my own woman over time, but every pigeon must return to the roost.

"Three days," I agreed.

He chuckled low in his throat—it took all I had not to smack him in the face at that—and then was gone.

So three days was all I had, if that. I wouldn't put it past him to change the terms once agreed upon. He had never been a man of his word.

Regardless of the details, there was one certainty. He would come back. I knew he would. It was only a matter of time, and he wouldn't hesitate to betray me if the money was better on the other side. He'd betrayed me before, selling me off to Charlie Warne, and cheaply at that. So much more rode on the bets we were making in wartime. My life meant more now, to me and to others. But with my father breathing down my neck, my time was running short.

Now, it was clear what I needed to do. I needed to find E. J. Allen, and soon. Whether he was in the city or not, I had no way of knowing. All I could do, at least for an opening move, was to cable the home office, using the code we saved only for the most dire emergencies.

SEND ME EJ ALLEN STOP HELL IS EMPTY

There was no response, at least no written one, several hours later. I despaired, pacing the tiny strip of floor between the bed and the couch, trying not to remember the room less empty. But after midnight, I heard a soft knock on my door. I prayed that it was the man I needed to talk to. It was.

I motioned him inside and locked the door behind him immediately, but I couldn't look at him. Not after what had happened.

"Warne," he said. "I'm so sorry."

I held up my hand, more forcefully than I meant to. "I don't want to talk about him. That's not why I needed to see you."

"Nevertheless. I am sorry. None of us wanted him to—"

"Don't say it!"

"But I wanted to tell you—"

"No! Nothing about him. Not a word. Only the business we must do. Understand?"

His eyes were full of sadness, but he said, "All right, Warne. Tell me what you're here to tell me."

"We must snare Mrs. Greenhow," I said. "And we must do it tomorrow."

The boss eyed me. I bore up under his gaze, only my rage against Greenhow keeping me standing. Without it, I might remember and collapse.

I wanted to plan with him, working together, like old times. But I could trust neither myself nor him. This time, all the ideas would have to be mine. I told him the part I wanted him to play and informed him what I would be doing. The only thing I needed from him was a suggestion for a trustworthy local apothecary, which he promised to secure. After that, success or failure would rest securely on my shoulders.

I could get myself invited into Mrs. Greenhow's house but only while she was there, and it was highly unlikely I could find the evidence I needed while she was present. That gambit had already failed once. We needed to be sure she was gone, and we needed to be sure we could gain access to the house during that time. We found a general who would welcome her company and feed her false secrets. How I wish we would have found him months before. But with his cooperation, we could be sure she would stay out overnight. Then, all we needed was a key. I knew the man who had one.

Getting it from him would be more complicated. That was where the apothecary came in. A sleeping draft would be easy enough to slip into his tea or whatever else he might be drinking. With him unconscious, it would be an easy matter to fit key to lock, enter Mrs. Greenhow's house under cover of night, and search at our leisure for evidence. Most of her servants did not live in, so there would only be Little Rose and one maid upstairs, and our experts knew how to be silent.

I knew her paramours and I knew her habits, everything I had seen and heard over the course of months in Washington, and I would use it all against her.

Of all the men she entangled herself with, there was only one who was allowed to come to her house. All the others, she met at their own residences or hotels, but for some reason, she had taken a shine to one particular gentleman. I knew this because she had told me. I knew every single thing about their relationship, including the fact that she had given him a key to her back door, which he availed himself of only when she gave him permission. He did not come and go as he pleased but as she pleased, she had informed me proudly. I had cooed at her confidence, praising her for taking the reins, and filed the information away until I needed it. I needed it now.

His name was Captain Bowditch. He had springy dark curls, an unkempt beard, and a solid belly curving out the front of his uniform. Had he not held a position as chief supply officer of the U.S. Army, I would have wondered what she saw in him, but with that, I knew. I had met him on several occasions and even engaged in some mild flirting, under Tim's watchful eye. With my husband supposedly out of town, if I were to approach him on some adventure, I thought the chances were good that he would offer to accommodate me. I needed to be certain though, and for that reason, I concocted a more detailed plan. I would pretend I had been assaulted and seek refuge at his house, as if I were fleeing an enemy. I knew his paternal instinct would get me halfway to my goal, and his lecherous manly nature should do the rest.

It wouldn't be pleasant, but it was necessary. And the draft that I'd been supplied with would keep me from having to fully engage him in the way my words and manner would promise.

And so the operation began.

Shortly after ten o'clock at night, a very late hour for visitors, I appeared on Bowditch's doorstep, disheveled, with my dress torn in a precise spot that would support my story of having been attacked, as well as revealing a generous view of my undergarments and the swell of my breasts above my corset.

"Could I... Would it be all right if..." I gestured toward the open door behind him, as if I couldn't bring myself to violate etiquette and invite myself in, even in my disastrous state.

"Oh, dear thing!" he said. "Please, come in!"

His house was modest, another factor that reminded me he must be of strategic value to Mrs. Greenhow, who was not known for valuing substance over style. Paths were worn in the carpets along the most-traveled routes, and the bricks around the fireplace were streaked with black ash from a fire that had been allowed to burn too hot, who knows how long before. All these details, I observed in a moment. I was there but not there, my mind separate from my body, despite the evening's importance.

I sat in his parlor and unspooled my sad tale, while he plied me with wine and made supportive clucking noises. His eyes returned over and over to the rip in my dress, and I leaned far enough over to give him an eyeful. Since becoming an operative, I had always been very conscious of my position relative to that of people regarding me, finding it important to view myself through their eyes. But I had never been so precise, so aware, of how every move I made led directly to a ripple of feeling in the person I was talking with.

I rubbed my ankle as if it ached, and he wolfishly followed the motion of my hand along my leg. I held my empty glass out toward him, and he nearly tripped over his feet in his haste to pour. So much depended on having his attention. I would do anything to keep it as the night unfolded.

The hour grew late.

Finally, after making it clear that I was afraid to go out in the street again after my experience, I waited for him to make an inappropriate offer, and he did not disappoint me.

"I must insist you stay with me tonight."

"I couldn't."

"You can, and you will. I have a small guest room that adjoins my own. Let me show you." He extended his hand, and I took it. In my other hand, he placed the wineglass that I had almost left behind.

In the room, he gestured to the bed and cabinets, saying, "You'll be comfortable here. But are you quite sure you should be alone? I would be fearful in your situation."

"I am…fearful, sir."

"Wait here just a moment, please," he said. He was gone

truly only a moment, as he had gone back to the parlor to fetch another bottle of wine, and he opened it quickly while I sat down on the edge of the uncomfortable bed and cast my eyes down at the carpet.

"So," he said. "Perhaps I should remain with you for a time. To be sure that you feel more secure."

I noticed that he did not phrase it as a question. I was unsure whether a refusal on my part would be graciously accepted. Not that it mattered, since I had no plans to refuse.

Silently, I nodded my assent.

I was in unfamiliar territory, but I could make educated guesses at what came next. I had to excuse myself for private ablutions, and he did too. While he was gone, I made sure to pour him another glass of wine and one for myself, though mine was just for appearance's sake.

I carefully took out the precious vial of liquid. Just a few drops should render him unconscious within a few minutes. Everything depended on the quick action of the anesthetic. If it took too long to work, I might find myself compromised, and that was to be avoided. But I'd been assured it acted with exactly the right speed.

The vial was slender and clear. The liquid inside was a pale yellow just this side of iodine. It felt fragile in my nervous grasp. I was just unscrewing the lid, hunched over his glass, when I heard the door handle rattle and the captain's voice call out, "My dear, are you quite ready?"

My hand twitched, and I fumbled the liquid, which tumbled down, down, down, and landed on the thick carpet. For a moment, I held out hope that the lid had still been sealed, but I could see at a glance through the clear glass of the vial that my hope was misplaced. Hungrily, the fibers of the carpet drank up what was spilled.

Every last drop was gone, and I was lost.

There was no time to mourn the error. I was still here, and my quarry was still just outside the door waiting for me. Something had to be done. This was my only chance to lay my hands on the key, and the key was my only chance to get into Mrs. Greenhow's household while she was out of town to search it. There had to be clues there. The Pinkertons would find them. But first, we had to get into the house, and to do that, I needed that key.

I forged ahead, and I did what was required.

Kicking the empty vial under a dresser and out of sight, I called out, "Enter."

He came into the room, and though he said nothing untoward, there was no ambiguity about what he intended, what he wanted.

A woman might take part in the sexual act for a host of reasons. Earlier in my life, I had done so out of sympathy and out of expectation. Recently, I had done so out of passion bordering on lust. With Captain Bowditch was the only time I did it out of patriotic duty. That didn't make it transcendent or glorious or indecent. It simply was. And then, it was done.

Afterward, he slept, and I got what I'd come for.

The key in my hand was hot from my flesh. Everything depended on it, on such a small piece of metal. For want of a nail, the shoe was lost, as they say; for want of this key, not much larger than a nail, a war could be lost.

Or, I hoped, won.

CHAPTER TWENTY-SEVEN

BRIGHT HOPE

A s we expected, Mrs. Greenhow stayed out all night at the general's, and a small team of our men was able to enter her house and search it thoroughly. I was not present for the initial search. As planned, I passed the key to an operative at Bowditch's back door. It was a surprise that the operative in question was Graham DeForest, and when I saw his familiar mustache and the understanding in his warm brown eyes, I wanted to cry out and collapse into his arms. It would have been a luxury. Instead, I pressed the key into his hand wordlessly, keeping my composure until I was back indoors.

Several long hours later, we repeated the operation in reverse, and I took the key back from him to replace it so that Bowditch would never know it had been missing. When DeForest returned the stolen key, he covered both my hands with his in a prearranged signal, the only thing that could put a smile on my face: they had found what they sought at Mrs. Greenhow's. Our work had been fruitful. I allowed myself a few precious tears of joy before I took the long steps back to the bedroom. Then I found the empty vial under the bureau and tucked it into my pocket, so I would leave no evidence. The spill on the carpet had already dried to invisibility.

My conversation in the morning with Bowditch was blessedly short, the span of just a few minutes. He left unmentioned the husband he thought I was returning to. He found several excuses to pat me possessively, touching my cheek, my hand, my shoulder. I steeled myself and did not wince. Then I returned to my hotel to scrub off the entire night's doings as best I could.

A few hours later, I went with the team to Mrs. Greenhow's house. Not having slept a wink, I was dizzy with exhaustion, but the importance of the day kept me alert. Dressed in a heavy nut-brown skirt and shirtwaist, sober and silent, I blended into the background. DeForest, without a word, stood next to me; I realized Pinkerton had brought him purely for my benefit, and I would have been grateful, if I had allowed myself to feel anything at all. Instead, I stayed focused on the proceedings. Pinkerton bore a civil warrant in hand, and we entered the spy's house legally, for the purpose of arresting her for treason and taking her directly to prison.

When we took her by surprise, Mrs. Greenhow attempted to swallow a coded message, but Pinkerton was able to grab it from her before she succeeded. The team was quick and surgical. They knew where everything was, so they were able to retrieve it in full view. They took her maps from the top shelf of the library and her cipher translation key from the drawer of the desk in the study. *If I'd only managed to pick that lock the first time*, I began thinking but cut myself off before I could finish the thought. Instead, I reached for DeForest's hand and squeezed it, and he stood by me, knowing only a fraction of what I was feeling but knowing enough.

Taylor came down from upstairs with Greenhow's diary in hand, and she tore herself free from the agent restraining her long enough to swipe his face with her nails. She even drew a bit of blood. But he laughed instead of cringing, infuriating her. We all knew this was the least blood that she had drawn, and hers in turn would be forfeit when the extent of her crimes came to light.

Like Mrs. Greenhow, I stayed silent during the entire enterprise. Hours later, once the arrest was complete and she was in custody, I had one more thing to say to Pinkerton.

Inside, I was burning with fury and grief; I did everything I could to keep both emotions out of my voice, making myself a creature of logic for him. Logic was always the hardest thing for him to say no to.

Arms folded, I said, "I want to interrogate her."

"Not necessary. We have enough to hang her regardless. Her testimony is beside the point."

"The point is different for me. Do I need to remind you?"

His voice was warm and fatherly, and it almost undid me. "It won't help. Will it?"

"Yes."

"Will it bring him back?"

"Don't be cruel."

"Sorry," he mumbled downward.

"I know it won't," I admitted, but I did not soften my stance. "I just want to see his killer punished. I'm shocked to see you might stand in the way of justice like that."

"I'm not trying to protect her. I'm trying to protect you."

"Like you protected me when you sent Tim to Richmond?"

"That wasn't about you."

Now, my anger was threatening to slip its chains. "Like hell it wasn't."

"Warne, I don't know what I can do to convince you."

"You can't," I said flatly. "What you can do is sign an order for me to go visit Mrs. Greenhow. My identity could be revealed at any moment, and I'll be useless here in Washington. Let me see her, and then let me go free."

"You've always been free."

"Have I?"

"Warne," he said, his voice weary. "I don't want to fight with you. I want you to heal."

"I don't know if I ever will," I said, "and that's the truth."

"I know. I know what it looks like when you lie."

"So you understand that when I say I need you to let me see her, my very life depends on it."

He sized me up in a long gaze that I refused to meet, knowing there could be pity in it. I couldn't stand to see him pity me. But he saw my resolve. "Yes. I understand."

"And?"

"Bring me a pen."

❧

The Old Capitol Prison, like the nation it served, was divided. The top half of the largest building was naked brick, but from the central line down to the ground, it was whitewashed. Long, low outbuildings, also white, flanked the square prison yard. It seemed quieter and more civilized than Castle Thunder, but I knew I was a biased observer. The difference was that in Castle Thunder, I had braved terror to see my friend, while at Old Capitol, I would flinch at no wrong as long as it was being done to my enemy.

They brought me to the door of the room and ushered me in. It was only a normal door, a normal room. No bars, no cages. She even had a window, with a view down to the street. The sun was so bright outside and the room so dark, I could see only her outline, but I knew her shape by now.

"Another lady to see you," said the young soldier.

Even before my eyes adjusted to the light, I knew Rose by her voice, as she instantly rejoined, "Her? She's no lady."

I stepped into the room and signaled to the young soldier to leave us. After a short hesitation, he did.

Mrs. Greenhow turned and saw me, and cold fury warped her features. "You shanty fast trick," she said. "Conniving bitch."

It wouldn't do to fly off the handle. If I used anger later in my dealings with her, it needed to be deliberate. I surveyed the room to delay my answer. The lady herself wore a fine gown, deep-blue silk with a skirt as broad as a bell, the same one she had worn that morning when I saw her carted off. Behind her was a bench. To my horror, I saw that a small figure was sitting on the bench, and she too was dressed for a parlor, not a prison.

"Little Rose," I said. "I did not think to see you here. Are you well?"

"Don't speak to her," snapped her mother. "Cover your ears, Rose."

The little girl complied. I wished she were gone from the room, but if this would be my only chance to speak with Mrs. Greenhow, I could not beat around the bush.

The spy went on, "Speak to me, if you must. And I imagine you think you must. Lapdog of the Union law. Whose are you? Whose dog?"

"No one's."

"We are all someone's dog, I suppose," she said. "Even me."

"I would not say that."

"No, you wouldn't. You never say anything untoward. You never say anything at all."

"Madam, I say a great deal."

"Empty words and outright lies. You said you were my friend."

"As you said you were mine."

She said, "But only one of us was lying about everything. Annie Armstrong. That's not your name, is it? I'd bet you're not even married to that man you said is your husband."

"Was."

"What?"

Despite my best efforts, my voice broke as I spoke the words I had not yet had to say out loud. "Was my husband. You killed him."

"I did not." She appeared genuinely surprised to hear the accusation, her denial sincere, but I would expect nothing less from her than complete perfection in her lies.

"You did. You told someone you suspected he was a spy, and they found him in Richmond, and they hanged him."

She folded her arms. "Of course I suspected him. And yes, I reported it. But I didn't have him killed. When you told me he'd been called to a base in Mississippi, that was the last news I gave my handler, because that's all I knew. I liked Armstrong, whoever he really was. Why would I do such a thing?"

"Because you're our sworn enemy. Because we are powerful agents for good, and you can't stand that."

"Good?" She laughed, throwing her hands up. "All you mudsills believe yourselves saints. It's disgusting. At least I know I am a sinner."

"And now the world will know. I'd like to give you the chance to confess your wrongs."

"Oh, are you a priest now too?"

"Not that kind of confession."

"You'll have no hope of either kind. I know when to keep my mouth shut."

"You seem to have gotten quite far by opening it. Among other things."

She bristled. "I did what I needed to do for my country. So did you. What's the difference between us?"

"I don't drag my child down into the darkness with me." I pointed at Little Rose, still with her hands over her ears, patiently following her mother's command.

"Don't you dare." Leaning forward, she brandished her finger at me, her cold fury growing hot. "I love my daughter. I'm trying to make a world where she can be happy."

"I think the happiest of all were the men you seduced."

"Shut your mouth. Shut it right now."

"If you can't bear to hear things told aloud, I wonder that you could bear to do them in the first place."

"You disgust me," she said, her voice a strangled shout. "Get out. I always knew there was something wrong with you; loneliness rises from you like a stench."

It was the truest thing she said, and it hurt more than anything else. I wanted to sob from the wound, but that was also what she wanted, so I had to deny her.

I cried plenty, back in my room, Tim's discarded socks still in the corner and the ashes of my father's burnt-up telegrams in the fireplace.

I would get no satisfaction from Rose Greenhow. She remained in the Old Capitol Prison, along with her poor daughter, awaiting trial. I desperately wanted to see her hanged with my own two eyes, but even in wartime, our justices insisted on process to fight off the madness. It could be months before she was brought to justice and sentenced for her crimes. I would have to content myself with her imprisonment for now.

I knew I could not stay. I would drive myself insane being in the same city with her, knowing she lived and breathed, waiting for the hammer to fall at last. Nor did I want to stay here for my father's wrath, whatever form it would take. I wanted him to come and find me gone, cursing himself for letting me slip through his fingers. No money, no daughter, no victim. He taught me the world was all winners and marks, so let him recognize himself as the mark for once.

But I did not know where to go. Chicago was my place of employment, and I didn't want to be employed there anymore. I had no home. No Tim, and no home.

I lay on my bed for hours, staring at the ceiling, wondering if maybe a jump into the swift-running James River would have been the best way to solve my problems after all.

Instead, I retrieved my horse from the stable and packed my saddlebags with a few of Annie Armstrong's belongings, leaving the rest behind. Pinkerton, or rather E. J. Allen, would come and clean up after me, I knew. I would leave him the mess. He had certainly left me one.

Riding for hours while the air grew colder and the sky darker, I bore due west until both the horse and I were exhausted. The country slipped past me, unobserved, while I kept my eyes only on the road ahead of me, without knowing where it was leading. I stopped for the night and rested. In the morning, we started again. I repeated the process until one night we stopped in St. Louis, and I knew anywhere after that would be frontier. I sold the horse. From here, I would stick to stagecoaches and trains, safer ways to travel. Without the protection of a roof over my head, closing my eyes to sleep west of the Mississippi was an act too foolhardy even for me.

That night, I stayed in a small roadside inn owned by a Polish couple, and I nearly wept when the wife served me a bowl of but-tered potato dumplings smothered in onions, the first pierogi I'd seen since I'd left Mrs. Borowski's boardinghouse. My path finally came clear. I would head for the Dakota Territory and wouldn't stop until I reached Bright Hope.

Mrs. Borowski was surprised to see me, to say the least. Eventually, I told her what had happened, though the telling of it was interrupted by tears and wailing and several sunsets. She had found a place for herself among the miners and frontiersmen. It seemed strange, in such a wild place, but I envied her comfort. The life clearly suited her, and the shaggy, unkempt men who pulled their chairs up to her table for the evening meal did so with quiet grace. She had obviously had an effect on them. The dinner included pasties, meat-and-vegetable pies in a delicious crust, which the Cornish miners especially seemed to appreciate, leaving nary a crumb behind. All told, her dinner guests were more polite and mannerly than many of those I'd observed in Washington. Civilization, I told myself, was not what it used to be.

She waved me away from helping to clean up after dinner

but invited me for a tumbler of plum wine once the dishes were cleared. I gladly accepted. She told me I could stay as long as I liked and did not press me for answers. That was good, since I had none.

The Dakota Territory was like nowhere I had ever been, which helped tremendously. It felt like the war was a world away. I came to love the wild hills, the miles of open space. I even loved the unrelenting brownness of everything. Brown dirt, brown clothes, brown buildings. Only the wide-open sky was blue and gray.

And for a while, I found a way to live. It wasn't the life I wanted, and most days, I didn't recognize myself, but it was something.

After a few weeks, I didn't wake up panting in the middle of the night, seeing Tim's dead body swaying from the gallows, deathly afraid my father would find and reveal me, even in this hamlet. I fumbled my way toward some small amount of peace, however fleeting, however small.

Unfortunately, that was just when I was found.

I had spent the day looking for work. My salary had added up to a pretty penny, but I wanted to keep my hands off it as long as possible. I would be easy to trace if I started communicating with the bank in my own name. I should have set up an account with another alias, one I had never used on a case, but I'd left in too much of a hurry. So I had gone around offering my services as a shop clerk, a bookkeeper, anything I felt I could do without needing to truly reveal the depths of myself. For a while, I wanted to be a woman without depths.

As I entered the lobby of the only hotel in town, I was looking forward to another night of falling asleep shortly after sunset, two fingers of brandy aiding my journey toward Morpheus. Alas, it was not to be.

"There she is now," said the hotel clerk, and the man waiting at the counter stirred and turned toward me with a look of expectation.

It was too late for me to run, and in any case, I wasn't sure what the right reaction was. I thought I had already run far enough. I thought even if he looked for me—and why would he?—there was little chance he would find me. But I should have known there was no point in hiding from the world's greatest private investigator.

The man in front of me, travel-worn and determined, was Allan Pinkerton.

I wanted to fall upon his broad chest crying, and I also wanted to cringe away from him like a disobedient dog. In a way, it was a relief. Now that he was here, I didn't have to fear his arrival. This new life I had begun to assemble was no kind of life. I was only wasting time. Of course he had come.

"Upstairs," I said quietly, not caring what the clerk must think. The rules were different on the frontier. Besides, now that I had been found, I doubted I'd be staying much longer.

But the weeks I had been here had made one thing abundantly clear. Whatever my feelings toward Pinkerton, I missed my life as an operative. I missed the feeling of being useful, of puzzling out an answer to a crucial question. I missed mattering. Now that he was back, perhaps that was on offer again, and even before we got to the door of my room, I had to hold myself back from throwing myself on his mercy. But I knew begging him to welcome me back was an insult to both of us. Everything had gone so wrong between us. I wasn't sure any of our former ease could ever be recovered.

I brought him inside and shut the door. He took off his coat—he was always more comfortable in his shirtsleeves, and the room was warm—and sat down in the chair. I perched on the very edge of the bed, ankles crossed neatly. The memory of the last conversation among him, Tim, and me hung so heavy in the air, I kept running my fingers across the bedspread beside me, hoping against hope to feel the solid warm bulk of Tim there next to me. But he would never be there again.

My melancholy made me abrupt. "Why are you here?"

"I came to give you the news," he said, twisting his hat in his hand. "I thought you should hear it from me. It won't be in the papers."

I knew immediately he spoke of Mrs. Greenhow. Nothing else, not even the daily movements of the war, could interest me. I hadn't gone near a newspaper since I'd arrived in town. There was nothing I wanted to know. "Hanged, I hope?"

"No."

"Then what?"

"They sent her back," he said.

I felt as if the floor of the hotel had fallen away underneath my feet and there was no longer anything solid in the world to stand on. Loss was the first feeling. The second was fury. My blood boiled. I struggled to find words besides profanities to express myself, but there were none. I leapt up. "That's all? No punishment? Nothing?"

"The exile was the punishment."

"Sent home? To the country she loves, where she'll be hailed as a hero? That's disgusting!"

"Kate."

"I'll go stab her in the gut myself," I said, "and I am not kidding." There was no room to pace, but I did it anyway, my fury too strong to stay in one place.

"I know you're not." He remained in the chair, looking up at me. "But, Warne, the last thing we need is for you to die too."

"Oh, is that the last thing *we* need?" I snarled at him, letting the full force of my anger loose at last. "Because I wouldn't mind it. I'm ready. Let's just call the game what it is. My life is a failure. The man I love is dead, probably because of me. Or maybe," I said, suddenly bold, "because of you."

"Me?"

I put my hands on the arms of his chair and leaned down into his face. "You sent him there. Because he told you we were engaged to be married. You saw we were in love, and you had to stop that. You had to take that away from us."

"That was not my intent."

I could not read his expression.

"Regardless of your intent. Or mine. If things had been different, if I hadn't loved him and you hadn't hated him..." I pulled away, pacing again.

"I didn't hate him! He was my best man."

"And you sent him to his death."

He was patient in the face of my abuse, especially considering how far he had come. "I sent him where he was most needed, for the sake of the country. I sent Hattie too, you remember? Was that because of you as well?"

My head ached, and I wanted to do something violent. Push him out a window or leap my own self. All this pent-up anger needed somewhere to go, now that it was flowing.

But something in me knew he was right. Tim had been his best agent. Pinkerton was nothing if not a logical, measured, deliberate man. If he had sent Tim to Richmond, he needed someone in Richmond.

He said, "I used to ask you to lie to me, to help you learn. I have never lied to you."

I leaned my head against the wallpaper, closing my eyes, wishing he hadn't come, wishing I'd never met him, wishing everything had been different all along. I couldn't bear the way I felt. I had no choice but to bear it. It was torture.

He went on, his voice more hesitant now, "But I came to tell you something else we discovered. That you need to know."

"Go on."

His next words were slow in coming. "It wasn't just Greenhow. If her word alone were enough, a dozen other people would be dead. Tim had someone else betray him."

I turned to look at him. I needed to see his face. "Not Hattie?"

"No, someone else. Someone we didn't foresee."

"Tell me."

"Mortenson," he said.

I'd barely though of Jack Mortenson a handful of times since he was dismissed for his poor behavior back during Hattie's early years. But as soon as Pinkerton mentioned the name, the image sprung instantly to mind, indelible: pale and awkward, always the odd man out, half ghost. Now, he truly was a sort of ghost, one who haunted us unexpectedly.

I sat on the bed again to steady myself. "But how? How was he there?"

Pinkerton rubbed his hand across his mouth and looked down at the rug. "He'd heard about the intelligence service, what we were doing for the railroads and the country, and he said he wanted to help."

"Oh no."

"He said it was all water under the bridge, how things ended. He said he could put aside his anger if I could. And we needed good agents, Warne, needed them badly. So I hired him back. And I sent him to Richmond, told him Tim and Hattie were there. But he was working for the other side."

I struggled to absorb the new information, to turn everything over in my mind. It made a kind of sense. The pieces of the puzzle snapped into place. Mortenson was the third agent who Van Lew's butler had mentioned, then. There had been three after all, one spelling doom for the other two.

Pinkerton sat quietly, his graying head lowered, clearly suffering under the weight of what he'd done. I wanted to touch him, comfort him. But the truth was too new.

I'd been wrong about his motives. I'd been wrong about Mrs. Greenhow's role too, or at least not completely right. We all had some part of the guilt, every one of us.

Only one thing didn't add up. "But they didn't hang Hattie."

"No. When it came to the final trial, Mortenson gave the damning evidence against Tim, but he wouldn't do the same against Hattie. On the stand, he said he didn't know anything about her being an agent of any sort. Whatever he felt for her before, it seems he feels it still."

"At least..." I couldn't complete the thought. It was horrible that he'd done what he'd done but not surprising he'd had a change of heart about Hattie. He hated her enough to put her in prison but loved her too much to sign her death warrant. Tim, though, he had no such feelings for.

"He fooled me," said Pinkerton, his voice thick with regret. "I shouldn't have let him. So I came to apologize to you, Warne. Because it seems Tim's death really was my fault, in a way."

"You couldn't have known," I said. "But you were so angry. In the hotel, when Tim told you about us. Why?"

"It wasn't because of your relationship. I was angry about that, yes, but not why you think." He looked down at his hands, knotted together. "If you'd gotten married, if you'd started a family, it would have been a disaster."

I made a strangled noise in my throat.

"No, no. Let me explain. I didn't want to lose you as an operative. The agency couldn't afford to. Your mind, your intelligence—it would have been such a waste, Warne. And I couldn't bear that thought. You took me by surprise. It's no excuse, but it's a reason."

I remembered DeForest saying something similar long ago. To the world, being a wife meant being a mother, which meant leaving the work. They didn't understand me, my circumstances. Pinkerton thought I was making a choice I wouldn't have made. We hadn't had time to explain ourselves, me to him or him to me. I put my head in my hands.

He went on, "And that upset me. Deeply, I admit. I didn't

want to sacrifice someone as extraordinary as you for something as commonplace as love."

I had to smile, a little bit, through my tears. "Is it so commonplace?"

"Happens every day."

"So you separated us because—"

"Because you could do more good apart than together. You'd ingratiated yourself with Mrs. Greenhow; you didn't need him there anymore. You both begged me to send you where you were needed. You remember?"

"I remember."

"I took you both at your word."

I nodded once, soberly. Tim had ridden off with no objections. Sad to leave me but dedicated to his duty. He had died in service of the country we both loved. A long and happy life would have been a better fate, but there were a score of worse ones.

Meeting his gaze at last, the few feet of stale air between us already feeling like untold miles, I said, "Boss, I'm sorry."

"So am I, Kate."

"When you know where Mortenson is, you know where to find me."

"I'd hoped to convince you to come back to Chicago."

"I'm not ready," I said.

"I can stay a few days—"

"No, you can't. You're needed. You've already been away too long, traveling all this way, just to tell me. Don't misunderstand. I'm glad you did, but you need to go. What I need from you is time."

"How much?"

"That depends. The only case I'll work is Mortenson's case. You let me know when it's time for me to start the operation."

He opened his mouth to say something else but then closed it and looked at me, really looked. I had forgotten the strength of that powerful gaze, of having his full attention focused on me. I wondered what he saw there. Whatever it was made him shake his head once, like a horse shaking off a fly, and relax into his chair.

We didn't sit and converse as comfortably as we had before, but it was at least something. We talked late into the night, about Mortenson and his whereabouts and what was known and unknown so far. By the time the sun touched the morning sky, I was determined that victory was within our grasp. One more clue would be enough, if it was the right one. It was just a question of when.

When he rose to leave, he said, "And Kate? If you want revenge..."

I braced myself for a moral lesson, but I was surprised at what came instead.

"I don't blame you one whit."

Then he was gone, leaving me spent and amazed and burning with new purpose.

CHAPTER TWENTY-EIGHT

THE CASE BEGINS

T wo weeks later, I had another visitor, and I didn't realize how desperately I missed her until she appeared.

Hattie stepped down from the rattletrap coach like a butterfly alighting, the scarlet lining of her traveling cloak winking bright as flame against the town's muddy backdrop. Smeared with dirt and plainly exhausted, she was still the most beautiful woman on earth, as always. I flung my arms wide, and she stepped into them. We both cried tears of joy and hung on for dear life.

We caught up quickly. She had been released from Castle Thunder at last in a prisoner exchange, forbidden from reentering the Confederate States, as if she would ever want to. She was thinner than she'd been, but she wore it well. It gave her a new air of seriousness, of substance, with little resemblance to the brash would-be actress who had first set foot in the Pinkerton Agency office.

I told her why I'd come to Bright Hope, of all places, and gave her a quick tour of the town, such as it was. We relished the illusion of normalcy for a while, chatting merrily like other women must, with little urgency. It was a luxury I wasn't sure we had ever enjoyed before.

We sat at the table in the town's only restaurant for hours, downing more steins of ale than ladies strictly should, making it clear to all around us that we were not ladies. The German brewer a few blocks down who supplied the Golden Goose did excellent work: his ale was strong, with a pleasant, bitter tang. There was intense interest in us—I credited Hattie, as I was a fixture already— but we made it clear we did not want further company, huddling our heads together, walling ourselves off.

As we pushed away our empty plates, Hattie sighed with contentment. At last, I spoke up on the topic I had avoided. "I know you didn't find me yourself."

She caught my meaning immediately and took it in stride. "No, I did not."

"His idea?"

"No, my idea, but he made it possible. I only had to ask him three times a day for eight days before he said yes."

I couldn't blame Pinkerton for giving in to her; though I had told him my conditions, he would know I would enjoy seeing Hattie again, seeing for myself that she was all right. "And what was your idea?"

"I needed to see you. To talk about what happened. Because I don't think either of us knows how to get past it otherwise."

I thought of her with Tim, just the two of them against the world in Richmond. They had played husband and wife, just as he and I had. I hadn't thought about how she had lost him too, and I wondered if we missed him in the same way. I said, "Did you... Did the two of you..."

"No," she said, but there was no surprise or shock that I would ask her. We were professionals; wild conjecture was merely our business. She smiled fondly, remembering. "He talked about you all the time. My Lord. He kept saying, *When this is over, when this is over.* He couldn't wait to hop the twig. You must have been so in love."

"For all the good it does me now," I said and raised the glass to my lips again, only to find it empty. I signaled for the next round.

She sat in silence, and I felt the need to reach out and pat her hand. It had been a lifetime since Chicago, since we'd rescued Carlotta Caruso, since we'd begun to understand each other. Before the war, a war that still raged but seemed so far away from this place.

"Hattie, we knew what we were getting into, didn't we? Being spies? Maybe I never should have hired you. Maybe you'd be better off if I hadn't. Probably married with a bevy of babies by now."

"I wouldn't want that. This is better. I only regret…"

"Regret what?"

She began crying then, in earnest, and the men around us began to stare—some openly, some with more tact. I shot a withering glare at the worst offenders, but there was little else I could do. I wouldn't tell Hattie to be quiet; I wanted her to be as loud as she could be, for both of us.

"I blame myself," said Hattie.

"For what?"

"If I'd talked to Mortenson, maybe he would have withdrawn his testimony about Tim, found a way to help get him free. Taken it back."

It broke my heart that Hattie thought she could have done something to change that monster's actions. He was the one who'd been responsible for Tim's death. Him and only him. I was done blaming anyone else. I knew Pinkerton felt himself partly responsible, but even his part, I had forgiven.

"Hattie, you couldn't. There was no way. You didn't even know he was in Richmond."

"Still," she said, her voice thin and weak, "if I'd asked the right questions, if I'd been face-to-face with him… I could have offered him something he wanted." She smoothed her plaid skirt over and over again. "I would have done anything."

"I know the feeling."

We rose from the table and embraced, holding on for a long time, sharing our lasting pain. I didn't feel better afterward, exactly, but at least I didn't feel worse.

&

Two weeks after Hattie left, I received my first and last telegram in Bright Hope.

THE CASE BEGINS

Frugal as ever, he had not signed his name, knowing I would intuit all that was necessary.

It was a matter of minutes to pack my suitcase and settle my bill with the hotel and not much more than that to bid farewell to Mrs. Borowski. It was a short walk to the station. I wasted no time. The train to Chicago only came past Bright Hope once a day, and I was on it.

Upon arrival in Chicago, I went to the office, letting myself feel like a stranger. It was too hard to think of myself when I was last there, so innocent despite all the deception that had been my life for years. I did not look at the faces of the operatives to see whether they were the same men or new ones. I drew no comparisons. The costume closet, no longer Tim's, I could not even acknowledge.

Seated across from Pinkerton at his big, oaken desk, as I'd been so many times, I prepared myself for a wholly new undertaking.

He began, "A bank teller's been murdered in Cincinnati."

"Poor man." But there was a tension under my sympathy; he knew the life I cared most about, and if the two didn't intersect, our conversation would be short indeed. I had come too great a distance, in all ways, for just another bank job.

"In the commission of a robbery. Successful."

"How much was taken?"

"One hundred thirty thousand."

I let out a low whistle. It was the largest sum I'd ever heard gone in a single stroke.

"So he had the vault open, and someone murdered him, then just emptied it all out?"

"Precisely. Struck with a hammer, back of the head."

"Poor man," I said again.

"Any suspects?"

"One. And I'd like you to go after him."

"You know I'm only willing to—"

"It's him, Warne."

With no hesitation, I said, "I'm on the job."

"He'll be hard to find," said Pinkerton. "He knows our ways. He knows how not to leave evidence. And now he has money."

"Most criminals slip up eventually. Weren't you the one who taught me that?"

"He's not most criminals."

"I know." I looked down at the scar on the edge of the desk, the deep cut in the wood I'd first noticed on the day Jack Mortenson was shot by counterfeiters so long ago. I had seen his blood. I knew he was human. "I'm not most operatives either, am I?"

"If anyone can do it, Warne, you can."

He reached into a drawer and laid my pistol on the desk matter-of-factly, with no fanfare. I retrieved it the same way. We did not say good-bye.

After only hours in Chicago, with the same suitcase never unpacked, I was gone again. I rode the night train to Cincinnati and committed myself to the investigation with a grim enthusiasm.

In the course of a few days, I visited the bank, talked to the manager, discussed the matter with the police, even viewed the body of the poor slain teller, who'd had no family to claim him. In a way, it was like any other case: I could only approach it methodically, one step at a time, and chip away at the lies and confusion and secrets until I reached the core truth.

It was a simple bank job in most ways, similar to countless other crimes of its type. The main differences were the fatality—most robberies of this type were perpetrated by masked men who left the bank employees alive—and the fact that a single man appeared to have taken on the entire job himself. No accomplices had been spotted, let alone named. He just seemed to walk into the bank one day, kill a teller, and make off with over a hundred thousand dollars. But of course, it couldn't be that simple. The things that looked the simplest were often the most complex. I knew enough to dig deep.

But it was hard. The first week passed, then the second. I returned to my hotel every night dizzy with impatience. There were days when I lay down sobbing with frustration when promising information lost its promise. There were more bad days than good. I only kept on because I knew what this man had taken from me and what I owed him in return.

I began to canvass the neighborhood around the bank in ever-widening circles, not skipping a single door. I spoke with clerks and lawyers, grocers and musicians, bartenders and security guards. At last, my questioning bore fruit: the watchmaker who had recently opened a shop in the storefront neighboring the bank had disappeared the day after the robbery. The timing was suspicious, and I began to search for the watchmaker, looking for signs that he'd been the accomplice no one had suspected.

For a second and third time, I returned to the Cincinnati morgue, hardly as large or as clean as the Cook County one I knew better, and I was again rewarded with more information. There were two unidentified bodies, bearing some resemblance to each other, with sparse brown hair, broad shoulders, and thick waists. It was hard to compare their faces, as both had been dispatched with a single shot to the back of the skull, but the similarity of the wounds was another clue I sorely needed. One was the dead watchmaker, William Hudson. Further inquiries revealed that the other was his brother, Carl Hudson, who had not been reported either dead or missing and whose last known place of residence was a row house near the harbor in Baltimore. It seemed likely that the watchmaker had been in on the robbery, slain so he could tell no tales, and his brother an unlucky casualty.

It was the slimmest of leads, but it was the only one I had, and I would not fail to follow it. I did not tell the authorities. I went in person, and I went armed.

Another train ride, alone, on the way to an uncertain future. The car swayed gently, but I couldn't rest. I hadn't been back to Baltimore since the events before Lincoln's inauguration. Tim had been with me then, but we hadn't known that we were wasting time not loving each other. There was so much we hadn't known.

I felt a pang when I rode past the abandoned cabin on my way into the city. I told myself that I would visit, thinking of Tim, once Mortenson was in custody. But I didn't know if I would survive the next few days, and if I admitted the truth to myself, my plans for Mortenson didn't involve custody at all.

Carl Hudson's row house was tidy and empty. I knocked on the door, and hearing no answer, I picked the lock and entered. Each small room was easy to take in at a glance, and when I stood in the last room, the kitchen, it was clear I would not find Mortenson here. I thought about searching the rooms for the money, which would prove his guilt, but it wasn't the money I wanted.

I knew he was nearby. It sounds odd, but I recognized the smell of him. Even after all the years that had passed, I knew he had been there. I weighed my options—Wait for him to return?

Call the local authorities?—and then I realized it was time for the noon meal. There was no food in the house's kitchen, and it had clearly not been used in months. Therefore, it was likely that he frequented the nearest saloon for his meals.

And indeed, I found him two blocks away, in a good-sized saloon called the Tender Heart, just steps from bustling Commerce Street. He sat alone at a table with a mug of beer and a ham sandwich. I almost laughed. It was as if he were any man, any normal person, and not a killer and a fiend.

The years had changed him. He was less pale, having clearly spent enough time in the sun to tan his skin a darker shade. But he was more wiry, less flesh and more bone, so even more like a skeleton than he had ever been. My body convulsed at the sight of him. Seeing him was the most welcome and most unwelcome sight possible, all at once. I was finally face-to-face with the person responsible for Tim's death, and the knowledge sang through every muscle, demanding action, demanding justice.

A smart woman would have called the police, but I would not wait. I strode over to his table and sat down across from him. He started—who wouldn't?—but quickly covered his shock with an ugly, oily grin.

"It's you," he said. "The girl."

"It's you," I said. "The traitor."

"I was faithful to my country. My country isn't the same as yours." His accent was stronger now, far more pronounced, a sharp Kentucky twang. He had stopped trying to hide who he was, who he wanted to be.

"Beyond that. You were a traitor to Pinkerton," I said.

"I should have venerated him for what? Was he loyal to me, when he kicked me out in the street?"

"You deserved that."

He laughed and took a long drink from his mug of beer before answering. Because he was sitting down, I couldn't be sure whether he was wearing a gun under his jacket. His hands were on the table, so I knew whatever happened, I could reach mine first.

As if it were unimportant, as if our conversation were just mere conversation, he mused, "Does anyone get what they deserve? Is that what you think?"

"Yes."

"Then I hope you sleep well at night on your lovely pillow of self-righteousness."

"I sleep fine," I lied.

"Without either Tim Bellamy or Allan Pinkerton in your bed?"

"Appalling, still," I said. "You don't know the first thing about my private life."

"Only that you're a whore." His voice grew more intent, colder. "And you never were a good agent."

I gestured at our surroundings. "Good enough to catch you."

"Ah, but have you caught me?"

"It would seem so."

With one long, slender finger, he pointed over my shoulder at the door to the outside. "I can see the exit. I'm faster and bigger than you. What are you going to do to stop me?"

In answer, I rose and brought my gun out of the folds of my skirt with both hands, pointing it straight at his heart. I'd never had to shoot a man in the line of duty, but I'd kept in practice. I'd also set aside the Deringer for a lightweight Colt Baby Dragoon, figuring that if things got so desperate that I had to shoot, I'd better have the option to shoot more than once.

The look on his face did not soften. If anything, he looked more defiant, not less.

Someone at the next table stood so quickly that their chair overturned. I could hear murmurings. It would have been better to corner him alone, but I couldn't take the chance at losing him.

He said, "That's a very small gun."

"The bullets are big enough."

He rose—seeming taller than I remembered—and backed away, edging past the table toward the open floor. I thought I saw the outline of a holster on his hip but couldn't be sure.

The crowd surged and swam around us, buzzing like a hive. For a moment, there was nothing but empty space between us, but there were too many people behind him, and I didn't have a clear shot. I should have waited. I hadn't waited. Now, one way or the other, we'd have our reckoning.

The crowd was thinning quickly as the inhabitants of the saloon stood and ran. A few ran between us, and I stepped forward to keep my eye trained on Mortenson. He grabbed at a woman running near him and missed, cursing as she slipped his grasp. Soundlessly, she kept running, and I cheered her just as silently as she escaped. I didn't want to hurt anyone else. Only my quarry. Only he deserved to suffer for what he'd done.

In what seemed like the space of a minute, it was just the two of us facing each other.

"You took that ring, didn't you?" It wasn't really a question.

He didn't have to ask which ring. He had tried to discredit me, to discourage me, so many years ago. Our vendetta had begun then; I just hadn't realized it. I wondered whether he had, when he took the snake ring from me on the streets of Chicago and slipped it back into the safe two days later, hoping to turn Pinkerton against me. It hadn't worked. At least on that front, I had won.

"Why does that matter?" he asked.

"Everything matters. You should know that, as a former detective."

"Former? Ah, Kate. You're such a fool sometimes. Once a detective, always a detective."

I let his words hang in the air, unanswered. We were done playing. Everything behind us was unimportant now. What mattered was that one of us would survive the confrontation, and it was time to settle which one.

"You won't shoot me," he said. "Whatever else you are, you're a lady."

His hand was on its way down to his holster when my first bullet caught him in the shoulder, spinning him halfway around. The recoil stung, but I forced my hand back up into position for a second shot while he struggled to right himself, his gun in his hand. He got a shot off in my direction, and with no time to aim, my second shot went wild. I heard his gun click in the silence, out of bullets. We both took a breath. Then he hunched low, clutching his shoulder, scurrying behind tables and between chairs toward the exit.

I went to take a step forward and fell. Only then did I realize my right leg wasn't working quite right. I looked down to confirm it. I should not have. Through the many layers of my skirting, I couldn't see the wound, but the blood was spreading quickly, and the fabric was already heavy with it. The stain radiated out from my thigh. The leg was numb now, but I knew the pain would come quickly, and I couldn't get ahead of it, no matter what I did.

I cursed angrily, loudly. I'd come so far; there was no chance I would let him get away.

I fired from where I was. My third shot missed. My fourth one buried itself in his back, and he fell. But then he was up again, faster than I was, and out in the street. I ignored the fire in my right leg and hauled myself up on my left, hobbling as fast as I could, panting. I had one bullet left. I prayed for the chance to use it.

He was waiting for me at the door and flung his body onto mine. We landed in the dirt with a shared grunt. My pistol skidded away.

The crowd held itself back, watching, as we scuffled our way into the street. Both of our guns were lost. He was bigger and stronger than I was, but he was losing blood faster too—at least, so far. He raised a fist to punch me, but I twisted my head away in a flash, and his knuckles pounded straight into the earth, stunning him for a moment. I thought I heard bones crack.

Then I looked around us, knowing that unless I did something, the next fist would take me out. Passersby stood gawking, not inclined to pick a side but willing to watch the scrum. I saw nothing within reach that I could grab to defend myself.

Only one thing stood out. I heard it before I saw it. We lay in the center of the road, people and animals surging in all directions, the bustle unceasing. A high-stepping horse, pulling a black wagon of heaped-up goods, was speeding in our direction, likely to pass close by us on the right side. I made the fastest decision of my life. I knew a weapon when I saw one.

I kneed Mortenson between the legs, wrapped my arms around him, and began to roll us both into the horse's path. He rolled with me, not knowing what I intended. How could he?

I heard the driver yell. I heard the horse whinny and rear. I heard the iron wheels of the carriage rattle and thump.

Then they were upon us, and I heard nothing after that.

CHAPTER TWENTY-NINE

INVESTIGATION

I opened my eyes to the pockmarked ceiling of a hospital room, the second time in my life I had done so. My broken body lay on stiff white sheets again. I felt my losses more keenly this time, knowing exactly who and what I had lost and when. I'd been barely more than a child myself when I lost my child, but that was not the only difference. I wanted to feel relief and joy. I'd succeeded in the hardest chase of my life. But mostly, I felt pain. Unrelenting, sharp, and persistent, everywhere.

"Kate."

I turned my head slowly, carefully, toward the voice. It felt like it took a year.

Pinkerton was sitting next to my bed, his chin propped and resting on one fist, as still as I had ever seen him. He was like a statue. When I stirred, a soft groan escaping my dry lips, he immediately turned his attention to me.

"Thank you," he said.

"No need."

"You did what no one else could."

I let myself drift a bit. Was it true? It might be. I wanted it to be.

His voice brought me back again. "I want to tell you—Warne, you're the best operative I have."

"Tim was the best."

He waited a moment before responding. "I miss him too."

I appreciated that the man was letting himself show emotion, but it was still an order of magnitude less than I knew I felt, deep down. Whatever satisfaction I'd achieved by hunting down Mortenson, the pain of losing Tim was still just as acute.

"But you—you have always been something special."

"Thank you."

"And we need you back."

"What?"

"Please. Come back. Work for me—work with me."

"It might take a while," I joked and would have gestured to my bandages if I could have moved.

"When you get better."

My brain was muddled. I wasn't sure whether the horse had stomped on it directly or whether the pain there was due to blood loss, ether, or other injury. Still, the answer came quickly to my lips. "To do what? I'm done spying. I can't, Boss."

"When the war is over, then. I'm going to need brilliant operatives of all kinds, and you'll be the star in the firmament. If you want to run an office, you can. If you want to start up the Ladies' Bureau again, train all my female operatives, you can. But I need you. This will be your legacy."

His use of the word stopped me short. I had been about to protest, but I didn't. Because I remembered what my mother had said, that a woman's family was her legacy. I had no family, but I did have a legacy. I had something else I could do with my life to make it worth living. In that case, I would be proud of what I left behind. And yet...

"I've done terrible things," I blurted.

He seemed to take it in stride. "Are you dead yet?"

"Boss?"

"Are you dead yet?"

I flicked my eyes down at my hospital bed and said, "It's not entirely clear."

"Warne," he said.

This time, I knew he was serious, so I answered, "No. Not yet."

"Then the balance of your soul hasn't been weighed. Yes, you've done bad things. We all have."

"Have you killed anyone?" I asked.

"Yes."

"And do you feel bad about it? Does it weigh down your soul?"

He considered this, rubbing his chin with one hand, thoughtful. "All the things I've done, good and bad, honest and dishonest, they stay with me. Always with me. But do I feel bad about them? It depends on the day."

It seemed a fair answer. I couldn't ask for much more.

He continued, "And you've done good things too. Saved lives. Brought justice. Come back to the agency. And do more good, for more of the world."

"Let me think about it," I said.

"Take all the time you need. The day the war ends, I want you to come to me and tell me your answer."

"All right."

He reached out for my hand. This is how I found out both of my hands were broken, swathed in white bandages. I shook my head a little, as best I could, and said, "Thanks anyway, Boss."

He laid his hand on my head like a benediction. His palm was warm and heavy. "Thank *you*, Kate."

Recovery was easier said than done. The physical injuries were bad enough: broken ribs, broken hands, a galaxy of scrapes and bruises everywhere the doctors looked. My attempt at sacrificing my life to take Mortenson's was noble, I told myself, but I should have been more thorough in the execution. This way, I was only half dead. Some days, it felt like more than half.

Even as the bruises faded and my bones began to slowly knit themselves back together under the skin, I lacked the spirit to move forward, a reason to get up and tackle each day. My first and last thought every day was how much I missed Tim, how large a hole he'd left in the world. Mortenson was dead, yes, but it changed nothing. Greenhow had slipped beyond my grasp; she had run the blockade to England and published a book about her adventures, raising money for her cause. I supposed I could write a book too, but there were so many things I never wanted anyone to know, I hardly saw how there would be anything left to write about.

Once I had the use of my hands again and the worst of the fog had cleared from my brain, I read many books while I lay in the hospital recovering. Hers was not one of them.

I'd hoped for a visit from Hattie or DeForest, but they were both on assignment. The war still raged on, though I could not see it from my bed. From time to time, I got a letter from one or the other. I could only tell which by the handwriting. Both sent highly creative letters—fake love letters sometimes, or a chatty missive as if from a gossipy aunt, all in code to keep things secret. One of Hattie's letters, full of atrocious doggerel written as if from a half-literate soldier to his unfaithful shopgirl, made me laugh so hard, I reinjured a rib. Those days were the best days. Unfortunately, the light always seemed to slip too quickly from the sky, my tiny window fading to blackness, abandoning me to the interminable nights.

I thought a lot about Tim, and I wondered what would have happened had he lived. Would we have burned bright or burned out? If I told him I would never bear children, nor would I ever walk away from my position as an operative willingly, would he still have wanted to marry me? I had no way of knowing the answers. There was no world where those things had happened, only the world where they hadn't. And I had to remind myself, every day, that I needed to be grateful I'd had his love as long as I had, even as short a time as it was.

Once I was able to walk again and to think without my head feeling like it was caving in on itself, I came to a decision. I would be a detective again, but this time, for myself. I would find my parents and make sure they could never hurt me. How I would guarantee that I didn't know. Life generally held no such guarantees. But I had shrunk my whole life from confronting them, and now that I was lost and alone, perhaps the best thing I could do with my Pinkerton training was to hunt down where I'd come from and the people who made me who I was.

They were easier than I thought to find. They were buried, side by side, in Charleston. The sun fought its way through the gnarled oaks to cast a dappled shadow over them.

There would be no reckoning, no confrontation. I had been cheated of it. The wounds Mortenson gave me in our final battle had mostly healed, but the wounds my parents had given me would be with me for life.

I moved back to Chicago. The city had settled a little in my absence and felt not quite so wild. The raising was complete, and the sewers worked well. The stink off the river seemed diminished. I selected a new boardinghouse and a new identity. Hattie had finished her assignments on the front and was based in Chicago again—a good sign both for the war and the agency. She offered to room together, and I was sorely tempted to have a friend so close by. But I had been on my own so long, I worried I wouldn't be suited for a closer living situation, so I told Hattie we would visit frequently, and she agreed.

I was glad for my privacy in October. Strangely, I didn't even remember how the shocking news reached me. Did I come across it in a newspaper? Overhear it in a shop? I only knew that my reaction to it was not at all what I would have expected.

Rose Greenhow was dead.

I wanted to be glad of it; I wanted to shriek in joy. Instead, I sat on my bed and examined the wallpaper, faded ever so slightly near the window, as the sun set outside and the room fell dark. My enemy's passing, which I'd once prayed and wished for, brought me no happiness. It only meant another motherless child, Little Rose, as I was now motherless. There was nothing to celebrate in that.

She'd almost made it home. On her way back from England, Greenhow's ship had sunk just off the coast of the Carolinas, blasted by a Union defender. It was not a direct hit, and from the story I heard, the ship sunk slowly. Nearly everyone else survived the sinking. She leapt into the water and might have made it to shore, but she was weighed down by gold bars sewn into the hem and sleeves of her dress. Against my will, I often pictured her as I fell asleep, the lace of her collar rising up around her face like seaweed as the hoarded gold dragged the rest of her down, down, down.

Chasing money was a fool's pursuit. Some women might leave a family as their legacy, but others had an effect in completely different ways. I paused, thinking about what her life had left and what my life might leave. I thought of Pinkerton's offer. I thought of what Tim would have suggested, had he been sitting there next to me. I thought of the line from Lincoln's inaugural speech—*the better angels of our nature.*

After that, it was only waiting.

CHAPTER THIRTY

THE END AND THE BEGINNING

When the day came, I misunderstood it at first.

It was only a few days short of the fourth anniversary of Fort Sumter, and when I first heard a boom from outside my window, I thought perhaps I'd missed a few days and that it was a salute being fired in commemoration. But no, it was the ninth of April, not the twelfth, and the boom was followed by other sounds, more difficult to identify.

The noise from the street was tremendous. It started as a roar, far off, and resolved itself over time into a chorus of cheers and shouts. As I listened, the voices came clearer.

And once I knew that it was the day I'd waited for—the day the war ended—then I knew it was time to follow through on the promise I'd made myself. Allan Pinkerton had offered me a position as an operative when the war was over, and this was the day I'd answer him.

I couldn't get to the office fast enough. I wasn't even sure he would be there or whether DeForest or Hattie or anyone else I knew might be, and in a sense, it didn't matter. I just wanted to walk through the door again. I just wanted to be among my fellow Pinkertons.

I could barely contain my excitement, and as I walked, it indeed spilled out of me, and the smile on my face became a laugh and then a yelp of joy. I must have seemed insane, but on this day of all days, I knew I would be pardoned; the whole city, the whole nation, was going mad with happiness, and we had good reason. The streets were crowded for the early hour, and it took much longer than it usually would to make my way to Clark Street, but I wasn't impatient. I was in motion. All was as it should be.

No one else was at the office yet. It was barely past six in the morning. They would all come later, I told myself, but for the moment, I was alone. The door stood silent, closed, but behind it lay promise.

Did I still have a key? I wasn't even sure, and it didn't matter. I desperately wanted to be back in that office, behind a desk, ready to throw myself into the work. I imagined the rows of shoulders of empty clothing in the costume closet, Pinkerton's immense, scarred wooden desk, the drawers full of manila folders, each keeping a case file's secrets. I had been away too long. Now I was early, but it was right and good. At last, I was just where I needed to be.

I tried to turn the knob. It resisted. The packet of lock picks was in my hand in a flash, and I worked quickly. I couldn't hear the click of the tumblers, of course, but I felt them yield.

"Someone has to be first," I told myself ruefully, joyfully, and swung open the door.

AUTHOR'S NOTE

Kate Warne is one of the most interesting people we know almost nothing about.

The real Kate Warne was indeed hired as the first female Pinkerton agent by Allan Pinkerton himself in 1856 after answering a newspaper ad. That much we know. Multiple accounts say she was a widow, though what happened to her husband is not clear, nor why she took the extremely drastic step of applying for a position that had never previously been open to women.

We're not even sure what Kate looked like. There are no confirmed images of her. Two photographs show up from time to time in discussions of her. Both date from the Civil War, and both show a person in men's clothing, so it's far from certain that we're really looking at Kate. For such an influential and pioneering figure, precious little information about her has been recorded and passed down. Then again, as a detective and a spy, that's probably how she liked it.

Everywhere we turn for information on Kate's life, there are blank spaces. Many of the Pinkerton National Detective Agency's files are kept in the Library of Congress, and those files are extensive; however, much of the material previous to 1871 was wiped out by the Great Chicago Fire, and Kate's entire career was previous to 1871. From those files, we know a few things: We know she was the first female detective, because Pinkerton wrote about hiring her. We know her work included befriending suspect Nathan Maroney's wife to gather evidence on the Adams Express theft case. We know she disguised herself as a medium to investigate a poisoning case at the behest of a Captain Thayer (whose sister and her lover were, in fact, trying to poison him, as the investigation proved). And we know she was instrumental in saving Lincoln's life on his way through Baltimore to his 1861 inauguration by pretending to be the sister of the disguised "invalid" Lincoln in his shawl and soft cap. Not a bad résumé, but there must have been so much more we don't know about. In a way, that makes her the perfect subject for historical fiction. I've had the freedom to imagine her, for which I'm intensely grateful.

As for the world I've drawn around her in these pages, I can say this: if truth isn't always stranger than fiction, it is at least a great deal more complicated. I have streamlined, combined, and edited many people and events from the historical record to serve my own purposes here.

Historical figures such as Abraham Lincoln, George McClellan, and Ward Hill Lamon appear here in positions they held in real life, though, of course, I have put words in their mouths. (It's my job.) As for the Pinkertons, Hattie Lawton and, obviously, Allan Pinkerton worked for the Pinkerton National Detective Agency during the years this book is set. Tim Bellamy is based on Timothy Webster, Pinkerton agent and highly skilled undercover spy for the Union, who was apprehended behind enemy lines in Richmond and hanged in April 1862. Many sources take it for granted that Allan Pinkerton and Kate Warne had a long-term affair, but there is no real proof of this. I've taken her romance in a different direction. This novel is really a love story between a woman and her work.

Students of history will realize that I took considerable license with the assassination attempt on Abraham Lincoln in Baltimore and the apprehension of the Southern spy Rose Greenhow; readers interested in more factual accounts can find them in the excellent nonfiction books *The Hour of Peril* by Daniel Stashower (Lincoln) and *Liar, Temptress, Soldier, Spy* by Karen Abbott (Greenhow). Abbott's book also gives a more complete picture of the fascinating real-life Elizabeth Van Lew and Belle Boyd, whose appearances in these pages are brief.

Kate's amazing career with the Pinkertons, which included supervising the agency's Female Bureau of Detectives for many years, was cut short by her death from a sudden illness in 1868. She is buried in the Pinkerton family plot. Perhaps fittingly for a woman whose life is so shrouded in mystery, her name is misspelled on her tombstone: *Kate Warn.*

READING GROUP GUIDE

1. Widowed and without job prospects, Kate answers a newspaper advertisement for a job as a Pinkerton operative. What do you think she would have done if Pinkerton hadn't agreed to hire her?

2. Kate is unsentimental about the death of her husband, Charlie. Did you find this surprising? What did you suspect was the reason for her unusual detachment?

3. When Graham DeForest meets Kate, he is flirtatious and solicitous, and Kate believes he is a ladies' man. When she follows him to practice her surveillance skills, she finds this is definitely not the case. Did you suspect his secret?

4. Kate has many good qualities that make her an excellent operative, but she is also impulsive and judgmental. What do you think her strengths and weaknesses are? Is there some overlap between the two?

5. Although the accountant, Vincent, is the one who has been embezzling money from the railroad, Kate considers his mistress "more guilty" because she initially suggested the idea and also threatened to blackmail Vincent when he wanted to stop. Do you agree?

6.   Kate draws a parallel between the roles she saw her father and other actors play when she was a child and the roles she's asked to play as a Union spy. What are the similarities between the two? The differences?

7.   Allan Pinkerton's wife, Joan, is highly suspicious of Kate, warning her, "You keep your grubby mitts off my husband. Don't think I don't know what you're up to with your late nights and your cases and your *work*." In truth, there was a widespread assumption that the two were having an affair. Do you think this was influenced by the fact that Kate was the only woman working among so many men? Would a woman in the same position today still be suspected?

8.   When her friend and fellow Pinkerton agent Graham DeForest proposes marriage, Kate is seriously tempted to accept. She thinks, "We could protect each other. Keep each other safe from what we both feared." Do you think this is true? As a gay man who had to keep his orientation secret, would Graham had been better off if she had married him? Would Kate?

9.   At Lincoln's inauguration, Kate reflects on what she and her colleagues have done to fight crime. "Deceived, lied, disguised, misled, threatened, entrapped, captured, hurt… Were we devils, even on the angels' side?" Do you believe it's okay to do bad things for good reasons? Did you feel Kate's actions ever went too far?

10.   Kate's relationship with Tim Bellamy evolves from mutual dislike to grudging respect and eventually into love, which is revealed when the two assume the identities of husband

and wife as part of an undercover operation. Do you think they would have discovered and admitted their feelings without this forced proximity? In some cases, can pretending something help make it true?

11. Two of the women Kate is asked to befriend under false pretenses, Catherine Maroney and Rose Greenhow, have young daughters. In both cases, Kate questions the actions she is taking to punish the women for their criminal behavior. Did you feel this was appropriate? Should their status as mothers have figured into their pursuit and punishment?

12. The real-life Kate Warne was among those who foiled the 1861 assassination attempt on Abraham Lincoln in Baltimore. How do you think things would have been different had the assassination succeeded? Did knowing this assassination was not successful affect how you felt while reading the scene?

13. Kate's parents threaten her with exposure and demand money to keep silent. Did you feel one was more dangerous than the other? Did Kate deal with them fairly? How did you feel when their fates were revealed?

14. In her final showdown with Mortenson, rather than let him escape, Kate rolls them both into the path of an oncoming carriage out of desperation. Do you think she expected to die? Was her revenge that important to her?

15. Kate's mother tells her "a woman's family is her legacy," and Kate thinks of this often as she considers what her own legacy will be. What legacies do you think are left by other women

in the story, such as Mrs. Borowski, Hattie, Kate's mother, and Rose Greenhow?

16.   In the author's note, Macallister calls this novel "a love story between a woman and her work." Did you find Kate's excitement about the end of the war and resuming her life as a Pinkerton a satisfying conclusion to the book? Did it feel like a "happy ending"?

ACKNOWLEDGMENTS

I can't even count, let alone name, all of the people to whom I owe a debt of gratitude for helping get this beautiful book into your hands.

Thanks to my guiding star, Elisabeth Weed, the best agent I can imagine having, as well as Dana Murphy and the partners of The Book Group. I'm thrilled to have some of the savviest agents in the business on my team, including Michelle Weiner of CAA for film rights and Jenny Meyer for foreign rights.

Thanks to the amazing Shana Drehs at Sourcebooks, whose keen editorial guidance and commitment to publishing the best possible book are equally impressive and appreciated. Sourcebooks has managed to pull together a huge team of brilliant, committed, hardworking individuals who also happen to be warm, fun people and are a pleasure to spend time with. Just a few of those I'm thrilled to work with include Dominique Raccah, Lathea Williams, Heidi Weiland, Stephanie Graham, Heather Hall, Sabrina Baskey, Carolyn Lesnick, Valerie Pierce, Sara Hartman-Seeskin, and Adrienne Krogh.

Thanks to the many amazing writers whose friendship, insight, feedback, and enthusiasm keep me going in the tough times and share in the celebration when news is good. There are too many to name, but I'm fortunate to walk this road with gems like Robb Cadigan, Stephanie Feuer, Pam Jenoff, Tracey Kelley, Kenneth Kraus, Allie Larkin, Ariel Lawhon, Sarah McCoy, Shelley Nolden,

Camille Pagán, Rick Spilman, Erika Robuck, Michelle Von Euw, Therese Walsh, and Heather Webb, as well as the Fiction Writers' Co-op and the Tall Poppy Writers.

Thanks to the indie booksellers who play such an important role in getting books they love into the hands of readers who need them. Your excitement and dedication is absolutely inspiring to see.

Thanks to my family, especially my husband, Jonathan, whose unflagging support of my writing is essential, not only to my career, but also my happiness. Because of you, I'm lucky enough to have both.

Last but not least, I want to express my boundless gratitude to all the readers out there. This wouldn't be worth it without you.

ABOUT THE AUTHOR

USA Today bestselling author Greer Macallister is a poet, short story writer, playwright, and novelist with an MFA in creative writing from American University. Raised in the Midwest, she currently lives with her family on the East Coast. Her debut novel, *The Magician's Lie*, an Indie Next and Target Book Club Pick, was chosen by guest judge Whoopi Goldberg as a Book of the Month Club main selection and optioned for film by Jessica Chastain's Freckle Films.